LEECHES and LIBERTY

LEECHES and LIBERTY

A Medical Historical Fiction

(1773–1781)

Richard H. Kennedy

TWO HARBORS PRESS

Two Harbors Press
212 3ʳᴰ Avenue North, Suite 290
Minneapolis, MN 55401
612.455.2293
www.TwoHarborsPress.com

ISBN-13: 978-1-936401-53-6
LCCN: 2011928302

Distributed by Itasca Books

Cover Design and Typeset by Madge Duffy

Printed in the United States of America

For Holly
The foundation of my inspiration
And the catalyst for this book

Preface

Medicine during the Revolution—for that matter all of the 18ᵗʰ century—was an ubiquitous practice mostly stalled in the theories and practices of much earlier times and proud of its traditions. Most practitioners adhered to the prevalent theories. There was little science in the colonies, no germ theory, no anesthesia, no stethoscopes, and no thermometers in common use. Doctors, mostly apprenticed trained, did what they thought best; they used what few drugs were available or that could be compounded from home gardens. They relied mostly on what had worked for some patients in the past. Therefore, medicine in the Revolution reflects the views of many different practitioners. Often the same procedures and medicines were used for very different diseases.

Good doctors were not ignorant. They applied what they knew and what they felt appropriate for a particular patient. Sometimes their ministrations worked. Often patients recovered in spite of them; some did not.

The names and events in this historical fiction, including well-known figures of the Revolution (Washington, Greene, others known in the Colony of Rhode Island), are reflections of the historical record. Dr. Carr is fictitious, my own creation of a typical village doctor of the period, but the names of his patients, neighbors, and friends are familiar names in the Village of Pawtuxet. Errors reported as historical fact are purely my own.

The herbal remedies described in this journal are well researched and were commonly used in colonial America, although considerable disagreement existed about what was most effective for a particular treatment. Some therapies will strike the reader as bizarre; they are. Doctors of the period employed what they had learned during their apprenticeship and repeated what seemed to work. Few kept records to support their suppositions.

History helps us to meaningfully connect with the beliefs, hopes, and worries of those who have come before us. The intent of these chronicles is to help us understand that those who shaped our independence had failings and fears much like our own uncertainties and suspicions.

We come to recognize our own struggle to realize our dreams, to better understand the evolution of medicine and the conduct of this most remarkable war.

—Richard Kennedy

The Medical Journal of Dr. Luke Carr
(1773–1781)

Introduction

Again, I had been a disappointment. I am always starting over. A melancholy dark cloud lingers over me. The vicar had booted me out and I could think of no other way to escape from my domineering brother. I had to get out of Kingswood—the most suffocating place imaginable. If I didn't flee soon, I feared that I would be forever trapped.

But, I had no money. My brother wouldn't lend me a shilling under any circumstance. My sister and her family were barely scraping by. Who would trust a young man like me with a loan? . . . A man who had abandoned his study of the ministry, had been thrown out by his family and had few prospects.

Although I had no interest in going to sea, I decided to sign on as an ordinary seaman (I had absolutely no skills to offer as a "jack tar"). I would sail for one trip only, if I could find such an arrangement; and once safely landed, I would stay in America. If the captain insisted on a round trip or a full voyage to wherever he was taking his ship, I would just jump ship and hide. I would make the best of a bad bargain.

America would be my destination. Going to Australia would be much too long of a voyage. The West Indies, I had heard, were too hot and full of diseases. When my brother would find out that I had gone to America, he would think I had sunken to a new low and would be glad to be rid of me. He would never try to find me.

No one in England ever pursued anyone who went to America. The only exceptions were wealthy merchants who couldn't bear to let someone cheat them by failing to pay debts. This was not my problem.

Why America? There was little thought that manifested this decision. I knew of neighbors who had sailed for America to make their fortunes or to escape the law. Because England had bountiful trade with the colonies, I knew there were frequent ships sailing from Liverpool.

Without any practical considerations, I packed up what little I owned and went to Liverpool. In a couple of days, I learned that timing was critical. If a would-be sailor waited until a ship was just about to sail or was overdue for a scheduled departure because the captain was short of the necessary crew, anyone willing to sail could sign on.

As Providence ordained it, I found such a ship. The *Sultan*, though fully prepared, was four days overdue for its scheduled departure. Just looking at the *Sultan* made me queasy. I did not like the smell of tar. I did not like the spiderweb of the ship's lines or the height of the mast. When I told the captain that I wanted to sail only one way, that I would work hard and cause no trouble, he had no intention of wasting time with me.

Although grumpy, belligerent, and hostile, he kept arguing with me and finally said that he would decide about leaving me in America once we got there, if I had not incurred any debts owed to the ship in the crossing.

Little did I know how serious a threat that could be.

I signed on.

1773

January 6

In Kingswood, the school master encouraged us to improve our writing so that we could record our outstanding accomplishments as adults. He insisted that all great men kept journals; and he said that by reflecting on our thoughts and actions, we would improve in the eyes of God. Back then I did not think that God was watching, and I never had much expectation that I would be counted among the "great men."

By deciding to sail to America I had already embarked on a great adventure. There may be some advantage in creating a record of my activities—certainly not a day-to-day diary—examining my thoughts by facing them on the written page.

January 7

I might have spent my life as a minister of the Gospel. That would have suited my father.

"Luke. It is way past time that you learn a trade or learn to serve some useful purpose." I can hear my father's pronouncements as clear today as when he spoke them. "You have shown no particular talent for business or any interest in following in my footsteps. My great hope and now my deep disappointment is that the Carr Grist Mill will not be run by both of my sons. I have begun to look for someone who will accept you as an apprentice."

Knowing full well that this topic was not open for discussion with him, I silently resigned myself to whatever that fate might be.

To a large extent my future was left to the whims of fortune. Because I would not train as a merchant, father could not use his connections with friends and associates to procure me an apprenticeship. Chance would dictate what I was to become. And as chance would have it, father encountered the vicar of our church. I am certain that father complained about how unproductive I had become. Perhaps, he just wanted me out of the house. Perhaps, he knew that I would need to be pushed into maturing and to accept responsibility. "I have spoken to

Vicar Wakefield," my father announced. "He is willing to discuss your reading for holy orders and will tutor you to that end."

Mother said nothing.

January 8

I was very near my fourteen birthday. Knowing that I was forever abandoning the family grist mill and because he just hated me, the torments by my brother increased. He yelled at me and threatened physical harm. He belittled my efforts and intelligence. He said that God would never let me be a minister.

February 9

Although I admired the aging vicar, he had been around the parish for as long as I could remember, entering the ministry had never crossed my mind. I couldn't imagine myself preaching—not that I didn't have something to say. A great unknown to me was what a minister did the other six days of the week. But I had no choice. He who cannot do as he would, must do what he can. Father wanted me engaged in some useful activity and out of the house. He was insistent, quite insistent.

February 10

I met the vicar today. He got right to the point. "Luke, have you been called to the ministry?"

Being called to the ministry had no meaning to me.

"All I know," I told him, "is that my father sent me and cautioned that I had better be attentive and learn well."

Vicar Wakefield laughed. "Well, Luke, I admire your father and if he sent you that is as good a start as any. Maude, my housekeeper, has made a room for you over the barn. Go put your belongings up there and come back. We will get started."

My corner in the attic had an old bed and chest. The attic was dark, moldy, and drafty. In the day's light I could see sunlight through the warped roof boards. In heavy rains, my corner got wet.

When I returned, the vicar outlined what he expected me to study and what he expected me to do. I had no quarrel about the domestic chores around his house, caring for the animals in the barn, and tending his herb and vegetable garden. I was less certain about dealing with the readings and how I was going to interpret them in light of my religious skepticism. Many questions that I had dared not ask at home troubled me: Why would God destroy his whole creation in a great flood? Why did he permit suffering and wars? How could Mary have conceived Jesus if Joseph was not the father? How could Jesus have risen from the dead?

The vicar told me that the House of Bishops had been arguing about the need for a prescribed course of ecclesiastical studies for the ministry and some day they would approve one in convention. But, for now the reading and the training was up to him.

"Your preparation for holy orders will focus on reading and rereading scriptures. You will have to be able to explain the design of each book and be able to interpret difficult passages. We will study prophecies, the divinity of Christ, church history, and examples of outstanding sermons." From his own library he loaned me Bishop Pearson's *Exposition of the Creed,* Bishop Burnett's *Exposition of the Thirty-Nine Articles,"* Dr. Wheatley's *On the Common Prayer,* and St. Chrysostom's *On the Priesthood.*

I soon had doubts about ever qualifying for ordination. I desperately tried not to make this show, but I found most of the reading not worth a button.

"We will concentrate initially," he pronounced, "on the Gospel According to St. Luke. Since you share his name, perhaps you should share his understanding of our Lord."

There was no choice. My own father would not have me back in the house. My brother treated me as an indentured servant. He thought my doing chores in a barn that stunk of cow manure was just what I deserved.

February 12

As my lessons unfolded I began to enjoy reading St. Luke, but I did not do well when the vicar probed my understanding. He tried to make me see deeper meaning and always challenged me to apply the lesson to daily living. I suspect he was preparing me to teach others, but I just didn't get it.

The vicar had to straighten me out about many stories in the Bible. For instance, I explained that the verses about the sower in Luke: 8 were to provide advice about farming—plant seeds only in good soil. He asked me what the lesson was in the story about the father and his prodigal son (Luke: 5) who squanders his inheritance while his brother labored; in this story, the prodigal son is honored by his father when he returns home. He wanted me to tell him what that story had in common with the one that described the Pharisee who had done so much good and the tax collector who was a sinner (Luke: 18). Jesus freed the tax collector from all blame. I was certain that I understood these stories. They tell us that life is unfair.

The vicar patiently explained, "My son, these stories are not literal examples but parables that were intended to teach us how we should behave. St. Luke frequently reported that Jesus did the unexpected, like celebrating the repentant prodigal son and the tax collector. These stories are about humility and forgiveness."

I think the vicar tried to make me feel less dimwitted by saying that often the disciples of Jesus did not have a clue what Jesus was talking about or why he did the things he did. However, I didn't feel better about my own confusion nor my being so wrong so much of the time.

February 16

Many people think St. Luke was a doctor because he recorded so many events in Jesus' life where he cured the sick. I marveled at these miracles and how it could be possible to cure the sick without the use of herbs, purgatives, or bleeding. Vicar Wakefield always took me on his visits to the sick. Since many of his parishioners never called for a doctor, the vicar treated them with herbs from his garden. He insisted that I memorize the name of every one of them and how to prepare them in teas, poultices, and salves.

February 18

Today we visited a man who had been bedridden for several weeks. His skin was covered with sores and ugly boils. With every movement he moaned in pain. The bedroom smelled of urine and rot. While I could barely breathe and had to look away frequently to avoid loosing control of the contents of my stomach, the vicar seemed to have none of these problems. He would sit on the edge of the bed, put his hand on the man's arm, quietly recite several prayers and listen patiently to whatever the old guy said.

When we left the old man's house, I asked the vicar, "Sir, how can you stand visiting Amos? He depresses me. He is unkempt, he smells, and he mumbles nonsense. Yet, you visit him faithfully every week."

"Luke, visiting the sick, the depressed, the suffering

is an important part of my work."

"I don't think I could do that week after week."

"Is Amos less worthy than other parishioners?"

"He seems useless to me. He doesn't hold a job, at least not for long. Most people would cross the street to avoid speaking to him—just avoid getting close to him."

"Why do you think Amos suffers?"

"I have no idea. He must have committed some sin that tortures him."

"In your reading of St. Luke's Gospel, do you remember any stories of Jesus tending the unattractive, sinners, those that other people shunned?"

"Well, yes. He associated with tax collectors (nobody likes them), beggars, people possessed by demons, foreigners, those who were not Jews, an outcast woman who had chronic bleeding and leprosy."

"If our Lord and Master worked with all conditions of men and administered to them, then should not we, who are his ministers, do the same?"

"I suppose so, but there is nothing we can do for Amos. If he wanted to take a productive role in our community, he could."

"Maybe not, Luke. We don't know what has caused his suffering and he might not be capable of just turning his life around. Our role is to show him that we care, that God cares. We can bring him food, visit, listen. We can pray with him and share his suffering."

"How long must we continue to minister to Amos? Must we help him until he gets better?"

"Luke, some people never get better. But we will try to help him beyond his current state. That is the work which calls us to the ministry."

March 10

Two aspects of my time with the vicar that I most enjoyed: tending his garden—mainly learning about the medical properties of the herbs he grew—and visiting some interesting parishioners. I dare admit that that I did not like visiting some of them.

March 12

Plants, I have decided, have an inherent magic of their own. They are a marvel of creation. They emerge from the earth with the first warmth of spring. They burst with rain into lush green or spectacular colors. Many have intricate designs and heavenly aromas. They are not confused as we often are about who they are or why they exist. They nourish us with food and flavor for our tables, tend to the sick and injured, lift our spirits with their beauty, and delight our souls with their wonder.

The vicar always brought herbs with him when he went to visit the sick. I would watch carefully what he did with them. But, most of what I learned about plants I learned from Maude. We often tended the garden together. She would get her rotund body in between the rows of plants, not crushing any of them, and hum some melody that she must have learned as a girl. While we worked she would quiz me on the names of plants and their uses. She would try to stump me. I quickly learned the differences in the shapes and textures of the leaves. Soon, she was able to randomly lay samples of plants in front of me and I could identify them even with my eyes closed by their aroma and the feel of the leaves.

Some were easy: the greenish brown anise seeds with their aroma of licorice; the citrus smell of lemon balm, the spicy scent of mustard. Maude would rehearse me until I knew their uses: anise for strong flavoring and useful for indigestion and colds; lemon balm for salads, tea, and steeped in wine for the sting of wasps and bees; mustard to rub onto roasting meat and made into a plaster for colds in the chest.

Other herbs were more challenging. I could not always distinguish just by their pale yellow flowers marjoram from thyme, but I knew that thyme could be used for shortness of breath and marjoram for nervous complaints. Maude could do marvelous things with both as seasonings in poultry dishes and soups. One day while I was watching her make soap using the crushed grayish-green leaves of sage, which she said "made it soothing," I asked her how she would describe its distinctive odor. "Sage is the smell of summer," she pronounced.

The timing of when to harvest roots, flowers, and leaves, Maude taught me, makes a difference in how therapeutic they are—roots of annuals should be dug up before the flowering period, perennials in the late fall or early spring, and leaves while the plant is in full flower.

She also showed me how to make infusions by steeping herbs in boiling water; for example, makinge mint tea for nausea. To treat a persistent cold I had she made a mustard plaster, spreading the paste on linen and putting in on my chest until my skin turned bright red. For the vicar, who developed leg sores, she made a poultice with bread on which she had sprinkled flour; she then stirred the bread into boiling milk and spread the paste on a rag. The paste was then set on the sores. When a neighbor's child, having disturbed a wasp's nest, got badly stung, Maude made a salve from onion and turpentine.

She told me she learned about herbs from her mother and grandmother. The vicar borrowed these treatments from Maude whenever he visited previously diagnosed parishioners. If he hadn't diagnosed a person, he just carried vinegar or garlic cloves to ward off miasmas and all sorts of infections, or he brought a jar of willow tea. He liked to apply sliced onion to the feet of the ill to draw out what was making them sick. Mostly, he listened, tried to improve their spirits, and told them about the cures reported in the Bible of those who believed.

The miracles of growing plants are fascinating. I am intoxicated by their rich colors and heady aromas. I love to be out in the warmth of the sun getting my hands dirty and my lungs filled by the freshness of the soil. I am most at peace when I am working in the garden.

Had I been confined to the laborious readings and strained discussions of theology, I would have run off a long time ago.

March 15

I have grown to believe that most of the sick visited by the vicar benefit more from the herbs than from his telling them about miracle cures in the Bible.

March 20

We had been discussing Burnett's *Exposition on the Thirty-Nine Articles* when the vicar stopped in mid-sentence. It was a painfully long moment before I looked up, suddenly emerging from my haze of inattentiveness.

"Luke, it is time we face your future. Your study has stalled. There is no life in your efforts—only shallow reasoning and meek understanding of what you read. We should terminate your preparation for ordination."

There was no anger in his voice—only disappointment and, perhaps, sorrow.

On the other hand, I was struck dumb with panic. *He is going to send me back to my father or, worse, to my brother*, I thought. I am a-dying. My life is over. I had best run off and hope to survive as a farmhand. At least I knew how to tend animals.

"What do your really want to do?"

I sat in silence unsure what to say. I didn't want to say anything that would anger him and cause my condemnation.

"The only thing that seems to interest you, Luke, is the garden. You have memorized every herb and its properties for both cooking and medicine."

It was true. He patiently drew me out to admit my lack of interest in the ecclesiastical readings and to acknowledge that I really didn't want to be a minister.

"You are young, Luke. You need to explore, to face challenges, to discover who you are. Perhaps, then you will know what you want to be."

I repeated these words again and again as I lay on my bed looking up through the cracks in the roof at the moon, whose light flickered on and off as the clouds moved across it. What did I want to do?

March 21

He asked me the same question again today. I told him, honestly, that I did not know what I wanted to be, but that I felt restless, confounded. I wanted an adventure, some excitement. I had to get away from Kingswood.

When he pressed me again, I thought I would shock him by declaring that I wanted to go to America. I hadn't really thought about it. And it didn't ruffle him in the least.

"Many have left England determined to find something new. I don't know what they found," he confessed, "but they rarely come back. The colonies are young and in need of everything, I hear. So, there may be opportunities there. You will have to find out how to get there and you will just have to run off."

I couldn't believe he had actually suggested this.

"My advice is that you don't announce your intention; your father would not be pleased. I will explain later to him that the Lord called you to America. You might be surprised to learn that James Blair went to Virginia as a missionary and started a college in Williamsburg. Timothy Cutler was ordained by the Bishop of Norwich and became the rector of Christ Church in Boston—of all the forsaken places to end up. I will write you a letter of introduction to Ezra Stiles who resides in the colony of Rhode Island. This might help you to get started. Reverend Stiles could have had a prestigious job as a minister in the Anglican Church in Newport but chose to become the minister of the 2nd Congregational Church instead. Almost anything can happen in the colonies. It might be just the place for you to go. I will write the letter tonight. You should make haste on the morrow while the spirit moves you and before I come to my senses and conclude that this is a bad idea."

The next day I was on my way to Liverpool without even a goodbye to Maude. With Vicar Wakefield's letter in my sack, America beckoned.

Once I had figured out how to sign on as a seaman, my goal was to reach Rhode Island. I liked the idea that

Rhode Island had functioned with extensive independence using its privileges granted by the charter of 1662. It had been founded on religious freedom and tolerance. I concluded that since the days of Roger Williams it must have attracted free thinkers, those who might be thought of as rebels. I fashioned myself at fourteen as one of those free thinkers, a bit of a nonconformist. Rhode Island sounded inviting.

As I stood paralyzed in place on the pier in Portsmouth, the *Sultan* loomed up before me. She was a monster, certain to eat me alive. I feared that I would not excel here but convinced myself that I would find a way to survive. I talked my way aboard the *Sultan* and set sail.

March 27

Some miracle intervened that saved me from certain death on this voyage.

I bore the torture of scorching sun and bone-numbing cold; of being constantly soaked, caked in salt brine, smelling like one of the rats that infested the ship, and worn to points of exhaustion that I never thought possible. I also had to succumb to the torments of ignorant officers and the crude and vulgar taunts of the rest of the crew. They did not take kindly to landlubbers who had no knowledge whatsoever of ships and the sea. The misery that I suffered was so destructive that I have blocked the memories until now. Perhaps, writing about it will purge the trauma from my mind and I can be free of the nightmares.

Storms at sea teach a man how insignificant he is. Nothing compares to this challenge to body and soul. Several weeks out, we began to experience the cold. I was certain that icebergs would suddenly appear and crush us. It grew colder and colder. Then we got bombarded with slanting sleet and hail. We could not furl the sail; our hands and feet were too numb. The rigging was coated with ice and the wind flattened us with every attempted step. Squalls came in succession and lightning bolted from the heavens. As the gale intensified the ship continued to be tossed, as if caught like Odysseus' ship in the whirlpool of Charybdis. The *Sultan* heeled to starboard until she appeared to be sailing on her side. The end of the yard arm was inches above the water. Spray flew over the ship. The masts were in grave danger of snapping.

The sea rose to fearful heights. It occurred to me that were I lost at sea no one would know or care. Only the anguish of the moment kept me from lying down at once to die. I was convinced some mindless force or Poseidon himself was determined to destroy the *Sultan* and was outraged that we had, so far, survived. My suffering could not have been more intense.

I was convinced that all that had been said about me was true. By running off I had hurt my father, was too ignorant to study for the ministry and had wasted the vicar's time and efforts. Now on board ship, I am not the man of action that I have imagined myself to be.

April 10

The most hateful event on this voyage was witnessing a flogging. When the cry went out, "All hands witness punishment, ahoy!" we had to assemble and face a cruel spectacle.

This time I knew the man who would be flogged, had battled the sea with him and eaten at the same table. Watching Sam being tied to the grating, his shirt stripped from him, I knew that the punishment could as easily have been mine. When you live under omnipotent authority, punishment is arbitrary. There is no appeal. The crime Sam was guilty of was fighting on deck. I can hardly write about this without trembling.

The cat-o-nine tails were whipped with full force against this poor man's back. The cutting, hissing sound was repeated again, again, and again, as the rest of us stood breathlessly silent. Drawn to and repulsed by the spectacle, I had to look away more than once. When the final blow was struck, Sam limped off, doubled up in pain.

The captain called for the next victim. He was a seventeen-year-old lad who had simply been caught in the midst of the fray. He pleaded with the captain to no avail. The boy howled with each blow as the welts and blood appeared on his back. The boy asked for salve to dress his wounds when the flogging was over; the captain denied this request. I can feel the boy's anguish to this day. I wished I had some herbs to help heal his wounds, but I had none. I did bathe his wounds with salt water to promote healing.

If I am going to survive, I have to swallow my arrogance. Nonexistent is the opportunity on this voyage to exert my mettle and prove myself worthy. I will hold my tongue.

April 23
Scared of living but miraculously still alive.

In a rolling sea, I responded to the command to haul in the fore-topgallant sail. Scrambling up the rigging and out onto the halyards, I was feeling confident, pleased with my increasing skill and newfound agility.

My confidence soon dissipated. The *Sultan* swayed like a hammock as the sea crashed against it from starboard, ripping across the deck. As I held on to the lines with all my strength, I heard a sharp cry just above me. Looking up I spotted Samuel about midway on the halyard, holding on with only his right hand. I could not tell for certain whether he was grasping a line or whether his hand was tangled. His body flapped back and forth like the sail he was sent to secure. He yelled for help. No one could reach him. As another huge wave engulfed the ship, he fell fifty feet to the deck. He made no sound as he plummeted but when he crashed upon a bulkhead the crack of his shattering backbones was undeniable. I stared, terrorized.

As I began to secure sail, the *Sultan* lurched, crashing down from a swell. I fell instantly from the footropes some twenty feet to the sheets of the fore-topsail below. By the Grace of God, my imminent death on deck was prevented as I found myself tangled in canvas and line. Disoriented, I knew I had to free myself before tumbling further. I was able to reach my knife and began to cut my left arm and legs free.

My left hand could now grasp a line and I struggled to cut the final line that held my right leg. The *Sultan* lurched again and my knife slipped and sliced deep into my thigh. I felt no pain until I was lowered to the deck and taken below.

Within hours every part of my body ached. I was certain that my ribs had been cracked. My hammock neighbor, Toby, wiped the blood from the knife wound and offered me a sip of rum. He alone showed concern.

In four days the wound was red, swollen, and festering. Some thought this a sign that healing had already begun. Between my aching ribs and nearly immobile right leg, I could do no work. No one with medical knowledge was on board; it didn't matter. There is little sympathy or attention on vessels such as this one. Doing your duty is what is expected.

In time, my ribs hurt less. More than once I opened the wound to drain the laudable puss. I am thankful to have been spared an ugly death from a fall to the deck, but I will carry the scar on my thigh forever.

April 25
By the Grace of God or some other guiding force, I am still alive. Neither the fury of the sea nor the *Sultan* herself killed me when I fell from the fore-topsail. But, I felt changed. My encounter with death has left me feeling that my true destiny lies ahead. I am no longer suffocating with despondency.

April 30
Except for an occasional Sunday, there is no break from work onboard. A regular "salt" is not expected to think for himself; he is relentlessly ordered—tar, grease, oil, varnish, scrape, scrub, furl, brace, make and set sail. The dirtier he looks and the worse he smells the more he is thought to be doing his share.

The first mate, or THE MATE as he prefers to be called, showed no regard for the men. Each man tows the mark or is severely punished. When the first mate is incensed at something or someone, he deprives the whole crew of whatever he wishes: a ration of rum or time below deck to warm up and dry off, even if after a double watch and saving the ship in a tempest. On land, he is probably of little consequence; but while at sea, he is Caesar, Attila and Hannibal combined.

Of all those in authority, the first mate was the most reprehensible. As a tyrant he was enough to make Job swear. While I avoided him whenever I could, he and I intensely disliked one another. He was tall with a nut brown beard and broad brow. His skin was dark as weathered oak. Each muscle was as hard as the iron in the ship's anchor. He never walked on the deck—he swaggered. Every rasping word was a grumble, a curse, and a challenge to intimidate, belittle, and convince you that you were stupid, lazy, and worthless. He found more for us to do than there were things to get done. Only the captain liked him, and many a day we were not certain of that.

He watched me for any excuse to use his handspike to motivate me with a knock to the side of the head or, preferably for him I am sure, to order me flogged. I soon learned not to seek redress of a grievance for anything— bad food, unfair work assignments, or refusal to provide free-time on Sundays. I learned never to ask him questions. He expected absolute obedience and deference. Any time I passed him, I was expected to look down and to doff my cap.

Such haughty arrogance riled me to no end.

Jack Tar is a slave aboard a ship. No convict in prison has fewer liberties, a harsher existence, or more severe punishment.

Our black cook, who, if he liked you, would do special favors like drying your shirt near his fire or permitting you to light your pipe. He warned me about the first mate:

"Don't cross the man, Luke. He play the devil with you, sure o' dat.

You might better be afraid. You think you knows, but I've seen him get his way."

The old cook was right. The first mate was insufferable, pompous, vane, and dangerous.

May 6
Standing the night watch is terrifying. Given control of the helm is an awesome responsibility for an ordinary seaman. My first few times nearly frightened me to death and left me totally exhausted.

When I had to face a storm, I felt the safety of the ship and its entire crew was in my hands. The officer of the deck was never far, but that brought me little comfort. Each time was a test of courage.

Moonless nights in a calm sea were worse. I felt utterly alone. When there are no stars to provide company or guide you, the mind takes you wherever it wants. I tried to conjure up pleasant images to distract me, yet I found that effort was more likely to take me deep within myself.

On such becalmed nights, the ship makes few sounds. Even the sea rests. The silence is overwhelming. At times I was certain that I was the only man alive in the universe. I was in a place of desolation—isolated. The darkness closes in, encouraging a dread of what lies just beyond the bow. The mind begins to imagine sea monsters swimming alongside the ship. Occasionally, a wave of effervescence washes nearby, further convincing the trembling soul that a sinister end is near. When the moon briefly breaks through the dense clouds, all sorts of grotesque shapes descend from above.

And yet, it is precisely on these nights that I experienced the most introspection. Activities on board normally prohibit any reflective thought. Life is nothing but reaction to the moment.

One discovery I made was that I was no longer suffocating. That is why I had taken flight from Kingswood, my abusive brother, and the vicar's boring lessons. I had come to realize that I might survive this voyage—in part as a result of my own wits. My destiny was not dependent on the stars. A real captain takes command of himself and then of his ship and crew. He sails on to his destination with whatever winds and storms come his way.

I stood alone at the helm on those nights, but I was beginning to feel fortified with purpose.

May 10

When I arrived in Rhode Island I made my way to Newport and delivered my letter of introduction to the Reverend Izra Stiles. He examined me for some time without saying a word. Whatever the vicar had said about me probably provided few answers to who I was or what I was doing there. However, Reverend Stiles kindly referred me to the minister at King's Church in Providence who arranged for me to stay with Mrs. Angell, a parishioner of his. She graciously provided me with board and lodging but insisted that I help tend her garden, feed the animals, and do other chores as she determined. I was delighted to have shelter and an opportunity to discover how I might be gainfully employed. She would have none of that, insisting that I was too young to take up a fulltime trade and must attend school. She was not moved by my protests.

May 22

My first days at Mrs. Moore's school convinced me that going to school was worse than studying with the vicar. I was the oldest among seven pupils. The youngest was only eight. Mrs. Moore was pleasant enough, but I was bored and needed to get on with my life. I spent most of my time plotting how to get out of going to school.

May 28

The need to make a living was paramount. But what could I do? What did I want to do? Was it time to do as my father had wanted for me and become a merchant? My options as I saw them:

Blacksmith—always a need but I am not strong enough.
Tailor—not much opportunity here except for

making common, everyday attire. More and more
colonists are importing clothing from England.
Printer—would have to move to the city, dirty work.
Bookbinder—would have to move but would have
access to lots of books. A possibility.

I could learn a trade by taking on another four- to
seven-year commitment as an apprentice. Was this an
opportunity to go to sea? Much might be learned by
going to sea, but after sailing here the only allure of the
sea was from the shore.

Feeling sanguine about this dilemma, I shared my
concerns with Mr. Fisher at his shoemaker shop. Dr.
Randall overheard and invited me to visit with him on
the morrow. After listening to my confused prattling,
he asked me if I were interested in studying medicine.
This possibility had not crossed my mind. I did know a
little about herbs from working in the vicar's garden. Dr.
Randall needed help and wanted to draw patients from
Pawtuxet, but he did not want to waste time in traveling
from Providence.

I hesitated, not wanting to take on a long apprenticeship, but I needed money. . . .

In a most generous offer, he said he would make me
his assistant. "I expect that you will do all of those tasks
required of an apprentice but I anticipate that I will soon
be able to perform minor medical services in the Village.
I will pay you a small sum and as business from the

Village increases I will continue to improve your wages." He committed to educating me beyond the normal scope of an apprentice and that in two or three years I might become his assistant. He tempted me with "inheriting" his practice, since he had no sons.

I was overwhelmed. Without weighing all of this, as I should have, I accepted on the spot. He drew up a standard agreement, writing in all of the provisions he had outlined, including the idea that I would be treated as an assistant. The agreement said nothing about inheriting his practice, but I believed he was sincere about this possibility, and I did not want to confront him about it. The agreement stated that he would teach me the art and mystery of physic or medical art and provide room and board in exchange for my services.

As was the common practice, we both signed the agreement, which was written in duplicate on a single sheet of paper. The agreement was torn in half with each of us getting a copy. I understand this practice protected both parties. If the agreement got challenged in court, the matching indentations proved the document to be genuine.

June 5

Dr. Randall suggested that I first accompany him on visits to his patients to be certain that I really wanted to study medicine. One patient I remember in particular. She had been sick for many weeks and was treating her stomach pains with sassafras.

When the pains got worse, Mrs. Barnes, a neighbor, had prepared her special poultice, which some say cures everything. It did not. Friends said Mrs. Briggs was growing weak, unable to eat much of anything. She drank only clear liquids. She took to bed with fever. Her husband feared that she was dying. In desperation he summoned Dr. Randall, who came in an instant. He told Mr. Briggs that he had to give her a purgative made from jalop and calomel twice a day for three days. During my visit to her with Dr. Randall, he bled her and ascertained that she was getting nourishment.

Miraculously, her strength began to return. Within a fortnight she was out of bed and performing her household duties. Whether by the Grace of God or Dr. Randall's interventions, I will never know for certain what caused the reversal of her misfortunes, but I believed, then and now, that it was the work of Dr. Randall. Perhaps, Providence had ordained him to tend the sick. I wanted to be like him.

June 10

Dr. Randall was true to his word. I began work and my medical education immediately.

I started to assist him in tending his herb garden, compounding medications, rolling out pills, cleaning his medical instruments, preparing bandages, treating ulcers and boils, changing dressings, preparing plasters, and restraining patients during minor surgery.

He suggested that to get a real medical education that I should attend medical school. There were probably only eight doctors in Rhode Island who had been university trained. Dr. Randall was not one of them. He suggested that I attend the Philadelphia Medical College or go to London or Edinburgh. I had no money do this; he could not afford to send me. "You are a perfectly good doctor," I told him. "What would I gain by a course of study at a university?"

University training might provide information about standard treatments, botany, and some chemistry in order to be versed in the composition of medicine. None of this sounded very practical. I might become "learned" but not of any more use to the citizens of Pawtuxet.

I was convinced that I would be bored sitting endlessly in a classroom when I could learn by doing. He laughed, knowing my disposition quite well. "I will teach you some very important principles of medicine. We will create a university education together. You will need to commit to extra time to read difficult texts and to discussing what you are learning with me. I will not tolerate your slacking off."

I agreed.

June 13

When Dr. Randall started my expanded education in the medical arts, he loaned me a copy of the *Aphorisms of Hippocrates.* Our discussions from then on were conducted by him asking me questions. At first, I felt I was being tested, as I had been in primary school as a child. I used to hate that because you either knew the answer or you did not. Often I did not. But with Dr. Randall, it was soon apparent that he was encouraging me to think critically and in greater depth.

Realizing that these sessions were of long-range value to me, I began to record our questions and answers in my notebook so that I could review them from time to time.

"Luke, what causes diseases?"

"According to Hippocrates, people get sick not because God punishes them, though people today pray to be healed just as the people of Hippocrates' time prayed to Aesculapius."

"What do you think causes people to get sick?"

"Bad air, miasmas, an imbalance in the humors."

"Let's explore those. Why do you think bad air or miasmas cause disease?"

"If there is a stench in the air, whatever created that could be harmful."

"Could you prove to me that there is something dangerous in the bad air?"

"No, because we cannot see the air."

"So, you guess that there is disease in the air. Tell me how you would conclude that bad air is the probable cause?"

"If a number of people who live near a swamp or near rotting garbage got sick, I would blame the bad air."

"You also said that illness is caused by an imbalance in the humors. How do you know that someone's humors are not in balance?"

"I don't know. I would assume that imbalance is the problem."

"We will talk more about assumptions later. If you see a patient who is flushed red and whose skin feels hot, what is your diagnosis?"

"An excess of blood."

"How would you treat this patient? "

"Bleed him, Sir."

"What evidence would tell you that your diagnosis was correct?"

"The patient gets well."

"If the patient does not get well, would you bleed him some more? If a little bleeding is good, is a lot of bleeding better? Would you take a pint? A quart? Several quarts?"

"I would continue to bleed the patient until he improved or showed growing signs of weakness."

"Are you following an aphorism of Hippocrates if you stop the bleeding treatment?"

"Yes. Hippocrates said, "First, do no harm.""

"Would you then do nothing? Does Hippocrates give other advice?"

"I would follow Hippocrates by being less aggressive

in my treatment or by trying other procedures that might prove helpful. Hippocrates cautioned that past experience is delusive."

"Because I have seen patients get better after bleeding, those observations might not result in a cure for this patient." He then said that judgment in medicine is difficult. "For instance, I don't think we have absolute guidelines regarding when to bleed or how much blood to take. You just have to try. I would watch the patient carefully. Hippocrates believed that sometimes the body heals itself."

"Do you understand the other three humors and their relationship to Aristotle's views?"

"Besides blood, there is black bile, yellow bile, and phlegm. These correspond to Aristotle's views of: earth, which is cold; air, which is dry; fire, which is hot; and water, which is wet."

"It is not enough to be able to name the humors. How would you recognize other imbalances?"

"Besides an excess of blood, which might make a patient very energetic and warm to the touch, an excess of black bile would make the patient depressed and irritable. Yellow bile would make the patient hot-tempered and violent, while an excess of phlegm would make the patient cold and dull."

June 16
Another educational session with Dr. Randall that had a

lasting impression on my thinking was based on Galen's *On the Uses of the Parts of the Body.* Thanks to the throne of God, Dr. Randall did not require that I read all twenty-two volumes of Galen's work based on his vivisection of animals. Galen's opinions were paramount for 1,300 years. In fact, he was considered to be the final word on medicine, and still is in the minds of many.

"Luke, what assumptions does Galen make in his voluminous studies?"

Dr. Randall never asks the questions that I anticipate. He is always catching me off guard. After some thought, I answered, "Galen says there is a divine master plan."

"Well, then as a doctor you really can't do anything to change what will be . . . ?"

"There is a plan and many of us believe today that 'God's will be done.' That does not mean that a universal force causes or cures disease."

"Do you think Galen made other assumptions?"

"Far be it for me to challenge Galen! But, I wonder whether all he taught us about structure of the body and physiology based on animal vivisection is totally accurate with regard to humans."

"You are wise not to be too vocal in criticizing Galen. Many who refuted him have been attacked as a result. They argue *ad hominen.* If Galen said it, therefore, it must be true. There is a lesson in being cautious with medical opinions. However, Luke, I encourage you to ask skeptical questions. While you may never collect as much data based on your observations as Galen did, taking notes and watching for patterns can prove very useful to your practice."

June 24

"Your patient comes to you with a distended stomach. She complains of discomfort that has lasted for four days. What do you do to make a diagnosis?" Dr. Randall challenged.

"I wouldn't need to do anything. She should be given jalop, calomel, or castor oil as a purgative."

"Slow, down Lukus." (He always called me Lukus when he was perturbed.) "Describe what you should do to get to know this patient."

"I would ask her what she had eaten."

"She tells you that she recently made a large tub of cheese for her family and had eaten a lot of it herself."

"That's it! She is constipated and needs a purgative."

"Isn't your conclusion *post hoc, ergo propter hoc*, since you reason that the latter must have been caused by the former? Are there other questions that you should ask?"

"I would ask her when she had her last bowel movement."

"Anything else?"

"I would ask if she had been drinking water. I would ask if she were pregnant."

"If you generalize the identity of a medical problem

or a treatment to apply to a particular patient, on what do you base your belief?"

"I would be following Francis Bacon in *Novum Organum*—the treatise you had me read."

"Elaborate on that. Can you explain your reasoning?"

"Bacon believed we could infer conclusions based on experience and observation. But he said you had to go beyond observation to really figure it out."

"Are there dangers in relying on the type of analysis that you have described?"

"We need to assure ourselves that the information we are using is relevant and that we understand how we have answered the questions that led us to the conclusion. Hippocrates, for instance, inferred that stagnant water was associated with malaria. He concluded that if you drank the water, you got malaria. Now we know that the cause of the problem is not the result of drinking the water; it is the bad air around the swamp. We should always consider a contrary point of view."

"In the previous case, didn't you immediately infer that the woman was constipated?"

"Yes, Dr. Randall, I did."

"What if the patient told you that she didn't want the treatment you had prescribed?"

"I would do what is best for the patient."

"Let's say a patient comes to you with a mangled hand. You tell him the hand must be amputated. He tells you he will never be able to apply his trade again. He insists that his hand will heal and refuses the amputation. Your previous answer would suggest that you would amputate anyway. Would you?"

"Yes, amputation would save his life."

"Do you have a moral obligation to follow the patient's wishes?"

"The patient's point of view needs to be considered, but my moral obligation is to do whatever needs to be done to save life."

"What if the man's wife agreed that the hand should not be amputated? What if the man's neighbor told you that he knew your patient well, that he is tough and that he would likely survive? What if the man's minister or another surgeon pleaded that you had no right to impose your medical decision? Would you amputate anyway?"

"Dr. Randall, you are raising many hypothetical challenges. But, I suppose other points of view need to be weighed. I need to think about this. I'm less confident about this amputation than I was a few minutes ago."

June 30
When I reread the notebooks that recorded the dialogue and comments from my apprenticeship and my education in thinking about medical problems, I am amazed at how much I had learned. Frankly, I left a number of sessions vexed at Dr. Randall's persistent probing and endless questions. Although I kept a stiff upper lip and an air of confidence, I felt impugned. He never told me

that I had gotten it right. He never even smiled or nodded his head to acknowledge my answer.

At the end of this series of educational sessions, I told Dr. Randall that I was grateful that he had given me so much information and so many answers to problems during my training with him. His response was typical. "I just asked questions. You knew the answers or you figured them out."

"The process of discovering answers myself," I told him, "has made the study of medicine, in retrospect, very exciting, and honestly, more challenging than I had expected."

Besides what Dr. Randall had helped me to understand about thinking through problems over my impetuous inclination to jump to conclusions, he also taught me to get to know each patient.

"Listen to him. Find out how long the symptoms have been present. Ask many questions. Many patients don't want to show more weakness by complaining. Touch. Feel for places on the body that are hard, or soft and tender, or that evoke pain. Observe a patient's breathing, skin color, how he walks, how his urine smells. He repeatedly told me that what the patient believes makes a massive contribution to his improvement or to his decline.

July 3
When I finished my formal apprenticeship and education and had been treating more and more patients on

my own, Dr. Randall told me that he had a gift for me.

Before getting to the gift, he couldn't resist reminding me that my thinking should follow a certain sequence:

1. Use experience
2. Link what you remember
3. Group the information into patterns
4. Reason
5. Propose tentative conclusions
6. Test them in your practice
7. Be willing to admit that while you might feel you have all the answers, they could be the wrong ones

The only tool he added that we had not discussed was intuition. He assured me that, while we had never discussed it, intuition can lead to the right answers. He also told me that he believed there was a power in intuition that should not be totally ignored. I had never seen him do anything based on intuition nor had he ever mentioned it.

Just when I thought that I knew Dr. Randall very well, that I knew how he thought, how he practiced medicine, what he valued, he surprised me again. He took from his pocket a box that contained a stone with a most unusual appearance. Roughly rectangular and only about two inches wide, it was the color of dried blood and sparkled with flecks of gold. A shaman had given it to him. (He had never mentioned any acquaintance with a shaman). He had been told the stone embodied fire, earth, sky, and water, and that it gave healing powers to the one who possessed it. He told me he also believed the stone had power to purify the spirit. This philosopher's stone, he attested, was not just a stone but a connection to the Creator and Creation and contained elements of positive and negative forces, elements of hot and cold, male and female qualities.

"Luke," he cautioned, "there is still much about the human body and about disease that we do not know. Some of the great alchemists, like Henrich Agrippa from the Middle Ages; the French alchemist Nicolas Flamel, who is said to have created the philosopher's stone; and Paracelsus, a distinguished forefather of medicine, learned about transformative processes and transmutations in the natural world. The stone, which I now give to you, will help you to learn, will give you new insight, and will make you more effective in your practice of medicine."

He had carried the stone since he was a young man and now he wanted me to have it.

July 11

Since terminating my studies with the vicar in Kingswood, I have had no interest in returning to the church. But, now I have decided to begin attending King's Church in Providence. Something is missing in my life.

Needed is a sense of community, something special to lift up the routines of ordinary days and my increasing self-centered isolation.

I have always thought that the order provided by Anglican services was comforting. The order of predictable words being said in the same prayers, the beauty of the language, and the repetition of the liturgical year, each leading inexorably to the next: Advent, Christmas, Epiphany, Lent, Easter; then the cycle returns. The established pattern is health-promoting. This worship unifies us with the mother church and England—its history and tradition.

I have procrastinated long enough. I am going to do this.

July 15

Rumors stream out of Boston like fishing boats leaving the dock. Some time ago, I can remember we got conflicting accounts of the so-called Boston massacre. Those traveling by stage suggested soldiers of the Crown had gunned downed eleven (some reported twice that number) innocent citizens in the streets. Eyewitnesses said that citizens had been taunting the British soldiers by calling them "blood backs" and "lobster sons of b–" and by throwing snowballs at them. We were told that the fire bells rang and many came out of their homes to see what was happening.

Captain Preston, who was on duty at the time, tried

to calm the crowd that might have consisted of four hundred people. No Riot Act had been read but someone fired a shot and some unknown number were killed or wounded—near anarchy erupted.

Many of my neighbors were outraged at the time. Rumor had it that Captain Preston would be put on trial. The occupation of Boston put everyone on edge. We prayed that we would not have to suffer a similar indignity here.

We must learn from these incidents. Rumors should not be treated as fact. High sentiments need to be quelled and put to rest.

July 18

I have been reluctant to commit to paper what I know about the *Gaspee* incident and my involvement. The fear of a charge of treason hangs over the Village. Dread of severe retribution caused us to take a vow of silence. Now it appears I can chance recording my participation in my private journal. . . .

Just when I think that I am personally safe from any political involvement of this colony in its disagreement with Parliament, I find myself right in the middle. They banged on my door well after midnight yelling, "Come, quick. He's been shot. Bring your kit."

Well, I had no idea of who had been shot, though I was soon to discover. There were several men with Ephraim Bowen, who had summoned me, but I could not make them out. Their hats were drawn low over their heads. That much I could see by the flickering light of the lamps, which they held as they led me through dark, moonless streets to the home of Joseph Rhodes on Stillwater Lane.

The patient turned out to be Lieutenant William Dudingston, Captain of the *Sloop Gaspee*. I knew him by the hateful reputation he had achieved since taking command of the *Gaspee* in 1768. He was propped up in a far corner. His blood had soaked through the sleeve of his left arm and groin area. He mumbled incoherently in pain.

As I began to examine Dudingston, I learned that he allegedly had been shot by Joseph Bucklin from one of our long boats that had carried our boarding party. He had lain bleeding on the deck bleeding, pleading for his life. The attackers had met earlier at Sabin's Tavern to plan this expedition. They rowed with muffled oars to the stranded *Gaspee* on Namquid Point, taunted Dudingston, ransacked the ship, and captured the sleeping crew.

John Mawney, one of the raiders, had stopped the bleeding. The wound to Dudingston's left arm did not look serious, though the musket ball had broken the arm. I cleaned up the wound with yarrow and comfrey and splinted the arm. Dudingston was still in considerable pain, cussing the "lawlessness of colonial, drunken sailors."

Other villagers in the room continued to keep their

identities hidden. A couple of them told me not to work too diligently on the Captain. He had been insulting Rhode Islanders by: stealing supplies for the *Gaspee*, such as pigs, poultry, and timber from local farmers; boarding, searching, and seizing merchant ships; and encouraging the impressments of Rhode Islanders into the British Navy all along the coast from Newport to Providence. He was hated, and some would have delighted had he died of his wounds.

I found that the bleeding in Dudingston's groin area had been the result of a musket ball having lodged there. Luckily for him (and perhaps for me) the ball had not penetrated deeply. I fished it out with a probe and my finger; then I treated the wound and bandaged the area with linen. The grateful Dudingston, not so arrogant in this situation, offered me a gold belt buckle, which I refused.

I then withdrew to have a much-needed tankard, too excited from the events to feel the exhaustion that struck me the following day.

July 19

Pawtuxet had been elated by the burning of the *Gaspee*, and no one more than I. Huzzah, huzzah, huzzah! We put one over on the Crown. The King does not rule in Rhode Island!

Considering that everyone seems to know every-thing about their neighbors in this Village, secrecy had been absolute regarding who planned the attack on the *Gaspee*, including the names of those who were in the boarding party and who participated in its burning. With over sixty people directly involved and many more who observed from their windows and from the shore, no one admitted to knowing anything about the incident. The Village has not been as united over anything as they have been over the burning of the *Gaspee*.

In fact, we defeated an eight-gun ship of the Royal Navy with a few muskets and brash courage. Credit goes to Captain Lindsay of the *Hannah* for brilliantly luring the *Gaspee* onto the sandbar, stranding the ship and crew until the change in the tide.

If there is going to be open rebellion against intolerable behavior by the Crown, it is fitting that it comes from Rhode Island. Those in Massachusetts Bay and in other colonies such as Virginia, who feel that they are more politically astute and culturally superior, are now discovering that we in Rhode Island can more than match them man for man. Our success has been widely reported in the newspapers throughout the colonies.

Despite all of this public bravado, there is fear of reprisal. Rumor holds that three regiments of redcoats are being formed to invade and occupy Rhode Island. There are those who call this high treason and that England will retaliate by revoking our charter.

The King issued a proclamation offering £1,000 lawful money to informers and offered a pardon to participants who would bear witness against the leaders of this plot. No one has broken ranks. Remarkable!

For now, we may have conveyed a critical message— Don't Tread on Me.

Our protests against the Stamp Act, the Sugar Act, and Townsend Acts—all of which hurt commerce and threatened our growing prosperity—had no lasting effect. Joining with other colonies on the nonimportation of British goods hurt both sides and could not be sustained. We had been able to ignore these Acts to some degree by smuggling and cleverly finding ways to trade with France, Holland, Spain, and the West Indies, until those fame-seekers like Dudingston, who were obsessed with harassing free shipping in the Bay, came along.

Once again, we have been disobedient, perhaps criminal, despite our just cause. If our vow of silence holds and the British insistence on punishing those responsible for the burning of the *Gaspee* fails, we will be long remembered and celebrated as heroes. If not, we all will be labeled as traitors.

August 13

She smiled at me and that is all it took.

Even at that moment I had been absorbed in Hymn 238: "Now thank we all our God . . ." I was joyfully singing:

> Now thank we all our God
> with heart and hands and voices,
> who wondrous things hath done,
> in whom his world rejoices;
> who from our mother's arms
> hath blessed us on our way
> with countless gifts of love,
> and still is ours today.

I just happened to glance behind me. I had never noticed her sitting across the aisle in the pew near mine. Not wanting to appear either irreverent or too bold in the middle of a hymn, I nodded politely and pretended to be absorbed in the words of the hymn. But, while my lips moved, I could not concentrate. The rest of the service, including a long sermon that, I think, was delivered with passion on a topic I cannot recall, was lost on me.

Later, I discovered from my neighbor where she lived. I am now attending King's Church more regularly.

I find all sorts of excuses to walk down Post Road, past her house, which is near the home of Sylvester and Mary Rhodes. With surprising regularity, we see one another and exchange compliments. Some days, I imagine that she compliments me with more respect than is usual or that I deserve.

Although I am bashful, I more than return the compliment. As I walk on, I rehearse all of the things I might have said—wanted to say.

September 12

Just when I was convinced that Hope's interest in me had waned, her mother invited me to tea. Although wishing this was a promising sign of Hope's interest, I am sure that Mrs. Tucker was expecting to appraise me as a prospect for her youngest daughter.

I am not much of a conversationalist, except with my patients and a few friends at the tavern. Otherwise, I am awkward, uncomfortable, and at a loss for words. Nevertheless, I had to be ready to make a positive impression. I rehearsed. I even wrote little notes of topics that I would bring up and answers I would give.

October 2

Hope is most accomplished on the pianoforte. To her surprise I recognized Handel's *Suite in A Major* and Haydn's *Sonata in C Major.* When asked how I knew Handel, since I did not play an instrument, I told them that Handel had first attracted my attention because his father was a barber-surgeon. I had heard that Handel's anthems were performed for the wedding of Prince Frederick and Princess Anne and his music for the coronation of George II. This was followed by questions regarding my views of Haydn. I do recall saying that I admired the power of his boisterous finales and how he had become an inspiration to others despite his relative isolation caused by his employment to the Esterhazys. I was fortunate that Hope had chosen to play works by Handel and Haydn, since I do not know much about other composers.

All in all, this was an agreeable afternoon. I pray that Mrs. Tucker was not just being polite when she warmly invited me, "Luke, do come to tea again—soon." I glanced at Hope, who looked directly at me with a glimmer in her eye.

Twenty-four hours later I cannot remember a single word that I said. What I do remember are the wonderful sweets and cakes that were served. More particularly, I have a clear image of Hope pouring tea. She is radiant and her smile melts my heart.

I did not sleep a wink last night!

December 21

Dumping over three hundred chests of tea into Boston Harbor was a senseless act of defiance. Harmonious dealing with the East India Company is vital to our prosperity. The Sons of Liberty in Boston are determined to have a fight at any cost. Radicalism is taking control. While we have been getting larger quantities of tea from Holland each year, we still need to trade with the mother country.

This "party" is not about liberty; it is about commerce. We hear that profits in the East India Company are in decline.

Who is behind all of this? Mohawk Indians? Not likely. A plot by Freemasons? More likely it stems from concerns by those like John Hancock, who is rumored to be getting wealthy smuggling tea.

What reprisals will King George invoke? Will any of us be safe now? Could our dispute with the Parliament of Britain be settled by adopting Franklin's Albany Congress Plan of 1754 with its forty-eight elected Grand Council members?

December 23

Moses Brown has freed his seven slaves. Perhaps, he intends by example to get others to do likewise. So far, none of his Quaker friends has freed their slaves. None have stopped consuming rum or refused to purchase goods like milled cotton fabrics that are dependant on slave labor.

Moses may be trying to demonstrate his moral superiority, claiming that enslaving Africans here is repugnant and punishable by God. His view is espoused by a tiny minority. George Washington—as fine an example of a virtuous character as we know—has not freed his slaves. Even Moses' brother John argues against manumission, asserting the right of every man to determine what to do with his property. Those who have been to Africa say that blacks are treated by their black masters there much worse than they are here. Especially in the northern colonies, slaves are cared for with greater Christian kindness than they are in the West Indies. They are better off here.

The Browns do not inspire respect. Despite the

development of manufacturing and the employment provided for the residents of this colony, Moses' brother John deserves little applause. He lords it around in his stately carriage, as much of a show of his person as the need to personally attend to his multiple business interests. Unlike most of us, who hold family above all else, John is not reluctant to embarrass Moses in any forum regarding his antislavery sentiments.

John is arrogant and vindictive. With a desperate need for canons that he could readily produce at the Hope Furnace, John has refused to sell them at any reasonable price to the Continental Congress. He would rather provide them to privateers. While others sacrifice and suffer, he prospers.

We have little chance of winning this conflict with England and of uniting these colonies of America with behavior like John's. We can't afford a merchant prince. I don't begrudge him the wealth he has earned, but we are here to create a new order that is free from the trappings and dispositions of royalty.

December 28

She accepted my proposal of marriage but did so against her father's wishes. He was always polite to me, but I suspect my lack of family and my trade were not, in his mind, worthy of his daughter. But, Hope makes up her own mind.

Our wedding was a glorious celebration. No doubt

this was due to Hope's and Mrs. Tucker's detailed planning.

We had, of course, published our banns at the church three weeks before. This alone stimulated a lot of anticipation among our friends for the party that would follow the wedding. While Mr. Tucker still harbored some hesitancy about the desirability of this marriage (he didn't think I added anything to the social standing of his family), he was not to be outdone in making this a memorable event. He also knew that Hope had made up her mind.

The ceremony itself from the Book of Common Prayer was traditional. The minister led a procession down the center of the Tucker's parlor, which had been nicely decorated with greens, berries, and handmade flowers. With her parents, Hope and I followed the minister; the bridesmaids and bridesmen followed us. Hope wore a lovely yellow dress imported by her father from London, and I wore a dark, new suit—the only one I own. I pledged myself with a ring; we exchanged vows and retired to the neighboring room to begin the celebrations.

There were two white cakes. Hope cut the first piece of cake to ensure fertility, so they say. We ate mine and, as tradition dictates, we saved Hope's cake, which we will sample after the birth of our first child and on each of our anniversaries.

We danced cotillions, minuets, and reels; partook of refreshments—small cakes; and endlessly drank cider, port, and wine. The festivities lasted long into the night, until we were all too weary to go on.

When we retired to bed, our friends followed. We would have been more than delighted to be abandoned at this point, but custom demanded otherwise. Each woman in our party threw a balled-up stocking over her shoulder at the bride, and each man did the same at me. Whoever hit either of us would be the next to marry. Hope's good friend Catherine achieved this honor to the laughter and applause of all.

Finally, we were blessedly alone.

1774

January 12

When Hope and I moved into our new house, one of my first tasks was to build our bed. I had planned for many weeks to make this piece of furniture special. The well-seasoned wood had been selected far in advance. It had once been part of the *Sloop Andromache* that had seen many successful voyages and had brought major profits for its owners. It had withstood great storms as it sailed the oceans of the world.

First, I created a heavy plaster of crushed sea shells, sand, water, and cow hair for the corner walls of the upper room. This was applied to further keep out cold drafts. The corner walls supported two sides of the bed. The posts for the other two sides were beautifully carved.

For her part, Hope had woven a warm, woolen bed carpet that would cover us. In time, we would have enough feathers for a bed sack to lie upon, replacing the one stuffed with hay and cornhusks. We would have curtains around the bed for winter nights.

With great ceremony, we hung a hagstone with a hole in it on the bedpost to ward off nightmares. The bed would always be a special symbol of our union.

January 10

Perhaps it was something I had eaten, but I don't think so. I had a vivid dream of a large black snake, larger than any I had ever seen. It sat curled on a rock in the middle of a path and stared at me. I froze in fright as its forked tongue darted in and out as if sensing whether I was food. Sweat immediately formed on my forehead. My hands became cold. I was looking for a stone to throw at it but, thankfully, it slithered away, this time.

January 24

Whatever is troubling Abraham Waterman has me perplexed. His symptoms do not quite align with any disease with which I am familiar. I have decided to consult with Dr. Carpenter, whose experience far exceeds my own.

Abraham is thirty-five and of a phlegmatic countenance. At one time I thought his sluggishness was an indication of despondency, but having found no cause for this by questioning him, I believe that it is his nature. He complains of shivering, thirst, pain in his back, and a swelling in his right foot. At times he cannot bear to be touched. My examination reveals a swelling so tight that the skin shines and is painful to the touch. I had thought he was developing gout, but the swelling has now appeared on his face. Pustules filled with water have closed one of his eyes.

Dr. Carpenter contemplated my description and agreed that some symptoms resembled those of the gout but that the disease was more likely Saint Anthony's Fire. I asked if the cause might be foul air.

"The likely cause," he told me, "was overheated blood. If someone gets overheated and then lies down on cold, damp ground, he invites St. Anthony's Fire. Cases that I have read about, which occurred in medieval times, were horrible affairs. The disease was similar to leprosy. It consumed people with a feeling as if they were burning. They were plagued with blisters, seizures, and spasms. The disease would destroy limbs—fingers and toes initially—and consume them in a most horrible way with a loathsome rot. The cause in medieval times was thought to be a fungus that infested rye and was ingested by eating rye bread."

"Tell your patient to avoid flesh in his diet, to drink cooling liquids such as barley broth, and to take cooling herbs and fruits. He must avoid strong drink, spices, pickles, and rye bread. He can apply soft flannel to his back and foot but should use no other external application. Give him a dram of nitre with five grains of rhubarb, which should be taken three times a day to keep his belly open. The disease is rarely fatal today, but it tends to reoccur. Your patient should avoid strong passions, exercise regularly, and take mild purgatives such as cream of tartar."

Grateful for his advice, I offered Dr. Carpenter my assistance whenever I might be of service.

February 14

Dr. Comfort Carpenter is a Mason. He often tells me about the enjoyable associations and friendships he has formed as a member of St. John's Lodge in Providence. Many leaders in the community are masons and probably predominate throughout the colonies.

Of late, I have been giving some thought about joining. I know only that they claim to be the largest and oldest fraternity in the world, dating back to the guilds of the Middle Ages. There might be some association with the warrior monks, the Knights Templar, and the Hospitalers; the latter helped to protect pilgrims during the crusades and, over time, became very wealthy and politically powerful. I am intrigued by the serendipitous connection to the order of the Hospital of St. John of Jerusalem (the Knights Hospitalers) that was formed in the 11th century during the crusades. Eventually, in another remarkable coincidence, their stronghold became the Isle of Rhodes.

I don't think there is any militant purpose in their Masonic lodges today, but their membership seems to reflect the politically influential. There is talk about how secretive they are, which makes me uneasy and uncertain. When I asked Dr. Carpenter about this cloud of secrecy, he assured me that it applied only to their ceremonies and ways of identifying one another. I remain skeptical.

They call the head of a lodge "worshipful master," which seems to me to denote religious implications. Dr. Carpenter says this is an old term that means "honorable" and the title of "master" refers to knowledge and leadership. Masons purport that they feel a responsibility for helping others. This is a noble purpose with which I can identify. In fact, I do know Masons that have helped widows and orphans. Mostly, I think, they help one another.

While Dr. Carpenter talks about Masonic activities frequently, he has never asked me to join. I understand the tradition is that no one is asked; you have to petition.

My reasons for joining might not be all that honorable. Although I would not admit it, I would join to be seen among the influential of this colony. I would join for the fellowship. I would join to make contacts for my practice of medicine and hope to get referrals from other Masons. These motivations are not very altruistic but certainly are practical.

I really do not belong to any organization other than the church. I will continue to ponder joining the Masons.

February 21

I have petitioned St. John's Lodge for membership. Dr. Carpenter reported that a group of Masons from St. John's met at Bowen Tavern on the 12th to discuss forming their own lodge in Pawtuxet. I know several of those present: Col. Ephrain Bowen, Jonathan Nichols, Pelog Rhodes, Jonathan Aborn, Christopher Rhodes, and Benjamin Smith.

Should this lodge be formed, it would be of great advantage not to have to travel the five miles to Providence in poor weather.

March 23

I have been accepted by St John's Lodge. My fear was that someone would blackball me. I will be installed or initiated, or whatever they call it, at their next regular meeting.

March 27

Drenched in sweat, I startled out of a restless sleep, shaking. "Luke, are you all right? Hope questioned with deep concern in her voice. "I have been shaking you for several minutes."

She moved closer. "Tell me what happened."

"This time there were three of them. They were huge, ugly, and menacing. They seemed to be conversing with one another, as if planning to attack me. They kept slithering toward me. I kept backing away, but I could not escape. I felt trapped. If you had not awakened me I might have died in my sleep."

"You frighten me, Luke, when you undergo these ordeals. Perhaps, you should talk with our minister about them."

"My panic over snakes goes back a long ways. I fear these dreams must be endured."

"Why do you think so?"

"When I was a child in Kingswood I started to have dreams of snakes. Perhaps, I tortured a snake in some childish game that I never could recall. My mother was not sympathetic and I would never have discussed it with my father who thought I was sapless anyway. Mother finally admitted one day that she had been frightened by a snake while she tended vegetables in the backyard when she was pregnant with me. "When a child is born," she explained, "after a mother has experienced this fear, the child will always fear the animal. Sometimes the baby will have a mark on his body that looks like the animal. I thought for some time that you had an image of a snake on your back."

"She was certain that this was the cause of my snake nightmares and that there was nothing that could change that fact. So far she has been right."

"I still think you should see someone, Luke."

She wrapped her arms around me and encouraged me to go back to sleep.

But I was too agitated.

April 4

Mr. Seth Ward is in exquisite pain from the gout. These fits most often come upon him this time of year. His agony is palpable. Typically, he is seized by pain in his great toe or heel. As the fit progresses he is tortured by throbbing anguish up his leg. He describes this as a burning, squeezing, and gnawing, as if his leg is being torn asunder from being stretched upon a medieval rack. His torture is worse at night. I have seen him with tears in his eyes.

He begs for a cure.

I keep telling him, "There is no cure for gout—only prevention. Only temperance and physical activity will lessen your periodic ordeal with this disease." Each time he pledges repentance and abstinence. These he conveniently forgets once the fit has passed. I would think that the excruciating torment he suffers would serve as a deterrent. As his rotund body attests, he is obsessed with rich food and strong wine. He cannot forgo these and so he suffers.

In response to his pleas, I give him laudanum to ease the pain. "Wrap your leg in wool cloth. Perspiration must be encouraged. Eat a thin diet and consume only cooling liquids. What can not be cured, must be endured."

Besides the reliable remedy of temperance and exercise, I tell him to change his behavior in preparation for spring. "Avoid intense thought, especially at night. Each March, begin a course of stomach bitters, taken twice a day, of tansy and burdock root."

We both know these suggestions will not remove the cause of his agony.

April 5

Just when I am convinced that I have found my way, I must serve yet another apprenticeship. This apprenticeship is unique—most unlike studying with the vicar back in Kingswood or as a surgeon. When I asked to join the Freemasons, I had no idea that there would be so much education involved.

I am a lowly apprentice again!

I waited in a small room outside the main lodge. When it was my time, I was blindfolded. While I had not noticed the temperature before, suddenly chills made me feel most uncomfortable. I felt isolated. A voice assured me that the blindfold was symbolic, and I would understand shortly. A length of rope was draped around my neck. This increased my anxiety.

The door to the lodge opened after several of my knocks and words were exchanged which I could not clearly hear. As the door shut with a slam my trepidation grew.

"As an apprentice," I was told, "you have much to learn. Tonight you will be sworn to secrecy and told about many of our customs and beliefs. In time you will master this knowledge and within this lodge pass it on to others. Are you ready to begin?"

I was not sure whether I was ready or not.

So much information was presented that I could not absorb it all. Someone escorted me to various locations in what felt like a large room. We stopped and made sharp right turns from time to time. Being blindfolded caused me to concentrate on the "journey" that I seemed to be taking and to the differences in the voices of those who instructed me. I had to kneel and take an oath not to divulge the secrets I was about to receive. The rope and blindfold were removed. As my eyes adjusted to the flickering candlelight I could see that three men sat on raised platforms that represented the points of the compass: south for midday, west for the setting sun, and east, where the Worshipful Master sat, for the rising sun. The room contained two columns and a table or altar was positioned in the center of the room with what appeared to be a Bible open upon it.

The officers of the lodge explained that the square and compass, once an essential tool in the building trade, should guide all of my actions. "Remember that one point of the compass always remains fixed while the other point moves to inscribe an arc or circle. Symbolically, the compass contains within its boundaries the principles of friendship, morality, and brotherly love. You are expected to live by these principles and to exercise charity."

There was a lecture about the building of Solomon's Temple on mount Moriah in Jerusalem. Legend holds that it housed fragments of the Ten Commandments given by God to Moses. No sectarian creed was suggested. Mention was made only about a Supreme Being or Great Architect. I answered several questions with the information that I had memorized. "With these answers," I was told, "you can visit any lodge in the world. You are now a in a long chain that has been passed down to you through the centuries."

"You had entered the lodge as an apprentice," the Master told me. "You came in darkness, but you have been given light. You are welcome here among your brothers."

Finally, I no longer felt cold. When the meeting of the lodge closed, a most enjoyable social followed. I look forward to the Fellow Craft and the Master Mason degrees.

April 12

The buckies, our river herring, are a most remarkable species. We would do well to imitate their drive, energy, and perseverance. Every spring the buckies provide us with entertainment and abundant fishing. They swim up the bay, into the cove, and under the bridge. They easily leap over the falls and continue to swim up the Pawtuxet.

They know exactly were they are going and return each year in order to make this pilgrimage to spawn. To achieve this goal, they must leave their natural environment—the sea—and adjust to the fresh water of the river. That also deserves our admiration.

Everything is at risk. Fishermen sweep up as many as can be caught. Once at the spawning grounds, success is still uncertain. Yet, their purpose is clear. Their numbers attest to a plan fulfilled. They repeat this grand adventure at the same time each year and remind us that we have much to learn from them as we renew our own lives each spring.

May 2

On a warm spring day like today, with new lime green leaves emerging with increasing numbers each day on the willows along the river, I am fully satisfied with my stay-at-home existence.

May 11

Over the past few weeks, I have had the good fortune of studying geometry with Jonathan Aborn, an officer of the Lodge. During the initiation ceremonies to become a Master Mason, I developed a fascination with the emphasis the Masons place on geometry.

In ancient times the difference between Master Masons and those of lesser reputation was the knowledge Master Masons had of geometry, which they used in their superior construction of great cathedrals and palaces. They closely guarded this knowledge in those days and, therefore, became known and feared for secrets associated with special symbols, rituals, words, and handshakes that were used to identify one another and for permission to enter the lodge.

My own knowledge of geometry—all but basic mathematics for that matter—has been woefully absent. I tried to read geometry on my own but could not comprehend it. Jonathan has made the study most enjoyable and has inspired me to think about its uses.

In discussing my study with Hope, she shed light on a number of uses of geometry that would never have occurred to me. In her quilting group, she says, they have to use geometry to figure out how much material they will need and how to construct the complex designs.

Her group makes birth date quilts with twenty-one diamonds in two colors, which surround seven diamonds in another color. They also like to create mariner's compass quilts based on a circle of eight isosceles triangles with their bases on the circle and another row of isosceles triangles going around the first. The whole process is baffling to me but the results are spectacular.

I know that geometry is used in land surveying, astronomy, navigation at sea, laying out complex gardens, and, of course, in architecture and building.

May 14

He simply won't listen. Every year I tell Remington that he must cancel Rattlesnake Day before someone seriously gets hurt or dies. His response, "Lukus, you are an alarmist. No one ever really gets hurt. We have been holding this event for years without anyone getting fatally bitten. The Village looks forward to this event."

I have repeatedly pled that he is tempting fate and eventually tragedy will strike. I have reasoned with him, challenged his social responsibility, and bitterly insulted his intelligence. He just gets angry.

"Lukus," he says, "snakes, especially rattlers, are a menace on our farms. They are a danger to our children and livestock. We hold this yearly reduction of snakes as a fun-filled community event to the benefit of all. I am tired of your complaining."

"At least, close the taverns until the hunt is over!" I shout back.

He dismisses me with a wave of his hand, turns his back, and walks away.

This is the last year that I am going to attend. Let them find someone else to provide medical care.

May 15

Rattlesnake Day started as usual at the taverns. The men drank heavily, perhaps to bolster their courage. They boasted of how many snakes they each had driven off the ledge into the bonfire below in the previous year. Each had a personal goal, and a few were determined to be the champion snake beater. There were promises of free drinks for whoever found the biggest rattlesnake.

The group of men who were filled with the reveries

swaggered to Rattlesnake Hill near the Joy homestead, where they formed a semicircle and began beating the ground with their poles—calling the snakes out of hiding.

I watched with concern from some distance.

We could see the smoke rising from the bonfires below the ledge.

When the first snake appeared, the excitement rose. The volume of shouts grew and the men got bolder, probing into dense vegetation. Some poked into crevices. A couple of intrepid "hunters" got down on their knees to better probe into holes and rock formations.

Abraham gestured to the others. He had provoked a huge rattler, probably seven feet long, out of a hole. The snake slithered off in a direction opposite from the ledge. The whole hunting group stopped to watch and to cheer on Abraham. He went after the snake with his long pole to head the snake off. Eventually, he cornered the snake against a rock formation. I swear the sound of his rattles could have been heard for miles.

Abraham moved to redirect the snake toward the ledge. The snake refused to move. The hunters began to chant, encouraging Abraham in this contest of wills. The snake held his ground.

Abraham moved closer. In an instant, the snake struck, biting his hand. Startled, at first, he yelled in pain. The snake moved off with several men in hot pursuit, intent now on killing the snake.

Suddenly, everyone was sober.

I rushed to Abraham's side. He was down on one knee, holding his bitten hand and already sweating profusely. I called him a dumb rascal.

Despite my attempt to rid him of his poison, his blood must have already been thick with venom from the snake. With his bile already so unbalanced there was nothing else to do. He was dead within two hours.

Certain was the revenge.

June 6

The smell of fear smothered me as I entered the house. Despite the warmth and brightness of the day, the front room made me shiver. The bedroom shutters were closed. A single candle burned in the far corner. I thought that I had arrived too late. Mr. J. Burlingame must already be dead. Light and life had already departed. The room was in mourning.

But he wasn't dead.

Mr. Burlingame's housekeeper insisted that the house should remain dark out of respect for the dying.

Mr. Burlingame would die, but he lingered still.

I had treated Mr. Burlingame several times in recent weeks for an occasional fever. He wavered having no fever for a couple of days and then it would return. I believed he had ague and that bleeding and purging him would soon rid his body of the disease.

I was wrong—terribly wrong.

When the fever would reappear, I increased the bleeding and the purgatives. Instead of getting better, as more of the disease was expelled from his body by the treatment, he got weaker. Some days when I visited he would be wrapped up in a blanket. He sat near the warm coals in the hearth even on days when the temperature in the house did not warrant a fire. He complained that his hands and feet were particularly cold. In my experience, chills are not uncommon when a patient is bled several times.

He took to bed and slept most of the time. His housekeeper, Hannah, lamented, "He will only sip broth and only when I feed him. He complains of an inability to swallow." I learned that he had contracted the disease, undoubtedly, from prolonged exposure to unwholesome air in the hold of a ship that he had been assigned to clean. The ship may have been used to transport slaves. He told me he stood for long periods in stagnant water and had uncovered the carcasses of scores of dead rats.

My remedy for Jabez Burlingame was wrong. I recently acquired a copy of Dr. William Buchan's Second Edition of *Domestic Medicine*. There is much controversy about some of Dr. Buchan's advice. Perhaps there is danger for those who do what he suggests if they know little about medicine. Contrary to my knowledge of how best to treat ague, Dr. Buchan recommends against bleeding and warns that vomits are only of assistance if used at the beginning of the fever. Nevertheless, the humors must be evacuated from the stomach. I did what I had been taught.

Had I known I would have administered other remedies.

I told Hannah to spend as little time as possible in Mr. Burlingame's bedchambers. "Madam, when he dies, everything in the room will need to be thoroughly cleaned and washed in vinegar. If you feel any symptom of the fever, you should immediately take a vomit and chamomile tea."

June 9

Mrs. Dutie Crandall and one of her daughters have been burning with fever. Both had been visiting New York City, where they say garbage has piled up. The decay and decomposition of rotting vegetables, pieces of fish, and butchered animal parts have created such a stench that passing by is nearly intolerable. They had covered their faces with scarves when in this area. Evil vapors find clever ways of entering us. Mrs. Crandall admits that the fetid miasma had nearly caused her to faint on more than one occasion.

They suffered from weakness and cold, clammy sweats. Dutie had powerful headaches, which made her extremely sensitive to light. Both were producing stools greenish and black in color, with a heady odor that assaulted the nostrils.

Following Dr. Buchan's new dispensatory, I administered a vomit of ipecac to both of them, which purged them of bile. I plied them with acids—lemons and oranges—in special drinks and had them lay out slices around the room. "Consume moderate amounts of red wine. Place this cloth soaked in vinegar at your bedside and inhale the scent. Also inhale the scent of tansy, rosemary, and rue." On the seventh day, I added a regime of mustard and vinegar poultices.

I am determined not to lose these patients to intermittent fever.

June 16

Hope thought it would be a grand outing to go to the circus in Newport. Friends of hers in the quilting circle she attends had seen advertisements in the *Mercury* that an accomplished equestrian was going to perform. The advertisements claimed that Christopher Gardner was incomparable—the best and perhaps the only truly accomplished equestrian with such skill in America. He had been trained by Jacob Bates, who is acknowledged as the best in Europe.

What Christopher Gardner was able to demonstrate on a horse was amazing. He performed on one, two, and sometimes three horses around an oval track so we could easily see each stage of his exhibition. He stood on his head in the saddle while his horse was at full gallop. He leapt from his horse to the ground, back up onto the horse, back to the ground, and back up onto the horse in such rapid succession that we stood in awe. To me this is a new form of theatre. The appreciative crowd was raucous, perhaps due to the numerous whiskey and rum stands nearby.

At a cost of a quarter of a dollar, the experience was well worth it.

July 7

While visiting with Mrs. Fisher, I encountered Mrs. Dennis inquiring about the health of the two Fisher children whose births she had attended. Sarah was born a year ago and Hannah two years before her.

This was a fortuitous meeting since I had been thinking for some time of expanding my practice into childbirth and was much desirous of having Mrs. Dennis instruct me.

She was, however, cool to the idea.

Mrs. Dennis has an excellent reputation in these parts but has rarely been called upon to attend births in the Village. Much of the professional literature from the continent and reports from the medical schools in London and Edinburgh indicate changes in the role of attending birth. I was interested in hearing Mrs. Dennis' views on these matters.

She protested that she was much too busy to meet with me (I suspect she knew instantly what my motives were). I enticed her to stay for tea and examine some medicinal plants I had been growing in my garden that had been imported from Scotland two years ago.

We wandered through the garden until she spotted the European creeping mint. She was clearly excited to discover this plant so close to home. I persuaded her to tell me how creeping mint or pennyroyal could be prepared in a hot pot for women to sit over during labor to ease pain. Then she quickly dropped the conversation about medicine.

Although delighted by my offer to send a couple of the plants down to her home in Newport, she was insistent on her need to be about her duties. When I told her that Mrs. Carr hoped to see her and that she had prepared tea for us, Mrs. Dennis consented (I think she had forgotten my previous invitation to tea).

Hope, of course, quickly dissipated Mrs. Dennis' coolness as they talked about the children and families. I remained politely silent until Mrs. Dennis got up to leave. Inquiring again about an opportunity to speak to her concerning her work, she agreed to meet with me when I brought her the wild pennyroyal plants.

July 14

I brought the wild pennyroyal plants to Mrs. Dennis today. She was most grateful and planted them immediately. I took this opportunity to ask her what the greatest challenge was with her patients. "I am seeing more patients who have lost confidence in giving birth as a natural process. Clergy like Cotton Mather and many others who warn women during their pregnancy that they would be near to death create terrible fear. In my experience, few women die in childbirth. Cleanliness prevents puerperal fever. Permitting nature to take its course resolves most problems."

I asked her about the many stories regarding images seen by pregnant women that produced bad outcomes. She looked at me in disbelief.

"What images?" she asked.

"I had heard that if a woman saw a frightening image of an animal, the child would look like it. And that if a woman saw a man without an arm, the child would be born without an arm."

Mrs. Dennis frowned silently, suggesting that no intelligent surgeon could possibly believe any of this. But, I went on. . . .

"If a woman longs for a particular food during her pregnancy—a common occurrence—but fails to satisfy the craving, the child will be injured and will be born with birthmarks."

"Simply, not true," Mrs. Dennis scoffed.

My timing was off. I foolishly asked her if I could observe her practice.

"Certainly not," she answered emphatically. "My patients would not permit a man in the room. Women do not want men to see them in labor and childbirth. Their modesty is extremely important to them and to their husbands, who also are not permitted in the room. Surgeons are called to births only when something is terribly wrong. If you are present, patients will suspect that I have been withholding bad news from them. Surgeons are also known for using sharp instruments, which most women would avoid at all costs."

Acknowledging her concerns, I then asked what she used to control pain. She advised that there was much too much talk about pain—all of which frightened women unnecessarily. "Pain," she pronounced, "shows progress in labor and is a natural part of the process."

After some probing, she said that many herbs were useful, such as amber, saffron, cumin, sage, and comfrey. She used bayberry to control bleeding and mint for nausea.

When I asked her how she knew when to break a woman's water, she responded in such a way that I knew my interview was over. "I don't break a woman's water except in most unusual circumstances. Your question reflects a typical attitude of surgeons and academically trained doctors who think they should be repeatedly intervening in the birthing process. What a woman in labor needs [the anger rising in her voice] is support from her family and neighbors, a midwife with years of experience, dexterity, and . . . ….patience."

Not wanting to be the target of any further scorn, I thanked her for answering my questions and bid her a good morrow.

Frankly, I was disappointed at not having learned more medicine from her, but I was grateful to have escaped any further confrontation.

July 16

The more that I have studied geometry the more I am convinced that there should be an application in medicine. As a surgeon, I rely on traditional theories, practices, and that which I have been taught by Dr. Randall and my colleagues. While many of these practices seem valid, I often feel that I am guessing at what might work for a particular patient.

Medicine needs a powerful mathematical tool that provides some certainty. Even the data I gather from actual cases—and many surgeons don't bother—I often don't understand how to make useful. If a pattern is not apparent, I am at a loss.

Experience in treating patients is useful but not sufficient. We all have a predisposition to do what we have always done. If what we do does not cure the patient, we try something else. We tend to remember what worked and, conveniently, forget what did not.

Those of us who pride ourselves on being good doctors also rely on intuition. Perhaps, our good intuition is a gift; perhaps, it results from being better at observing our patients, better at listening to what they tell us, or better at matching our knowledge and experience to the case at hand. In the end, all of this is very imprecise.

Nothing is imprecise about geometry. The properties and relationships of points, lines, angles, curves, surfaces, and solids can be measured and calculated. The theorems are applied; there is no guesswork.

Since geometry can explain the way different parts of something fit together, the application of geometry to the human body could be most beneficial.

What a difference it would make if I could actually calculate how much medication should be given to a five-year-old child who weighs fifty pounds compared to a 150-pound adult. Currently, I estimate but tend to prescribe less than I might because I don't want the child to be given too much.

Could geometry help to calculate the amount of medication in the body after several doses or the amount of bad blood that should be removed to rid a particular body of what is causing the illness? If I understood the geometry of the bone structure, might I be able to help patients recover more quickly from broken bones?

Despite all that I have learned from Jonathan Aborn, he cannot help me with how to apply the basic theorems to the human body. I need to find someone who is a surgeon and who has also studied mathematics.

July 23

What a disgrace! Lafayette has been appointed as a major general. Are we so bereft of talent that we must turn to France to lead us? We have our own Nathaniel

Greene, Benedict Arnold, Ethan Allen, Nathan Hale, Israel Putnam, and James Varnum. How can we possibly claim to win independence if the French are to do the fighting for us?

We will never be able to hold our heads high among the nations of the world. We will owe the French, and they will own us. What other motive could the French have but to get back what they lost to the British during the Seven Years' War? They want empire, at least, as much as England.

We cannot trade one tyranny for another. Let the British hire mercenaries and bribe our slaves. We must stand alone. Making the Marquis a general is outrageous.

August 15

Treated Jabez Burlingame today for a painful toothache, which he has bitterly complained about for weeks. I had told him to hold cloves in this mouth, but this provided only fleeting relief. He also tried holding tobacco in his mouth; still he complained.

Last spring, Caleb, our blacksmith, had fashioned me a toothkey for pulling teeth, which I sharpened as best I could for this surgical procedure. When Jabez saw the toothkey, he refused to permit me to use it. But, he had been in such pain for so long that he finally consented. I did have to urge him on by challenging his manhood and by calling him several uncomplimentary names.

While Jabez broke out in an anxious sweat, I inserted

the toothkey into the gums under the offending tooth and gave it a quick yank. He shouted in pain. The tooth was out. With great bravado, Jabez will tell everyone he knows about his courage and this amazing instrument that I have for removing teeth. My growing reputation as a tooth puller may convince others to ask for services.

I advised Jabez to use quills to get lingering food out from between the few healthy teeth that remained and to rub his teeth with ash. Knowing Jabez, he will ignore these suggestions. In time, he will be back to see me.

August 19

The more I thought about the possibilities and opportunities for adding manmidwifery services to my practice, the more determined I became to improve my knowledge. My preparation as an apprentice under Dr. Randall had provided no information on childbirth. Perhaps, Dr. Randall did not see attending birth as part of a medical practice at all.

However, I have been reading about a group of doctors—William Dewees of Philadelphia, John Vaughn of Wilmington, and (led by) Dr. Benjamin Rush of Philadelphia—who believe that giving birth is no longer a natural process in the civilized world. They argue that luxury, indolence, lack of exercise, and poor diet have created changes in women's uteruses, which make their labors long and painful. Apparently, this is not true for African women, Latin American women, or for Irish women who have large families. Their labors are comparatively easy and nearly painless. Even Mrs. Dennis said that she was seeing more patients who thought that birth was not a natural process, though she clearly thought this was wrong. Rush, Dewees, and Vaughn, on the other hand, concluded that the process of giving birth was a disease, as evidenced by the tedious and painful process of labor. They proclaimed that it was reckless to leave childbirth to nature.

If Mrs. Dennis is not going to be helpful, I need to find someone else.

September 2

My colleague here in Pawtuxet, Dr. Jason Bartlett, suggested that I write to Dr. James Lloyd in Boston. His childbirth training had been in Europe with William Smellie. Dr. Smellie had studied at the University of Glasgow as well as in London and Paris, and he was the best-known man midwife in Scotland. According to Dr. Bartlett, Dr. Lloyd had established a lucrative practice in Boston among the wealthy.

Dr. Lloyd graciously responded to my letter and invited me to spend a day with him, which proved most informative. He was confident that man midwives would soon replace women midwives. Contrary to Mrs. Dennis' view, he believed that superior intelligence, education—especially in anatomy—and willingness to provide much desired intervention would rapidly promote this change.

"The use of forceps," he proclaimed, "distinguishes us." He insisted that the timely use of forceps, which were now frequently used in Europe, resulted in faster deliveries with less pain for the woman.

"Also, women midwives never practice copious bloodletting, but we know the procedure is often necessary to reestablish a systemic balance in the body. Bleeding a patient is also useful for swelling in the legs, tension in blood vessels, headaches, and plethoric—suppressed menstrual periods."

In just a few minutes I had already learned more from Dr. Lloyd than in my entire conversation with Mrs. Dennis. Over dinner at the Sherborn Inn, originally the most agreeable home of Colonel Samuel Bullard, Dr. Lloyd spoke more candidly. "Women midwives," he argued, "are guilty of interfering mischief. They like to have women walk endlessly around the room, wearing them out at a time when they need all their strength. They use butter or hog's grease to help relax the woman's soft parts. While the women midwives claim this permits stretching for the birth of the child, such measures are totally unnecessary. I don't know why women put up with such rubbish."

Shaking his head, he sarcastically told me that women midwives are also inclined to use magic rather than science. He had heard of the use of Eagle Stone, which claimed the power to pull the child out. He thought this was witchcraft.

I told him about Mrs. Dennis' general belief that pain was a necessary part of giving birth. Dr. Lloyd agreed that giving birth was certainly not painless, but wondered why women midwives were oblivious to this pain. "Men are more sympathetic and genteel." He said that he often used labor powder concocted of date stones and oil of amber or cumin seeds beaten together in an ale. "This brings immediate relief. Little else is needed."

September 4

I spent a couple of days with Dr. Lloyd in Boston during a week when he anticipated attending a birth. When we were summoned to the home of a woman in labor, I did not anticipate that so few family and neighborhood women would be present. I was introduced as a surgeon and invited, without objection, into the room. The woman, who had been laboring for some hours, was initially relieved to have Dr. Lloyd present.

I learned a great deal from silently observing him. He waited to be invited into the room. His examination of the patient was most discrete. He touched her only under the blanket, which covered her despite the heat of the room. He was polite, perhaps overly so, in asking questions and responding to those asked of him. When he had a question of an intimate nature, he would often ask it through one of the other women in the room. What appeared to me to be an unnecessary circumlocution was apparently welcomed by the patient. He kept the room dimly lighted; he even moved a candle to the far side of the room.

Her women attendants had placed an axe under the bed to cut the labor pain, but this stratagem was not working.

While the birth occurred quite successfully within a few hours of our arrival, neither the patient nor some of the women in the room were content. Possibly, the woman had been in labor longer than was reported. The women attending kept whispering to Dr. Lloyd to do something to relieve the pain and to speed the process along. Dr. Lloyd was polite but, essentially, ignored them. The patient was not at all polite. She was stubborn, demanding, petulant, and generally disagreeable.

Later, Dr. Lloyd explained, "Women in labor are irrational, in fact temporarily deranged. They do not remember the following day what they have said. Their pleas and demands should never influence your decisions of how to proceed."

My patients in Pawtuxet are not always compliant with my advice. Yet, rarely have they openly challenged or argued with me. I have never been called a disrespectful name. The behavior I witnessed with Dr. Lloyd is uncommon in my experience . . . and troubling.

October 8
Nothing saps strength and vital energy more than the

quickstep. Normal duties cannot be performed. Those so afflicted must remain in close proximity to the necessaries.

The punishment for consuming overripe fruit or meat that has begun to decay is most unpleasant and should caution against ever repeating the error. However, hunger tends to overcome the memory of the last encounter with the flux or quickstep.

Fortunately, the body rids itself of this affliction with no intervention. My neighbor, Horatio Slocum, asked if I might provide something to give him relief. He was not amused by my jokes.

I prescribed boiling comfrey root in milk or an ounce of rhubarb root in a pint of water. To speed the process along I suggested, "Grease your hard belly with lard and apply hot cloths. Eat some chocolate to restore your strength."

October 24

As a young man soon after settling here, I remember the great pleasure we had raiding the Harris apple orchard. We loved apples and could hardly wait until fall when they hung in abundance from the trees. The sweet smell of the blossoms in spring got us planning our mischief. When the time finally arrived, several friends and I would pick a specific day for our raid. We believed that we could calculate the exact time when the ripening was at its absolute peak.

Sneaking into the orchard when no one was in sight, we posted our sentries, who were instructed with secret "bird call" signals in case the enemy appeared, and designated who would flank to the left and who to the right. No military maneuver was more carefully planned.

We gathered more apples than we could possibly carry and ran off at top speed to our hiding place, as if being chased by a militia of farmers. Then, we would devour more apples than any of us could safely consume. Of course, we were not hungry and could not even pretend to eat dinner. Shortly thereafter, we would be sick as dogs from having eaten too many apples.

There would be no sympathy. We would pledge to be more moderate next time. We never were.

I have loved everything about apples, still do: the rows of trees; the opulence of the fruit covering the branches, seemingly much too heavy for the tree to bear; the heady smell of ripened fruit; and the russet of the leaves after harvest. I loved the apple jelly, the sweet cider we drank much of the year, the wonderful aroma of burning apple wood, and the inviting cinnamon smells of baking apples pies.

But, most of all—I loved stealing them!

November 6
Beginning to take hold in Providence is the celebration— if one can call it that—of Pope's Day. On November 5th, there is great feasting and drinking to commemorate

the aborted attempt by Guy Fawkes in 1605 to blow up Parliament. The event is marked by as much derision of the Pope as can be generated by the participants until inebriation clouds the minds of observers. The other hallmark of the day is a reversal of the social order. The lower class "rules" for the day. Perhaps, this flaunting of all convention is what generates so much gaiety and, undoubtedly, explains its growing popularity. Those in positions of authority and whose status usually demands deference, at least in appearance, detest Pope's Day. But artisans and laborers make no pretext of appearances on this day.

The wealthy are solicited to help fund the festivities, which they dare not deny under a risk of damage to their property. They wisely stay indoors.

This celebration has not reached the crescendo that has been seen in Boston. There, as is typical of them, everything is taken to extremes. Generally, the good-natured behavior here has been viewed with bemused toleration. In Boston, however, various artisan groups, who have a certain rivalry among themselves during the rest of the year anyway, use the excuse of Pope's Day to invade each other's territory for general lawlessness. It is hard to see this as anything other than mob warfare.

Boston's extremists aside, Pope's Day seems to me to be an appropriate leveling of arrogant class distinctions that are held so dearly in the mother country. More importantly from my perspective is the assertion of the

value of artisans and the contribution of common laborers to the general welfare of the community.

Nel never mentioned anything to us about observing
Pope's Day. Perhaps, she was reticent because she has
been a domestic in our household only a few months.
Nevertheless, we gave her the day off.

November 17

Much to my astonishment, I was called to the village
home of Aletta Clarke by her midwife Sarah Fisher. Sarah had succumbed to Aletta's urgent request to call in a
doctor. I may have been the only one they could reach.

When I observed Mrs. Clarke, she had obviously
been struggling for many hours. She was pale, weak,
and experiencing severe pain. Sarah rehearsed with me
what she had done to try to comfort Mrs. Clarke: walked
her, placed her over a steaming pot with sage to encourage dilation, provided her with saffron tea and comfrey,
and covered the perineum with fern paste. . . . Labor had
not progressed.

This was clearly tedious labor—evidence of a dis-
eased state, which Drs. Rush, Dewees, and Vaughn
argued had rendered childbirth no longer natural for
women of the civilized world. It was reckless to leave
childbirth to nature. At least, in this case, Sarah Fisher
reluctantly agreed.

I had to do something. . . . I was expected to do something. . . . I was not there to do nothing.

Could the infant's head be too large? Was Mrs. Clarke's pelvis too small? Did the infant need to be turned in utero (a procedure that I did not believe I could accomplish)? Then, I began to fear that the infant was already dead or that, if some corrective action was not taken soon, Mrs. Clarke would die.

My set of forceps was quietly tucked in my medical bag. They were the last, desperate option I had. Reluctant as I was, I decided to bleed Mrs. Clarke, taking a few ounces of blood. I waited. The room fell ominously silent as everyone watched for some sign. Nothing happened. I rejected bleeding her again.

Seaman's *The Midwives' Monitor* had suggested a low dose of ergot, which was believed to be a miracle drug. John Moultrice had sent me a small packet of ergot, recommending that I try it should I encounter an "exhausted, stubborn uterus."

I gave Mrs. Clarke thirty grains of ergot in a cumin tea. Almost immediately, contractions began. A handsome boy was born within an hour much to the delight of everyone in the room and much to Mrs. Clarke's relief.

The baby was washed with milk and water. A flannel cap was placed on his head. I wrapped the umbilical cord in linen and placed it on Mrs. Clarke's belly (The cord would drop off from the baby by itself). I encouraged Mrs. Clarke to drink water in which fish had been boiled to ensure that she had sufficient milk to feed the baby.

A successful birth is a thrilling experience. Such joy is without parallel. However, I was soaked in perspiration, drained of energy from nervous apprehension . . . and uncertainty.

November 23
I have been called to several births—three to be exact—but have yet to be comfortable with my assisting in childbirth.

At Dr. Lloyd's suggestion I had purchased Valentine Seaman's *The Midwives' Monitor* (from David Hall's Market Street Printing in Philadelphia]. The forceps are a frightening metal device and are of prodigious size. I see why Dr. Lloyd had advised they remain hidden from the patient. He had also recommended that I purchase Smellie's *Treatise on the Theory and Practice of Midwifery,* but no copy could be located.

Despite the Seaman's reference from which I learned a great deal, I remain uneasy during the various stages of labor. I worry about not knowing what might need to be done should something go wrong. I fear being challenged with mismanagement and ruining my reputation. I am abhorred by the thought of performing a craniotomy or having to choose to save the mother's life by destroying the infant. Interacting with a woman in labor and with other women in the birthing room is different from my ordinary practice and not always pleasant.

I have exchanged correspondence with John

Moultrice, who practices in Charleston, South Carolina. While he has an outstanding reputation as a dependable man midwife and has offered me several useful suggestions, I can't practice being a man midwife through correspondence.

December 14

We have no hospital here for persons of insane and disordered minds. The only one I have heard of in the colonies was mentioned in a letter I received from Dr. Pasteur, who spoke of the facility in Williamsburg. Perhaps, there are many in need down there in Virginia.

Praise be to God, we have few in need of such services here. The people of Pawtuxet are too engaged in their daily work and respectful of Divine Providence—even if they fail to attend church—to permit their minds to wander. I must admit, however, that our current political climate might deprive any one of their senses.

This day, Mrs. Felicity Ward brought her sister Constance for my examination. Mrs. Ward feared that her sister had lost her senses.

I observed Constance, who sat passively across from me. She was pale and listless. She kept her head down, apparently examining the grain of the wooden floorboards. As I spoke to her, she steadfastly refused to make eye contact with me. When she looked up from "examining" the floor, her stare was vacant, withdrawn.

Mrs. Ward reported, "My sister has been suffering

from this malady for several months. When her husband went off to fight with the Continental Army, she cried for weeks and then seemed to withdraw from the world. Constance refuses to speak, eats little, and rarely moves from a chair."

Mrs. Ward had taken her sister into her own home but was now beyond her patience or hope of restoring her sister's health. At first she kept Constance near her in the house. Out of embarrassment, eventually, she confined Constance to a back room.

My diagnosis was melancholia. Constance was not violent, nor dangerous to others.

"We believe," I told Mrs. Ward, "that those who suffer from disordered minds choose to do so. The loss of her husband may have triggered this condition, but she can and must decide to brighten her days and rejoin the routines of daily living."

"What can be done?" Mrs. Ward wanted to know.

"Her body is out of balance," I answered. "We must evacuate her bowels, cup both sides of her neck to draw out what is poisoning her mind, and use scarification and leeches to bleed her."

If Constance heard me, she made no response, no reaction to my treatment plan. Mrs. Ward, however, swooned and nearly fainted. "Must this be done?" she pleaded.

"My dear Madam, indeed, it must. We can start now. You will need to bring her to me every day for the next week until the melancholy is released. At home, you must talk to her frequently. Insist that she sit in a room such as the kitchen where there is a lot of activity. Make her do household tasks; better still, get her to work along side you in the garden. At least take her outside into the air for walks. We never know how long these treatments will need to continue, but together we will convince her to reconsider this melancholia she has chosen."

December 16

Thankfully, I have not been called in recent weeks to another birth, not since the one I attended with Aletta Clarke. Being the "hero" of this birth was a wonderful feeling, yet I don't think the travail should be as hard on the doctor as it is on the mother.

There does not seem to be as much demand for man midwives in the village as I had anticipated. Villagers think that males who practice midwifery are more costly, and these times do not permit expenses that can be controlled.

A few years ago, families in the Village were growing at a rapid rate. Families with seven births were not uncommon. The war, its uncertain outcome, and the struggling economy of the colony have all restricted the desirability of bringing children into the world.

Once again, my timing may be off.

1775

January 2

Noah Robinson came to me to plead for attention required by his cousin, Jeffrey Benedict. Noah whispered his cousin's need as if he were afraid someone might overhear. I have known of Jeffrey's lament and did not want to visit or treat him. Noah appealed. Not concealing my disgust for the matter, I finally acceded. Noah was embarrassed to accompany me.

"You can find where Jeffrey is staying by following the river upstream from Aborn's, past the Healy Homestead and then right at Josiah Westets'. Turn just before you reach Josiah Harris' old place and look for a sign, 'Big Chickens for Sale.'"

Concerned about the troubled lines forming above my brow, he assured me that he was almost finished with his directions. He droned on. "You will see a slightly used path next to a field where cows used to graze. Follow a little distance up Sackanosett Hill. Jeffrey is staying in a cabin not far from Goody Collin's place. You can *not* miss it."

Jeffrey is guilty of immoral behavior; he is not remorseful. Yet, he wants me to cure him. I have been struggling with ethical concerns, with my obligation as a doctor and with my personal belief that I should curb such unseemly behavior not only for the patient's own well being but also for the public good.

Jeffrey has syphilis, the French disease, or the great pox. He has come to me before with this discomfort but has refused to curb his appetite for illicit liaisons.

When I left Aborn's fortified for this ordeal, a refreshing salt breeze swept up gently from the cove. That was the last pleasant thought I had. The rest of the journey took me further from the Village and deeper into my troubled thought about Jeffrey.

When I finally reached Jeffrey's cabin and examined him, he had the same rash that I had seen the first time I treated him. He had lesions on the moist areas of his body, complained of a sore throat, malaise, and weight loss. He said he was staying in the cabin because he hardly recognized his own personality. I assured him that I had come only at the urging of his cousin, and I had no intention of treating him again.

Jeffrey swore, "I do not have the great pox. It must be some other disease because I have abstained from any immoral conduct for months." He lied. As he prepared us tea, he took out two cups and poured the tea into only one, which he gave to me. A few moments later he realized that he had not poured his own and had to retreat to the stove.

Refusing to admit to having the French disease he, nevertheless, asked what treatments were possible. I recited in the most graphic terms possible a litany of "cures" that I had read about:

> Moses has suggested that sufferers be put to death.
> Patients could be infected with malaria and treated with Jesuit's bark.
> Patients could undergo salivation where the disease is sweated out by rubbing the body with mercurial ointment. The patient is wrapped in flannel and confined to an exceedingly hot room until the patient has salivated 2 ½-3 pints per day.
> The patient is likely to loose his teeth and maybe his nose.

"Jeffrey, you are beyond the point where bleeding, purging, blistering, or taking an emetic are of any use. Even when skin lesions clear, your blood carries the offending humors, which will flair up again. The pox can appear up to six months from the time you reinfect yourself. A flair-up from a previous dalliance can occur in a year or in several years. You may forget, but Divine Providence does not. The course of the disease progresses from obvious external symptoms, like the rash and lesions, to your internal organs. You will become confused, disoriented, and probably insane."

He had steadily lost what little color he had when I arrived and slumped pathetically in his chair. Without the table in front of him, he would surely have fallen over.

"Jeffrey, you are on the precipice of a fatal calamity. You will never be cured and may die from this episode. I implore you to follow the maxim—a burnt child dreads the fire."

"Is there nothing to be done?" he implored. Tears welled. His nose began to drip obscenely. Frankly, I had no sympathy for him.

"Try the following:

An old Indian remedy is to sprinkle sulfur on your feet and shoes.

Go to the apothecary or send your cousin and get a supply of mercury. It is the only drug that has been reported to help but can cause tremors, sleeplessness, and hallucinations.

If you must continue to practice lewd and licentious behavior to the further destruction of your body and damnation of your soul, wear an English raincoat."

I knew he would ask. "Colonel Condom, an English army officer, invented a device made from the intestines of lambs, which are dried and rubbed with almond oil. This envelope goes over your penis and prevents you from spreading the disease."

"You have done yourself irreparable harm, Jeffrey.

May God have mercy on you."

January 10

Dr. Lloyd invited me to visit and consult with him in Boston. We had a productive time swapping case histories and remedies. I brought him some herbs from my garden and he gave me a bottle of Mrs. Winslow's Soothing Syrup, which he had recently acquired by some stratagem from Scotland.

We spent the evening at the theatre. The American Company of Comedians was in town. The scope of entertainment was much more extensive than we get in Rhode Island. Besides the main production, which was a satirical portrait of married life called "The Way to Keep Him," by Arthur Murphy, the evening's program included dances, lighthearted songs, and instrumental music played on the fiddle, the recorder, and a stirring melody played on the harpsichord. We were also treated to a short lecture on the history of comedy and a puppet show. All of these were entertaining, if not exhausting, since the program lasted four hours. You need to be well rested to attend the theatre in Boston.

"The Way to Keep Him" was filled with foolery that made sport of marriage, friendship, and the French, and contained the inevitable confusion of identity and misdirected letters. Lovemore and Mrs. Lovemore were well acted by Mr. Beadle and Mrs. Ely. The widow Belmour (Mrs. Elliott) sorted out all of the mix-ups to bring the play to a happy and moral conclusion.

The asides made exclusively to the audience cut through all of the hypocrisy of the "public" views expressed amongst the characters. The audience was fully engaged by cheering and jeering, hissing and applauding, to express our approval or censure of the characters' motives.

The theme that a wife is out of date and that there should be no expressions of mutual love between husband and wife was happily contradicted in the end.

I am most grateful to Dr. Lloyd for his invitation. Without concerts and the theatre we would live a most melancholy existence.

February 7

On my way today through the Village, I strolled by Mrs. Moore's house. I recalled happy times and a few not so happy times spent under Mrs. May Moore's tutelage. She would begin each day with a reading from l Psalms, the 13th verse of 1 Corinthians, or some other favorite passage of hers. She taught us reading, spelling, history, and arithmetic and never failed to recite the Golden Rule. Because we never questioned anything she told us, our beliefs may have been shaped to a greater extent than we were willing to admit.

I did not much like going to school since I was the oldest in the class and didn't go for long. In retrospect, Mrs. Angell with whom I was staying was probably right in making me go. She was right about everything.

February 8

I was thinking again today about Mrs. Moore and the short time I had spent attending classes in her house. She liked to rate each of us on a five- point scale—five was excellent. When the roll was called, we answered with our name and announced our rating. Unless a point or two had been taken off for mischievous conduct, I would answer, "Lukus, number five." How proud we were to be counted among the excellent.

Occasionally, we could get an extra point if she observed us sitting up especially straight, if we demonstrated extra good manners, or if we were unusually studious.

What a happy day when I could say, "Lukus, number six!"

Life was simple then, when we knew that we were number five and surely destined for heaven.

March 3

Not to be outdone by Boston's Tea Party, we held our own in Providence. No one bothered to dress up like an Indian.

Church bells proclaimed the start of the event as the crowds gathered. Instigators claimed that three hundred pounds of tea were taken from ships and burned. Women brought tea from their homes and added it to the flames that were fueled by newspapers endorsing the Tea Act. Even the door from the Crown Coffee House was thrown on the fire.

Boston suffered punishment from holding its little tea party by having the port closed and the overwhelming occupation of troops.

For a largely symbolic act here in Providence—one that will have no economic impact on the East India Company—we may have invited far more devastating retribution.

March 19

Coughs are a common ailment and most are treated with home remedies that have been in families for years and passed down from grandmothers. For most coughs these remedies work fine.

We know that coughs result from pores that are blocked by bad humors and are evidence of a struggle of nature to dislodge the enemy. Therefore, we do not want to eliminate coughs before they accomplish their intended purpose.

Like the cures from grandmother's garden and those I learned from Maude at the vicar's residence there are many treatment options that I employ. My preference is to use liquorice root with honey or to use boiled turnips. Many patients have received relief from taking teaspoons of molasses and lemon or a combination of sugar, brandy, and sweet oil. One of my favorites is a syrup made from the inside bark of a pine tree and sweetened with honey that is boiled down and taken warm. This combination is most soothing and the one I take myself.

For very stubborn coughs I provide paregoric, an opium from poppy seeds, when I can get it from a peddler.

March 21

Peleg has had a bad cough for a week. He would never ask me for treatment unless he were fearful of dying. His limp might have been prevented if he had gotten medical attention years ago when the injury occurred. He never asks for anything.

Peleg must have been born with the gift of laughter. His disposition and practical jokes make him a pleasure to be around. Without trying, he makes me laugh with his clumsiness. He frequently drops whatever he is carrying and is always bumping into tables. Since he does not watch where he is going, he bumps into others. He adds to his comical appearance with his dark red jester's cap (the only one I have ever seen in that color), which could easily double as a night cap. Since he never takes it off, I suspect he sleeps in it. He tells me "Tis the becomingest cap in the whole world."

Now that I think of it, tomorrow I will bring him some pine bark and honey syrup for his cough.

April 18

The pastor at King's Church is not the sort of man I

would invite to the house for cider—or even tea. He does not project a neighborly demeanor. Like many other ministers of whom I have an acquaintance, he has deep, penetrating eyes. His face is marked with authority. His voice—grave, solemn, and strong. What he says and how he says it defies contradiction. I cannot imagine holding a real conversation with him.

While I certainly don't accept everything he says, I would not argue with him, either privately or publicly! Yet, within the congregation, he is esteemed, respected. Perhaps, it is his total focus on things spiritual. He almost seems unaware of the politics that surround us. Never once has he mentioned the burning of the *Gaspee* from the pulpit. I recall a recent prayer he offered on our behalf:

> Almighty God, you proclaim your truth in every age by many voices: Direct, in our time, we pray, those who speak where many listen and write what many read; that they may do their part in making the heart of people wise, its mind sound, and its will righteous.

April 26
We are fond of symbols as if they, somehow, create in themselves a goal we wish to achieve. . . .

Only hard work and divine Providence make success possible.

We have a liberty tree in Providence, in the yard of Joseph Olney's public house. In prideful contrast to the one in Boston, ours is grandeur. It has steps leading up to a fixed seat that is twenty feet above the ground, where, I guess, the Sons of Liberty can go to contemplate the Great Cause.

Silas Downer, when he dedicated it, is reputed to have said that all who saw this elm should be "penetrated with a sense of their duty to themselves, their country, and their posterity . . ." Downer, as only a great orator could, used every rhetorical device known.

On this occasion, he reminded us of our natural right to trade, but protested that Parliament had "restrained, perplexed, and fettered" it. Besides choosing words that would inflame—"fleecing the merchants," our being visited by a "plague" of British ships—and evoking the threat of a British military government in each town, he appealed to the trust imposed on us by our ancestors. By the end of his oration, he was referring to the tree as a "sacred elm," and making comparisons through Biblical allusions that we should grow stronger like the house of David.

The liberty poles, which are sprouting up like stalks of corn in every town, are another hopeful symbol. The pole itself seems to have no significance, but it is topped with a Phrygian cap that has symbolic meaning going back to ancient Greece. Former Roman slaves wore them after being emancipated by their masters, and the three magi are depicted wearing them. Comparing ourselves to either Roman slaves or the magi is haughty. I doubt that many of my neighbors know the significance of the cap. Most think it looks like a red night cap at the top of the pole and simply call it a "liberty cap." The Whigs are inclined to win the minds of those who know little by reducing complex issues to simplistic concepts.

It will take a lot more than liberty trees, liberty poles, and grand public orations to inspire a consensus to break our ties with England.

May 1

After our regular meeting of the Lodge, I joined Captain Oliver of the *Daphne* and Captain Nathan of the *Wanderer* who often attended whenever they were in Providence. They are usually engaged in transporting Rhode Island rum to the West Indies in exchange for molasses, sugar, and slaves, which they bring to New England.

It did not take many tankards of rum before we were focused on the slave trade. Captain Oliver expressed his fear, based on the discipline that he thought necessary on board his ship when carrying slaves, that Negroes were always on the verge of mutiny and would revolt given the slightest opportunity. He told harrowing stories about putting down violent outbreaks by killing those involved and dumping their bodies into the sea. He thought we might again see the same behavior that erupted in 1741 in what has been called the Great Negro

Plot. Blacks set fires at Fort George and dozens of other fires to destroy the property of whites. To put them down, seventeen slaves were hanged and thirteen others were burned at the stake.

"Blacks are simply inferior," Captain Nathan added. "The evidence is in the Bible. Noah's disobedient son, Ham, was black and, therefore, his progeny was marked as slaves forever after."

Captain Oliver added, "Some assert that God created separate races. Blacks had weaker minds from the start. Thomas Jefferson believed that black inferiority 'might be an unchangeable law of nature.' Bringing them to America provided them with productive, useful lives."

From my own reading, I know that Dr. Benjamin Rush, our best known physician, had concluded from his studies that inferiority had been caused by a mild strain of leprosy that had turned their skin black, their hair woolly, and resulted in their being less sensitive to pain.

I asked if there were some inherent inconsistency between our struggle to be free and independent and our trading and keeping slaves? There was silence. Apparently, freedom applied only to white males.

For the sake of the discussion, I challenged, "Well then, is not slavery out of keeping with our belief as Masons in brotherhood and that liberty and equality go together?"

Both of my seagoing friends protested that Master

Masons, for thousands of years, had used what amounted to slaves to build the great cathedrals and castles of Europe. They insisted that slavery was part of the natural order. If trading in slaves and keeping slaves were acceptable to revolutionary notables who are Masons like John Paul Jones and General Washington, then there can be no inconsistency with Masonry.

Thinking that we had said all that could be said, I hoped we might move on to another topic. But, both of them wanted to know what they could do to keep blacks alive during the long and often arduous voyage to America. They said that they lost 10 to 20% of their cargo as a result of delays in sailing and in the six weeks or longer that it took to cross the Middle Passage.

My advice was easily summarized:

"Provide enough food and drink.

Bathe them in vinegar.

Insist on periods of exercise, especially something vigorous like dancing on deck."

They thought that bathing them in vinegar and making them dance was peculiar but agreed to test my suggestions.

May 8

Such humiliation I have never witnessed before. But, I must confess he deserved every excruciating moment he was forced to endure. We could have hanged him but may not have achieved as great an effect as we did.

Just how I got swept up into this I cannot explain and pray that I will not have to explain. In the end, I was glad to be counted among those who say that just retribution was achieved.

Unpopular under the best circumstances, Jesse Saville, whose responsibilities require that he collect tax revenues for the Crown from ships of trade docking at our wharfs, was discovered having been charging inordinately excessive fees. He pocketed the difference between what he owed the Crown and what he charged, thus creating his own personal treasury.

I am outraged at the audacity of his cheating us for however long this vile act may have been occurring. While we certainly did not consider him a member of our community, he frequently attended services with many of us at King's Church and attended Lodge. We trusted that he was only performing duties dictated by his appointment. Yet, we discover that he is vile, contemptible, weak in character, devoid of Christian morals, a wolf lurking among us, a bird of prey.

Once exposed, he was fair game for our civic action. We seized him at his home on Post Road and dragged him into the street. We were intent on teaching him a lesson that he would not soon forget. He was stripped nearly naked. Others heated the tar. The crowd began to gather to enjoy the spectacle. His exposed body might have been of considerable anguish in itself and insult to his dignity, but that did not stop us.

The tar was poured over him. He shouted in pain and pleaded for his release. This only goaded us on. Next, we covered him with feathers and demanded his public confession. He gave none. I think it appropriate that the feathers were from geese since now he clearly resembled a silly goose. The swelling crowd berated him with foul names and again demanded a public apology. He refused, protesting innocence. Some in the crowd took candles and tried to set him on fire. This had little success, but surely began to strike terror into his soul.

When he refused to confess for the third time, Mr. Saville produced a halter, which we hung around his neck like an animal of burden and paraded him around. The crowd cheered and mocked him. Swine dung was thrown at him—again fitting since pigs are the lowliest of the farm animals. Someone suggested that we hang the miscreant. As we began to lead Jesse off toward the nearest suitable tree, now shaking in fear, he made his confession. We insisted that he shout it repeatedly so that all those assembled could hear. We set him free after he repented.

Should the Crown foolishly decide to leave Mr. Saville assigned to this Village, he will forever be shunned.

May 24
They got it wrong.

The light described in John 1:9 is not an "inner light." Why the Quakers cling to this mistaken notion that each of us has direct knowledge of God's will based on this fourteen-word Biblical verse shows a most ignorant interpretation. St. John equates "light" with "life," not with divine knowledge. He also is talking about Christ, not about all the rest of us. A group that builds its foundation of belief on this verse has no foundation at all.

It is blasphemy to claim that everyone has the same inner voice as Christ. The real Biblical revelation regarding the image of "light" does not make us wade through hundreds of pages and thousands of verses. Genesis: 3 shows us that God commanded, "Let there be light: and there was light." There is nothing mystical about this. God separated the day from the night. The "light" is understood to be literal. It was the first day and "it was good." In Genesis we are given our understanding of creation.

I might be more tolerant of the Quakers if they did not have nearly everything else wrong as well.

Even before the mention of light, St. John tells us:

"In the beginning was the Word, and word was
With God and the Word was God."

But the Quakers, who are sparing in their determination that words are needed at all in worship, contend that each of them is equal in hearing the word of God. Without the benefit of clergy, who have studied and considered the Bible for many years, how many of us would understand the word of God? Few! Is truth somehow magically revealed by silently sitting at a meeting full of Quakers? Is consensus among those present—if that is what they achieve—more reflective of God's message than that presented by educated clergy? I think not.

God has not "called" so many to the ministry because He thought we could fully understand his mysterious ways on our own. Why would we "tremble" or "quake" at the word of God as the Quakers are said to do? Surely, God does not expect us to live in fear of what He wants us to believe and what He wants us to do. As Adam and Eve so miserably failed to understand, we are expected to listen and to follow. God does not rule, like King George, through fear and threats.

June 3

Bawdy, politically irreverent, cynically honest!

We were treated to John Gay's "The Beggar's Opera" last night at Hacker's Hall in Providence. Rarely are we provided such theatrical entertainment so close to home.

This play breaks all the rules. Its characters are far from the classical nobility portrayed in Greek or Elizabethan theatre. This one turns the world upside down, entertaining us with criminals, beggars, thieves, whores, and jailors. Gay has plenty of criticism to spread across the social spectrum. All get satirized: lawyers, husbands and wives, military officers. All are corrupt.

The Beggar himself tells us:

" . . . it is difficult to determine whether (in the fashionable vices) the fine gentlemen imitate the gentlemen of the road, or the gentlemen of the road the fine gentlemen."

"Sacred" institutions are ridiculed: marriage, loyalty among friends, the courts, and management of prisons. The music is far from operatic. The songs are more appropriate to the tavern—lively, ballad tunes.

No wonder it has been so popular! We are a long way from the criticism that the play was intended to ridicule Robert Walpole, but its social satire speaks loudly to us and to these troubled times.

How grateful I am to just enjoy the sumptuous costumes, the irrational plot, and the celebration of the comic.

General Greene, with his own biting satire, responded to the criticism of this play as being subversive to morals because it shows criminals in a favorable light and it ridicules the social order:

"Ring the bells backward," he quipped, "cry fire, the church is in danger!"

Sometimes we need to round out our views of the nature of man and our concept of the social order. We wrap ourselves in erudition and blind ourselves with sobriety.

No one at last night's performance left in fear that the underworld was about to take over or that the play should be banned here as it was in England.

Of course, the Quakers were not there. They condemned it without seeing it and threatened perdition for those of us undisciplined enough to attend. Their criticism probably increased attendance.

As for me, I welcomed this short retreat.

June 12

It was the most amazing medical miracle I have ever seen.

For years I have heard about the bonesetter Sweet family of South County. Numerous rumors claimed that the Sweets had extraordinary powers to set bones. I had talked with Joseph Turner, who years later remembered as a young man having had his broken leg set by James Sweet. Others had tried to make Joseph whole, but he had walked with an awkward limp until James Sweet attended him.

I was suspicious that some sort of chicanery was at work. Did the Sweets use a trance to make patients think they had been healed? Was there some quackery afoot to make the Sweets wealthy?

I had heard that Job Sweet set bones for years in Newport. Francis, my neighbor on Fair Street, knew Dr. Job and asked him if I might observe his treatment. Job was reluctant; he said he did not perform for an audience.

Because I was a surgeon, I guess Francis convinced Job to speak with me.

Like all previous members of his family, Job practiced bone-setting as a sideline. He earned his living as a craftsman. The only money he took—when he took any—was to pay his travel expenses to get to a patient. Dr. Job also did not claim to have some divine gift—just a talent that he had inherited from his father.

I was totally confounded by his humble attitude. Not all of his family, he told me, were bonesetters. But, some male in each generation had this special skill. This includes three generations since his great grandfather came to Rhode Island from Salem in 1637.

Something remarkable was going on. A growing reputation over three generations does not just happen.

Dr. Job told me that he handled fractures, sprains, dislocations, and breaks. He had no idea of how many people he had helped; he kept no records. When I asked him what he actually did to achieve such success, he told me he did not know; he just did it.

Again, I sensed something was amiss.

My request to observe him was, again, denied. I was certain now that some trick was involved.

As I was about to leave, a young woman who was in great pain with a dislocated hipbone was assisted into his house. Without hesitation and oblivious to me, he spoke tenderly to her and asked if he could place his hands on her hip to locate the trouble. In tears, she consented while we all watched. After a few minutes, he told her "walk around the room." She did, and without apparent pain. I stood there with my mouth agape. She smiled, hugged the doctor and with her companion, left.

When I could recover my voice, I asked Dr. Job what he had done. He said that he could "see" every skeletal bone, and so he could manipulate the dislocation back into place.

Much to my chagrin, this skill was not something he could teach me. Perhaps, it was indeed a special gift. What else could you call it? Perhaps, this was not innate but had been learned from years of observing his father.

To me this was as close to a miracle as I had ever seen.

June 24

As is the custom, St. John's Lodge processed from the Lodge to church to sacred services and to listen to a sermon.

It is fitting that we observe St. John's Day not only because the lodge is named after him, but also because his is only one of three feast days that commemorate birthdays: the nativity of the Lord, the annunciation of Mary, and St. John. The Lord said of John, "there hath not risen among them that are born of women a greater than John the Baptist" (Matthew 11:11). It is appropriate to reflect on this day what we know about John. His remarkable birth precedes the birth of Christ by six months. His father, Zacharias, was struck dumb when he learned that his wife Elizabeth, Mary's cousin, would bear a son; she was barren and in her old age. When the priests circumcised Zarcharias' son, they called him Zachary, but his father and mother insisted that he be called John. So, both his birth and his name were unusual. None of their kindred had been called by that name.

We would all be comforted to know that our purpose in life was as clear as John's—to prepare the way for Christ:

> "Every mountain and hill shall be low
> And the crooked shall become straight
> And the rough ways plain."

How I would rejoice in knowing that I had such a predetermined mission.

John also exemplified humility, which we all need to emulate. He made it clear that he was not the Light but had come as a prophet to bear witness to the Light of Christ.

Comparisons with Christ are also illuminating. John is conceived by a barren, older woman and was not expected to be born. Christ was born of a young virgin and his birth was long anticipated. For us in this new world, our understanding of St. John is particularly important. John represents the old, born of an elderly couple, and he heralds the new as a prophet. His celebration is marked by the summer solstice when the days become shorter, while Christ's birth is marked by the winter solstice when the days become longer.

I am particularly respectful of this greatest of prophets. The Knights Hospitallers used St John's Wort, which was hung over doors and windows to ward off evil and as a tonic for depression, tension, and rheumatic pain.

One of the historical celebrations of St. John's Day was the building of bonfires, perhaps as a symbol of bringing light into the darkness. While we in Rhode Island light bonfires on numerous occasions, the eve of St John has not yet become one of them.

Appropriately, the sermon on this day was taken from Colossians III.14: "And above all these things, put on charity which is the bond of perfectness." The Reverend addressed the lodge directly throughout his remarks, reminding us that Masonry is founded on the grand principle of charity. He spoke of how a truly charitable man must be a faithful friend, and the commandment "to love your neighbor as yourself" is exemplified in the lodge where friendship and brotherly love abound, and where differences are amicably resolved in our commitment to serve one another. Reverend Andrews made it clear that our obligation must go beyond the members of the lodge to our friends, to everyone in the community, and ultimately to extend beyond those confines to reach the utmost limits of human nature.

Being a Mason himself, he spoke freely in the language

of the craft about the Grand Architect, who laid the foundation of the earth and fixed the chief cornerstone. He drew a comparison between the Grand Architect and the official structure of the lodge where we learn from the Grand Master. Reverend Andrews reminded us of the special knowledge that had been given to Masons: the love of geometry and architecture, which distinguished Master Masons in ancient times. He urged us to use the bonds of Masonic brotherhood from which we enjoy happiness to promote the good of others.

His was a message powerfully delivered to our satisfaction. We retired to the lodge following the service.

July 18

No one seemed to recall when she had arrived in the Village. No one knew where she had come from or how she managed entirely on her own. Nevertheless, she was known for her herbs. While I never spoke with her, it was said that she could break fevers when others failed. None of my patients ever admitted to having taken her advice.

The Village boys taunted her by knocking on her windows at night, shouting "Out witch," making a game out of her being a withered old woman. On the night before he was to go to sea one of the older boys, Seth, decided on a final visit to the witch. She spotted him and somehow knowing that he was going to sea shouted, "You! Take a good look at your home before you sail. You will never see it again."

On his return, when the ship was off Namguitt Point with many Villagers there to greet them, the lad climbed high up on the mast and gleefully proclaimed, "She said I'd never see home again but we're here, we' re home!"

He lost his hold, fell to the deck and died. The old woman was avoided thereafter.

July 28

Walked today many miles up the Pawtuxet Road to Pomecansett and Fields Point and through the fields. The scents of rockweed and hay mingled, making them pleasantly indistinguishable. Over the hill the aroma of sweet clover gently reminded me of the wonders of the Almighty's creation. 'Twas a thoroughly refreshing morning hike.

August 2

Treated the young son of Oliver Rhodes today who had broken his leg from a terrible fall while trying to balance on a rock above a cliff. He was bruised and in pain but had suffered little other damage.

His left leg, however, was of considerable concern. Bone fragments had pierced the skin, which did not portend well for the likely success of setting the bone. I suggested to Oliver that he consider taking his son down to South County to get assistance from the Sweet family, but Oliver felt that he wanted me to do what could be done.

With his father holding him down, I removed what bone fragments I could and reduced the fracture, placed a poultice of wheat bran over the open wound, and an eighteen-tailed bandage on the leg. I provided a small dose of laudanum for the pain.

I whispered to Oliver that full recovery was unlikely and that the best we might anticipate was some mending. His son will, at best, walk with a pronounced limp the rest of his life.

Such a tragedy for this young lad.

August 29

After years of abuse, Mrs. Paine overcame her reluctance.

"Why did you not come to me before with this problem?" I challenged.

"I did not think his drinking was as bad as it is. Besides, I didn't want anyone to know how abusive he was at home. This is a family problem."

"You should have come to me sooner or to your minister."

"It is my obligation to keep the family together. I didn't want the embarrassment of others knowing about Mr. Paine's problem. Up until now, I have always been able to keep him from hurting anyone. He's not such a bad husband, but he is not always reliable. I've had to help him when he was too inebriated to harvest apples. I've run the cider presses myself when he couldn't get out of bed."

"Mrs. Paine, you have needed help with Sylvester for some time."

"If he knew that I was telling anyone about his binge drinking he would be furious. It was better to have others believe that everything was harmonious. He would leave me, I am certain, if he knew that I had talked to you. Then, what would I do? I would be alone. There would be no purpose in my life. I am too old to start again. I used to be able to control him, not now."

"While I am willing to help you, there is little I can do for Mr. Paine. If he insists on besotting himself, you can try a few things in his diet. In your cooking, give him bitter almonds, cabbage, wormwood, and the roasted lungs of animals. This may discourage some of his drinking. But, his real problem is not with a disease. I am a doctor, not a member of the clergy. Ask the help of your clergyman."

"We do not often go to worship. Mr. Paine never goes. I know what the clergy would tell me anyway. I would be told that Our Savior worked a miracle in the wilderness to feed 5,000 with a few loaves and fishes and that He did this without providing wine. He would say that the demon rum has enslaved Mr. Paine, that he cannot make moral decisions and has fallen into debauchery, idolatry, discord, fits of rage, and selfishness. I have heard it all before.

Threatening Mr. Paine does not help. The minister

will say that this is the work of Satan, and God will, in
the final days, punish Mr. Paine with everlasting destruction. He will admonish us to pray for deliverance. Mr.
Paine is more interested in rum than prayer, more interested in deliverance by strong drink than in some future
salvation. Please, come to see him," she pleaded.

"If I could cast out the spell that he has fallen under
by commanding *deletrius* or by weakening the grip that
is suffocating him by waving my hands over his body
and demanding *expello*, I would do so. You need a power that is not encompassed in my medical training. But,
I will come for your sake. You need to know that it is
useless to treat him for one episode of befuddlement.
When he is willing to moderate his binging, he will be a
healthier man."

September 4

Reluctantly, I visited Mr. Paine at his wife's urging. As
she had described, he had taken to bed but somehow
had continued to sneak a bottle of alcohol into his bed. I
could smell it on his breath and night shirt. His countenance was ghastly, his skin cold and clammy, his speech
slurred.

He seemed to recognize me. I told him that no kind
of poison kills more certainly than an overdose of ardent
spirits. "Do you want to die?" I asked. "Do you want to
leave poor Mrs. Paine all alone?"

He mumbled through laborious breathing, but

otherwise showed no sign of concern. He seemed to like being stupefied.

"I will treat you for this current state of befuddlement, but I will not attend you again unless I am given reports that you have reformed your behavior."

The contents of his stomach had to be purged. I thought to induce a vomit but suspected he would spit out anything I gave him. Having given me no option, I drained ten ounces of blood from the nape of his neck by means of cupping glasses. He moaned as I applied the glasses but appeared too weak or too indifferent to protest. I then inserted a clyster of six ounces of milk and water mixed with two ounces each of sweet oil and brown sugar to which I added two tablespoonfuls of common salt. I told Mrs. Paine that this would soon produce a stool. Finally, to empty his belly, I injected smoke of tobacco into his bowels by using a hand bellows. While each of these treatments was unpleasant, Mr. Paine was too apathetic to care or too numb to notice.

"Mrs. Paine, your husband's continued drinking might result in his hands trembling and delusions that would even frighten him. Some men in this condition see snakes crawling all over their room, rats running about gleefully in their beds, and believe that the devil has come to take their souls. Having sunk in degradation he is mired in the devil's muck."

Nevertheless, Mrs. Paine was grateful that I had come

to treat him. But I cautioned her that she needed to seek help from someone else. I would not be back.

September 16

Not possible. Most unlikely. An absurd allegation. But, could it be true?

Hot talk at the tavern, where truth and fiction sit side by side and often commingle, was that the British were infecting blankets with smallpox and giving them to the Indians. The alleged plan was to send the sick Indians for treatment to colonial towns or to encourage them to join military units with a rumored promise that Americans would reward them for joining.

Lord Jeffrey Amherst had been guilty of the practice of infecting blankets that were then given to Indians during the so-called French & Indian Wars. According to "tavern experts" letters between Colonel Henry Bouquet and General Amherst attested to this practice, which created epidemics among the Indians.

The British have often referred to Indians as wild beasts. But, certainly, such a practice as intentionally infecting others with smallpox is as barbarous as any Indian atrocity. This possibility is not inconsistent with accounts we have received regarding conditions on British prison ships, which have been described as "more cruel than common murder." They confined John Brown aboard one of their ships and a Baptist pastor on a ship in Newport.

Could the British in their desperate attempt to win the war stoop to such vulgar tactics?

October 7

Rhode Islanders are healthier than many who live in the southern colonies. One might suspect that long, cold winters would inflict more coughs, colds, and chest congestion, but there is no evidence of this. In fact, I am convinced that the many storms that track across Rhode Island, bringing so many weather changes year round, cause our citizens to adjust rapidly to the constant changes between heat and cold, wet and dry, high winds and calm.

This strain makes us stronger and more resistant to disease. We are repeatedly rebalancing our bodies. Except for southern farmers, we spend more time out in the open air. Rhode Islanders also have the advantage of cleaner air from breezes that come off our miles and miles of beautiful coastline. How fortunate we are.

Someday, if the data can be acquired, I will prove this thesis by demonstrating that Rhode Islanders live longer.

October 9

Hope's condition has been arduous. Her sickness in the morning has gone on and on. Some say the nausea goes away after three months. This did not happen for Hope. She is uncomfortable lying down and getting up. Sleep is fitful and so she is tired most of the time. She craves strange food combinations like turnips and chocolate, which she eats any time of the day and night. And yet, she bears all of this with stoicism. I think she looks beautiful as her belly has blossomed, but she does not think so.

October 21

We had calculated a potential birth date for what we wished would be a son. We were anxious about creating a large family, but with the looming war we thought that growing our family might have to be postponed.

Two weeks before the anticipated date, Hope began to labor. She told me to rush to our nearest neighbor but that I should return immediately. She believed the baby was on the way. I ran over to ask Mrs. Hannah Brown to come quickly, but she was not home. I sent her son to find her. I rushed back to be with Hope. She told me that the labor pains were now coming more frequently. "You might have to help, Luke. The midwife and the neighbor women may not get here in time."

"Me, help?" I thought to myself, trying not to show too much panic. I had given up catching babies. Nevertheless, I began to sweat from every pore as I prepared the rags and blankets.

Hope's breathing accelerated, taking on a rhythm of its own, as did her exclamations that the baby was coming. I thought that this could not be. But some things are going to happen in a hurry whether we are ready or not and despite our desire to slow them down.

Daniel was born into my waiting hands just as two neighbors burst into the room. What an indescribable thrill it was to catch my son as he announced his arrival into the world. Thank goodness, the neighbor women took over from there.

Birth—especially of your own child—is such a miracle.

October 30

Serving as a surgeon has its surprising moments. Patients come with all kinds of questions: common complaints, difficult symptoms based on nonspecific or contradictory evidence, puzzling ones for which I initially have no answer whatsoever, embarrassing ones about private matters that require a great deal of delicate professionalism, and occasionally a witless question.

Today, someone came with one of the latter.

His complaint, for which he wanted treatment, was that he was losing his hair.

"Seth, I can't imagine why you have come to me with this."

"Doc, I respect you as a surgeon. You must know about such things."

"Are you just trying to add a little humor to my day?"

He got quite indignant. "Well, I **thought** I could talk to you. No one thinks this is serious. My brother laughs at me; he isn't losing his hair. My wife smiles and tells me she still loves me, but I think she loves me less."

Reluctantly, I decided that Seth did need someone to listen to his concerns. "Are there other members of your family who are bald," I asked, "your father, for instance?"

He admitted that his father was bald and a couple of his uncles and a cousin. But his brother was not going bald. When I probed deeper, I was able to deduct that he identified having a full head of hair with his manliness. The image of Sampson in the Bible was clearly in his mind. He was certain that he was growing weak and would be feeble long before his time.

He could not be reassured that hair loss was almost always a natural process and that he had nothing to worry about. He insisted that I treat him. When asked if he was concerned enough to permit me to bleed him, he readily assented. Obviously, he was troubled.

"You are not at a point where you need to be bled. I once read in the *New England Almanac* that a cure for baldness was to rub the spot on the head with an onion until the spot got red and then to apply bear's grease." I cautioned that I had never prescribed this "cure" and had doubts about whether it would help.

He seemed not to care. He left with a renewed animation in his step. The frown was gone from his brow.

November 14

Banners and flags are beginning to appear at all major events to rally pride in the colony and our cause. Even the Rangers have added a flag to our company colors. The most popular banner is one with a rattle snake on a yellow field with the motto, "Don't Tread on Me." The bright eye of the rattle snake, which itself is unique to America, may be esteemed as an emblem of vigilance. The snake does not attack without provocation and communicates a clear warning. But when it strikes, it does so with a deadly bite and never surrenders.

The Colony of Rhode Island has its own flag with thirteen stars, an anchor, and the word "Hope." It is well designed but a lot less rousing than the rattle snake flag. I like it better, nevertheless.

Perhaps some day there will be a true national flag of the united colonies, if all of the colonies could ever agree, but I do not see us giving up our Rhode Island flag.

November 24

Unlike the structure of the Continental Army, the Pawtuxet Rangers function with many of the elements of a democratic government. The regulars of the army are aghast that we elect our officers and do so annually. British officers, in particular, think that this leads to a lack of discipline, insubordination, disrespect, and sloppy and ineffective soldiering. The Redcoats often malign the colonial militia for these reasons, declaring that these soldiers are the very reason the colonies will never win the war.

Thomas Paine derisively called us "summer soldiers" because we go home to tend our crops in the fall. General Greene said that since we were not properly trained that we could not deal with the grim realities of a long military campaign. Even General Washington, we were told, complained to John Hancock that we were hurtful to the cause upon the whole. Yet, we do not buy our way out of serving, leaving the responsibility to the poor and the very young.

While members of the militia are more independent and freer to go home when they decide to do so, many take great pride in their ability to shoot. After all, many of us are excellent hunters and are particularly committed to defending our towns and those interests that we hold most dear. In fact, Pawtuxet is much more secure because the Rangers are here, and they protect the River from their forts on the Bay.

The original charter issued by the General Assembly in 1774 recognized "the Preservation of the Colony, in Time of War, depends, under God, upon the military Skill and Discipline of its inhabitants . . ." So far, Pawtuxet and Providence have remained safe because the Rangers are here.

Other militia units have quickly responded when they were needed—at Concord, at Breed's Hill—greatly swelling the numbers in the Continental Army and providing a formidable adversary against the British. Was it not the presence of such a force on Dorchester Heights that forced the British to abandon their occupation of Boston? The militia helped to accomplish that without a shot being fired!

The militia units are better because they elect their officers. There is accountability for leadership. Why would Rhode Islanders want to give up their say in how they would be led or engaged in any conflict? The defense of individual rights is the reason we are fighting in the first place.

December 25
Usually, we anticipate the Christmas season will be filled with traditional activities and merriment. Our mood is damped this year by the war. Yet, we are determined to enjoy ourselves as fully as possible this year, anticipating that much could be curtailed in the year to come.

As always, we attended church on Christmas Day. To our great satisfaction, the minister preached a sermon that never mentioned the looming conflict or what conditions might befall us here. While thinking that we will be spared is foolish optimism, why dampen an opportunity to celebrate the Christmas season?

He pointed out that a sullen heart is not a sign of Grace and that rejoicing in the Lord "maketh a merry heart." Many of my neighbors believe that somber sobriety and sorrow are Christian obligations, and we are closer to

God when we deny temporal joys. For once, the minister and I were in full agreement. Experiencing comforts and conveniences are healthy, not a bar to our striving for holiness.

He cautioned us, of course, against intemperance and told us that our joy must be founded on right principles. We must, he reminded us, keep our expression in its due compass.

After all, "unto us is born this day a savior." Glad tidings are in order. Much uplifted, we greeted our friends as we left the church. At home we began our celebration of the twelve days by decorating the mantel and front door with pine boughs, boxwoods, and flaming-red wild berries. The smells of the season filled the house. Then we sat most contented by the fire and sipped a glass of brandy, which we had been saving all year.

December 26

Our thoughts are occupied by the fear of occupation. We are increasingly aware of deprivations. No goods are being imported from England. We are making our own tea from materials that are locally grown. Our "liberty tea" consists of rosehips, lemon balm, raspberry leaves, and peppermint. It is tolerable but not very good. Some women are making tea from evergreen needles. It is worse. Our former success in obtaining goods from other colonies, the West Indies, or even from Africa through privateering is nonexistent. Even Hope's father cannot get good linen or finished clothing. Hope does not complain about wearing homespun. She is constantly sewing and mending. Our dinners these days are simpler. We are eating a lot more turnips and walnuts. Part of our patriotic duty is not to eat mutton—a favorite this time of year. The wool is needed for clothing.

Hope has organized neighbors to collect blankets and to make shirts for our soldiers. We share all we can. Our prayers in church were primarily for their safety and welfare. We also prayed that, if it be God's will, and we assuredly believe it is, that George Washington and General Greene will soon see victory. It has been a long time since we thought our Cause was about to triumph and peace would be at hand. Perhaps, this year.

Despite all of this, we give thanks for the birth of the Christ Child. As best we could, we observed Boxing Day by giving gifts of small clothes and food to the poor, the widows that are my patients, and to Nel the servant who helps us—now only occasionally—with work around the house. They were all most grateful and our hearts were warmed.

Yet, as the year draws to a close, I am troubled by what I am doing with my life. Have I been complacent, too comfortable? Am I missing my opportunity to distinguish myself by making a real contribution to the Cause? Glory will not be earned by tending the gout, toothaches, baldness, and spider bites. Others will have exciting stories when they return to the Village. No one will honor me for curing earaches and measles. Yet, I cannot fake enthusiasm for this war and for what may have to be endured and pledged just to wear the uniform.

1776

January 10

Zuriel Tower is a hateful scourge to this village. I had, yet another, angry confrontation with him today. He and I might have had a profitable partnership; that will never happen now. Our disagreements on the ethical practice of medicine have turned into acrimonious shouting and name-calling. I called him a snake, a quack, and a pretender. I can't record what he called me; I wasn't listening. He criticizes my work both publicly and privately, I am told. He will pay dearly.

He has no useful purpose in Pawtuxet. We do not need him. If he had any skill at compounding medicines, he might be of service. He has neither knowledge nor skill. He urges people to come to him to get compounds that they could easily make themselves with herbs from their gardens. He should simply advise them and not charge.

Most reprehensible is his fostering of expensive patent medicines upon gullible neighbors who will be poorer for their purchase and not healthier as a result. Zuriel imports Daffey's Elixir, Turlington's Balsom of Life, and Anderson's Pills. No one has ever been helped by these elixirs, despite their popularity. I could create an elixir much better than any of these.

Manipulating people's fears when they are most vulnerable is censurable. That is exactly what I intend to do. The Continental Congress made a big mistake by separating apothecaries from surgeons when making appointments. This gave the apothecaries a baseless legitimacy.

If there are apothecaries in the colonies worthy of practicing their trade, I do not know of them—not a single one. I can do what Zuriel does without opening a separate shop. I can better advise and follow-up on treatment. The big difference—I do not demand unwarranted charges.

January 15
The behavior of the Quakers continues to confound my patience and tolerance. They are not even tolerant of one another.

Members of a Meeting spend an inordinate amount of time and effort cleansing their ranks by enforcing rules around dozens of misdemeanors. These offenses include:

- Using colonial currency that is "tainted" because it is used to pay the army.

- Marrying a nonmember.
- Attending an innocent diversion such as a puppet show.
- Participating in a lottery, which we frequently conduct as the source of funds for such necessary civil projects as building a bridge.
- Failing to contribute funds to those who someone else decides is suffering and in need. Charity is not an individual's choice.
- Failing to attend Meetings.
- Deviating from using plain language, for which Jeremiah Wilkinson was harassed.
- Possessing furniture or clothing that is embellished or crafting the same for others.

For a denomination that promotes that each member is free to understand duty as revealed by God through "inner light," they repeatedly send committees to "labour" with the transgressors until they confess their errant ways, or in refusing to do so, they are disowned. These "labouring" visitations are intended to intimidate. Visits are reported back to the Meetings to serve as public embarrassment. Failure to comply results in banishment. Noncompliance results in denial of interaction with or any assistance from other Quakers.

This is not what faith should be about.

February 23

"We are properly Britons." So began the continuing debate at the Aborn Tavern last night. Copies of Thomas Paine's *Common Sense* have been circulating among us for some time.

The newspapers, especially from Boston and Hartford, have published provocative pieces with regard to our deteriorating relationship with the Crown. But, Paine's pamphlets are better reasoned, filled with less inflammatory rhetoric, and yet more inviting to debate.

And, debate we had!

Peleg did not take long to open the discussion with his, "We are properly Britons, gentlemen. Our culture and customs are British. Our families are English. Many of us were born in England."

Arnold countered immediately by complaining, "If we are properly Britons, then why are we not afforded the natural rights of all Britons: fully representative participation in Parliament, right to formulate our own laws, and the right to impose appropriate taxes on ourselves?"

And so we were off to another serious round.

In our previous exchanges, we had already plowed this field, so Peleg moved on. . . .

"It is preposterous to declare an open and determined independence. We are not prepared. We would be foolish to think we could prevail against the world's greatest navy and army. Reconciliation is our only hope."

Using Paine's arguments, Arnold declared that we were as ready as we were ever likely to be and that the time was now to foster union.

I reminded them both that our attempts to persuade the Crown with emissaries and protestors had proven ineffective in the end. "However, I agree with Peleg that it is unlikely that we can win a war. Too many lives will be lost in this uneven contest."

"We have already lost lives at Lexington, Concord and the occupation of Boston," Arnold protested.

"What have we gained by those losses?" I asked. "What did we gain by getting the Stamp Act revoked? It was just replaced by another restriction."

Warming to the task at hand, Peleg insisted that we needed British protection against European powers.

Arnold thought this was preposterous. He felt we could create a navy of our own and that we could easily raise an army much larger than the British could transport here.

I agreed. "We are excellent ship builders right here in Pawtuxet." I asked them to recall my comment after the burning of the *Gaspee*, "Distance from England and our river are powerful weapons in our favor."

"Well then," Arnold countered, "we need British protection for our commerce."

That comment raised immediate responses from both of us and also raised the volume of our voices.

Arnold: "England acts only from their own interest.

We can trade on better terms."

(Myself): "I agree. The record shows that Pawtuxet has prospered with trade arrangements that we have made ourselves, even when prohibited from doing so!"

Peleg: "A declaration of independence will divide the colonies," Peleg shot back. His comment might have had some impact had he not, in his excitement, knocked his own pipe out of his mouth. It smashed on the floor, disturbing us all.

Arnold: "Protecting our right to trade with whom we please will ensure our growth and will be a strong bond to unite us. The opportunity to trade is one right we can agree on."

Peleg: "We won't get any help from Europe. We can never stand against the Royal navy and army for long."

Arnold: "England has fewer friends in Europe than you think. Parliament cannot afford to buy German, Irish, Scottish, and Indian mercenaries for long. Our independence might be just what the French would find advantageous. Don't rule out their hatred for the English after the Seven Years' War and their lust for greater influence around the world."

(Myself): "What alternatives do we have?" I asked. "Reconciliation? It is already too late. We are pegged as rebels, especially in Massachusetts Bay and Rhode Island."

Peleg: "We have no plan for independence. Even

Paine argues that we need government to give us order and sincerity."

(Myself): "Do you not mean 'order and security?'" I corrected.

He nodded.

Arnold: "Paine has proposed an outline for representative government. He would have us implement a new experiment based on natural rights, not on a monarchy created by usurpation, heredity, and divine right. Why should this vast territory consent to be ruled by an Island?"

(Myself): "I agree with Paine on this point," I added. "What does a king give us? Kings are inclined to wage war for their own glory and gain. Then they give away the plundered treasures to their friends and tax the rest of us to pay for the war. We need a central government but one based on simple principles, not on one that is as complex as the English system, where the Crown is overbearing. My understanding, based on what I know about medicine, is consistent with what Paine says, ' . . . the more simple anything is . . . the easier repaired when disordered.' God knows, governments get disordered. That is how I look upon the human body and medicine. Balance within the human body and the body politic is what we need."

"Huzzah, Luke," they both echoed. "Do you have anything in your medicine chest to resolve this or do we just have to bleed them to achieve the balance?"

"Best I can do for now is to order you two another tankard."

February 27
With the recent publication of Thomas Paine's *Common Sense* and the heated discussions surrounding it, I was struck by a prayer offered last Sunday by the pastor at King's Church:

> Almighty God, who has given us this good land for our heritage, save us from violence, discord, and confusion, from pride and arrogance and from every evil way. Defend our liberties. Empower with the spirit of wisdom those to whom in thy Name we entrust the authority of government. In the day of trouble, suffer not our trust in thee to fail.

Why this prayer was chosen, I do not know. It would be most appropriate were we close to open conflict. I worry that the pastor, with all of his social and political connections, knows that the British are planning a new crackdown on the colonies. While he never includes political topics in his sermons, his selection of this prayer is ominous.

March 7
Pardon Slocum came today for his semiannual bleeding.

He wants to be bled in early spring and autumn to relieve congestion and to purify his blood. Sometimes he appears without any symptoms of ill health, but that does not alter his demand.

He is convinced that the bleeding makes him feel better within several weeks.

I have argued that feeling sluggish after a less active winter, changes in the air that come with new growth in spring, and the changing of leaves in the fall are all natural. These, I tell him, have an impact on his body and he will adjust anyway within a few weeks.

But, he will have none of my analysis of seasonal patterns. He knows what is best for him, so I bleed him twice each year.

Some people cry out when I cut them. Some just flinch. Others turn their heads as far away from the procedure as possible, gazing into vacant space. Not Pardon. He holds out his arm in ritual sacrifice. I always go to his modest home at the end of Remington Street where he lives alone. He insists that his semiannual bleedings be done at his own table. I can tell he has purposefully cleared the table. Stacks of his collections—odd-shaped shells, pieces of rope, huge pinecones—are scattered on the floor. Pardon's body appears to have been designed by a committee of Parliament who couldn't agree on any specifics. His head is too small for his broad chest and short, stout legs. His hands are huge with fingers twice the length of my own, but they hang on his arms that do not look as if they could support them. His hair is neither brown nor red—mixed like a salad. He cannot control the tone of his voice. At times it resonates like a rich baritone and then suddenly slips two octaves to that of a prepubescent boy.

"Should we use leeches this year or are you certain you want to be bled in your right arm this time?" I inquire. "Would you prefer that blood be drawn from your right leg or your neck or even, for a change, from your left arm?"

"No, Doc. It must come from my right arm," he dictates in his best baritone voice.

There is considerable debate about which location to choose in order to do the most good. For Pardon, however, his complaint is a vague notion of sluggishness and he just wants to be purified. In order to please him, I proceed with some drama. He sits upright, shoulders squared like a private about to be promoted to sergeant. He rests his right arm on the table as I place the copper bleeding bowl under his arm. I study his arm, touching it in various places as I select the all-important spot for the incision. I have watched other doctors study their patients for five minutes or more, pondering this decision. This, I believe, is just for show, but patients value their surgeons based on intangibles: deliberate actions, confident tone of voice. I am learning to be better at this.

With a certain flourish I take the linen covering off my small collection of bleeding instruments. My hand wanders over the scarificator, but I don't select it. Pardon and I have the same discussion each time I bleed him about the use of a scarificator. "The sarificator," he protests again, "is too quick. I hardly know that my skin is being punctured and the bleeding is too slow."

I take the scalpel and draw it across the spot selected, inserting it deep enough so that he can clearly feel the cut. Pardon grows silent as the blood begins to drip into the bowl. He watches in fascination as his bright red blood begins to cover the bottom. As it accumulates ounce by ounce and darkens, he breathes deeper. His ritual at these bleedings is to loudly exhale as if he were pushing out the bad air from his body along with the bad blood. His breathing is distinctive.

When the bowl is half full, he looks up at me to indicate that he thinks that is enough. His whole body looks relaxed. I put some lint over the wound and wrap a bandage around the arm. He will wear the bandage for days longer than necessary to announce to all that he has been bled and is now well. He is a walking advertisement for me. While I feel guilty bleeding Pardon, who really is not sick, if others would come to me earlier, they could preclude becoming more seriously ill.

He smiles. "I feel better already," he announces. But I notice his voice is softer, like that of a young lad who is uncomfortable in saying anything to his school master and he clearly steadies himself by holding onto the table as he gets up. "Come back in six months," he tells me.

I prefer to bleed Pardon than to bleed many patients who struggle through the whole procedure. They cry and complain of pain. Some turn pale as if they are about to faint. Yet, all of them will tell me later that they are grateful.

March 25

Dr. Peter Tenny and I decided we would bring the professional medical controversy regarding blood letting to the fore by staging a medical lecture in one of the buildings of the College of Rhode Island. Although each of us had an opinion regarding the usefulness of copious bleeding, our intent was not to resolve this argument, but to stimulate thought and consideration regarding its application among our colleagues. We decided the most provocative format would be a debate:

Proposition A: Copious bleeding has been shown historically to be a primary cure for disease and should be aggressively practiced. (Dr. Tenny would present this view.)

Proposition B: Copious bleeding is an uncertain cure. The difficulty of making a sound decision and the knowledge required to safely administer this treatment is so complex to be beyond the scope of only the most experienced doctors. Bleeding should be done only in moderation and with the greatest caution.

Our announcement of the debate drew a room full of practitioners. Dr. Tenny began:

"Since the time of the ancient Egyptians and Greeks, doctors have drawn blood to aid the healing process. Twenty-five centuries of success cannot be denied. The lancet is probably the most effective medical instrument ever created. Many other medical practices have been tried; many have failed or should be employed sparingly because no other is as effective as blood letting."

I responded with my introduction:

"Dr. Tenny, you begin this serious discussion of the relative merits of blood letting with a series of exaggerations. If blood letting alone was so effective we would have no pharmacopeia, no tonics and elixirs, no trepanning—which, by the way, goes back to ancient Egypt—no need for amputation, no purgatives. . . . I could go on. The point is that if blood letting were the answer to so many problems the practice of medicine would be a simple art. It is not. Even blood letting when used appropriately is very complex."

He paused only momentarily before responding, "We have the advantage of the founders of our profession—Hippocrates and Galen—who recommended blood letting for nearly every known malady. Phlebotomy, first administered by the clergy, has been and continues to be trusted by doctors and patients alike and with good cause."

"Let us get specific, Dr. Tenny. Our audience did not come here to hear generalities. Blood letting has limited application. It should not be used:

- In hot weather.
- When the patient is already phlegmatic, having been weakened by the disease.
- In the treatment of infants and children.
- At the time of menstruation.
- During pregnancy.
- In people of advanced age.
- When the patient is experiencing coldness of the extremities.
- When the patient is sweating.
- After the fifth day in pleurisy."

"Dr Carr, all of these objections can be readily addressed. Imbalance in the humors (blood being the paramount humor which carries our vital spirit) is most often a profusion of bad blood causing the problem and must be eliminated. Excitability in the blood vessels demands blood letting. There is ample evidence in the 2,500 years that this treatment has been practiced that none of the concerns you expressed are restrictive."

I responded. "The danger, I am convinced, is a tendency which you have just expressed to think that bleeding is *the* answer, the only answer, to the treatment of so many diseases and problems. Each of us knows that the human body is resilient and often heals itself. As physicians, we tend to remember when our patients recover and not to think about those who do not. Because so few medical records are systematically kept, we simply do not know how successful bleeding our patients has been."

"Dr. Carr, your concerns reflect a pessimistic view of the unquestionable achievement we have attained throughout the ages. Our theories are well considered and have stood the test of time unchanged. Our practices—most especially in bleeding patients—are grounded in tradition. We should take pride in this and continue to practice our art with confidence."

I countered his enthusiasm. "We do take pride in our profession and should promote our skills for the good health of those who come to us for treatment. Yet, all doctors are not equally skilled. All doctors do not have the extensive knowledge required to draw blood in such a way to ensure a favorable outcome."

"What are you insinuating?"

"Does each of us know the optimal bleeding site? I have heard much disagreement about what vein should be opened and on which side of the body. How much blood should be drawn: for each disease? . . . for a particular patient? . . . and over how long a period of time? Should all patients be bled until they faint? How do we adjust for: the season of the year? . . . the age of the patient? . . . the state of the patient's pulse? . . . the corpulence of the patient?"

"These are appropriate concerns, Dr. Carr, and are not to be dismissed lightly. As doctors it is our sacred duty to learn all that we need to know to serve our patients well. We are sworn to 'first do no harm.' You are quite right that there is much we need to know. Experience teaches us well. . . .

"My final concern is with regard to other standard treatments and where these fit into treatment regimes which you would like to see dominated by heroic measures of bleeding. Do we abandon opiates, emetics to induce vomiting, purges to cleanse the bowels, restrictions to diet, sweating and salivation?

"Each of these has its place, Dr. Carr. However, bleeding should be our primary therapy. With the exception of diet, which the patient either does or does not follow, each of the treatments you have mentioned is disagreeable to the patient. These treatments are often violent insults to the body and leave the patient feeling depleted. Each of these can be useful but the body automatically reacts to the substances given, removing bile from the bowels or stomach. The physician has no control of the quantity expelled. Opiates are, of course, useful to help the patient cope with pain. Sweating creates few objections but is slow. Throwing off disease this way or through salivation is often ineffective. Only bleeding permits us to measure precisely the amount taken. We can observe immediately the patient's response. Bleeding is not painful, and unlike these other treatments, is not disagreeable. It should be the treatment of choice."

Dr. Tenny and I took pleasure with this debate and apparently so did the members of the audience. We retired to the tavern, where a lively discussion continued well into the night.

March 28

I would not have planned to attend, even with an invitation from General Greene, if Hope had not been so wildly excited about accepting. His Excellency and General Greene would be en route from Boston to New York with their wives and were planning to stay one night in Providence.

A special dance had been planned as the entertainment. I suspect there will not be many of these events should the war continue for some duration. I do not like to dance and neither does General Greene, so we may be able to secret away for a private conversation; I suspect that is why he invited me.

Hope loves to dance but has had so few opportunities. Caty Greene also loves to dance and is rumored to have charmed his Excellency and the Marquis de Lafayette on the dance floor. General Washington, I understand, will dance well into the night whenever he can.

In truth, I would like the honor of meeting General Washington, though engaging him in conversation already sets my knees to shaking. I will have to practice a few lines so my mind does not go blank at the crucial moment, and I appear to be a total fool.

Hope has had preparations for our attire underway for weeks.

April 2

His Excellency General Washington chose him with exceptional care and insight. General Nathanael Greene has already honored us in Rhode Island by being commissioned by the Continental Congress as the youngest brigadier general in the army and acknowledged as General Washington's second in command.

He happened to be en route from Boston to New York when he and I attended a puppet show in Newport. We saw "The Creation of the World." Besides diverting our thoughts with such irreverent scenes as Noah and his wife dancing on the ark, we could not miss Punch's political message. He mocks the law and kings and pokes fun at everyone with impunity. We love to see him wield his slapsticks to defeat the very authority figures sent to bring him to justice. His opponents—the Policeman, Beatle, Jack Ketch—are bullies who he overcomes. Even the devil himself is outwitted. Punch gets away scot-free and we cheer with him, "Huzzah."

Many of us retired to the Sign of the White Horse where the tavern proprietor, Jonathan Nichols, greeted us all most cordially. Much to his torment, General Greene has had difficulty with his leg for many years as well as continuing bouts with asthma.

Discovering that I was a surgeon and his being troubled by current pain in his leg, General Greene sought me out and asked if I would privately meet with him. We found a quiet room and sat by a warming fire where a waiter filled and refilled our glasses with a most delicious port. Weary from his duties in Boston and recent travels on horseback, General Greene was, apparently, more than content to escape the social amenities of the evening and to sit and chat with me. How fortunate for me. His clear, liquid blue eyes, which kindled with excitement as he spoke, captivated my attention.

I quickly learned what medications he often took when his leg was particularly painful and assured him that I would provide him with an ample supply for the remainder of his journey to New York, including my own special elixir of apple cider infused with rum and sweetened with molasses. I promised to deliver these to him in the morning. He was excited to try my elixir, which, of course, for me provided a rush of appreciation.

He wished to be brought up to date on recent events in Rhode Island, especially whatever I knew about happenings in Coventry where his family continued to live. Mrs. Greene was expecting a child, and he was concerned for her because his new military duties took him away so much of the time. He also questioned me endlessly about the political climate of Providence and about the sentiments of citizens regarding the war. A Rhode

Islander himself, he clearly understood the reluctance to put at risk the provisions of the Rhode Island charter and our hesitancy to join too closely with the Sons of Liberty in Boston.

We discussed our mutual participation with the militias in Rhode Island; he had helped found the Kentish Guards. Without equivocation, he encouraged my continued service with the Pawtuxet Rangers and urged rigorous training. "One day we may need every able-bodied man in Rhode Island," he predicted. "The better prepared the militias are, the greater service they will be. In the end, Luke, we are not likely to win this war relying on the militias. We face the greatest army and navy in the world. Even with a well-trained and committed Continental Army, our challenges will be formidable. Consider using your talents to directly support those who fight. I would be pleased to have you in my headquarters."

His invitation took me by surprise. I made no response but my stomach began to shudder.

He also urged me to observe carefully the incursions on the rights and liberties of all colonists. "We must begin to think of ourselves as bound in protest by these arbitrary acts of Parliament and unite with one accord to oppose them."

When I inquired, he told me of his deep adoration for General Washington, which is why he had agreed to join the Continental Forces now stationed in the Colony of

Massachusetts Bay. He said that Washington was an outstanding leader who cared deeply about the men who served under him. "General Washington commands respect by his very presence. He has an intuitive sense of how to confront the better-equipped and immeasurably better-trained British forces. We desperately need his patience and superior judgment if we have any hope of victory. We will have to outsmart General Howe and the others. We will have to fight a very different war than the one to which the British are accustomed." He smiled as he sipped his port and suggested that we might just have to wear them down.

He told me that we would likely need many surgeons like me to care for soldiers in the field, at brigade hospitals he planned to establish, and in our homes.

Feeling freer to engage him—perhaps several glasses of the excellent port had helped to fortify me—I asked what philosophy or tenets of religion drove his commitment.

He explained that he was no longer a Quaker, having found their dogmatic adherence to certain rules unacceptable (I knew immediately why I had been drawn to this man). But he elaborated, "We do have an inner light that can help us to know what we should do. Trust your instinct, Luke, in your own medical practice. I have learned already from General Washington that we must eschew arrogance over every military or diplomatic triumph. We have a rightful cause and Divine Providence on our side, but the British will not abandon these colonies without the exercise of their great power. They have the resources to sustain this effort for a long time."

I sympathized with his having to leave his growing family and the management of the family forge. He sighed, the thoughts bringing to mind the sacrifices. "It would have been happy for me if I could have lived a private life in peace and plenty . . . but the injury done my country . . . calls me forth to defend our common rights."

Despite the pleasantness of our conversation and the comfort of our surroundings, his remarks were sobering. However, I am thankful that we have a man of his character and humility to lead our soldiers. I feel privileged to have experienced the blessing of this conversation.

April 5

His Excellency General Washington rode into town with a great flourish, escorted by General Greene. He will lodge at the home of the Hon. Stephen Hopkins. The steps of the houses along the route were crowded with women. The hillsides were covered with men. He was met outside of town by the First Col. Little's Regiment, followed by Col. Hitchcock's Regiment, the Company of Light Infantry, the Company of Cadets, the Governor of the Colony, who rode on the General's left hand—a grand and exhilarating parade.

April 6

I was not invited to dine with the party at the house of the Hon. Stephen Hopkins, but I did see his Excellency again today at an elegant entertainment at Hacker's Hall, where dinner and a number of patriotic toasts were drunk.

General Washington must be over six feet tall, handsome, dignified—almost regal in his military uniform. His presence is commanding. He is the center of every room he enters.

April 24

Many a tankard was lifted tonight at the tavern at the news that the statue of King George had been pulled down on Bowling Green in New York. This statue fully reflected his imperial arrogance. It displayed him as a Roman emperor, a full one-third larger than life. It seems to me that he was large enough without increasing his height and girth. The statue stood fifteen feet high on a pedestal of white marble and was highlighted like his coach and everything else he "owns" with gilt and gold.

The 4,000 pounds of lead that had created this craven image was sent to a foundry to make musket balls. Yankee ingenuity at its best!

April 27

At the meeting of the Rangers tonight we were told that Gilbert, Malloy, Barnes, Currier, Holtz, and Lynch had enlisted in the Continental Forces and were headed south. There had been no talk about members of our militia abandoning their duties in Pawtuxet to serve elsewhere. No one, not even Colonel Arnold, had urged any of us to go off to war. Yet, six of us were already gone and, frankly, there were nods of admiration by several members when Colonel Arnold made his announcement.

When I told Mrs. Carr, she said she had heard already that several men had joined General Washington and that others were being recruited. I put it to her directly, "Should I join?"

She hesitated. "If you went to war, I would worry about you constantly. But, your medical skills could be desperately needed. Besides, you would look handsome in a new uniform."

With that our awkward discussion ended. My stomach was suddenly as distressed as it had been when General Greene had invited me to join.

May 9

My respect for T. Paine grows. Not only does he present his ideas with reason, backed up with historical facts and precedent, but also with logic. He is not mired, as are many of my medical colleagues, in what he calls "the defense of custom." In *Common Sense* he argues, with passion and without regard to his personal safety, concepts that are unpopular in many powerful circles. I respect him for this, even though I am not ready to enlist in the Continental Army.

Besides, in the Appendix to *Common Sense*, he takes on the Quakers. In his "Epistle to the Quakers," he challenges their recently published, *The Ancient Testimony and Principles of the People Called Quakers*. While he does this with some politeness, there is no doubt that he is attacking them at the core.

He asks if "all sin was reduced to, and comprehended in the act of bearing arms," then why do the Quakers not challenge the British as well? He thinks this position, which they use against rebellion in the colonies, as grievously inconsistent with what they claim to be in conscience. He wants an explanation of how they can pretend to have such strong scruples against violence while so many of them are profiting from the conflict. He calls this "hunting after mammon." There is nothing equivocal about that language, and it is an argument that I have often used myself.

I admire the way Paine starts his "sermons"—slowly, disarming his opponents' natural defenses and then marching in with flags unfurled and drums beating. He ends by loudly asserting, "Ye do not believe what ye profess. Ye ought not to be meddlers in politics," and that this testimony, "serves only to dishonor your judgment."

I wish I had his linguistic skill.

May 21

Standing on the bridge today watching the waters wash over the falls, I was consumed by the timelessness of this place. The bridge: crossings, connections, separations. Below is no gurgling brook. The river is assertive, untamed, changing. The mysterious light flickers and dances—never the same. The waters connect us to all that is upstream. We are the hosts, welcoming the flow into the Bay and the great ocean beyond.

Here on the bridge, we are in transition.

But we are grounded. Slightly above the current, we are connected to all that has come before, sensing the same stirrings felt by all those who have stood on this spot, standing on the edge of a continent, shaping a future of infinite possibilities.

Whatever the truth may be, we do not simply pass over the bridge.

We pause. Saluting the past, in a moment of reflection we make the present less tense. This fascination feeds the soul; it is why we live here.

June 11

We do not know who he is. We suspect he is a deserter but he won't talk to us about what unit he served with or where he has recently been. What we do know is that he has malaria, and we are not pleased that he has landed in our Village.

There is a custom here and in many locales where

undesirable persons are encouraged to leave. While not a very Christian practice, it has developed in the community interest. Someone who wanders into our Village without any connection to others who live here and who has no apparent means or inclination to support themselves becomes a burden on the community. This practice is not intended to apply to those who become widowed, are incapable of working due to injury or disease, or even to those who happen by the Grace of God to arrive here sick.

Yet, malaria is certainly not a disease we want introduced here; nor are we comfortable with this mysterious and uncommunicative stranger.

Nevertheless, we will treat him, pray for his timely recovery, and then we will send him on his way.

June 18

My malaria patient still is not talking. His wandering fever has followed several stages of progression. He shivered initially and nodded when asked if he were chilled. I gave him another blanket, yet his feet remained cold to my touch. In the second stage of the fever his skin became red, his pulse quickened, and his urine became high colored. I asked Mrs. Randall, who was caring for him, to wipe his brow, hands, and legs with cool water. I am certain this provided some comfort but did not dispel the fever. When he entered the sweating stage, I predicted his body was eliminating its poisons.

Despite his unwillingness or perhaps his inability to speak to me, I talked to him about the causes of malaria. Cases often occur in summer and during rainy periods, and most have been found in proximity to poisonous vapors or swamps or from the effluvia of stagnant water. Some people have insisted that malaria was related to astrology, but that may be because it most frequently appears in the summer.

I treated this stranger with what I had. Much success has been reported by the use of cinchona or "Jesuits' bark." I read where sick animals had been observed chewing on this bark, which appeared to speed recovery. The dispensatory says that patients are reluctant to drink an infusion of the bark, which is bitter to the taste and difficult to disguise by adding rose leaves or wine. Under the best of circumstances the bark is difficult to obtain; I had none.

There have been many bold, foolhardy experiments that have been tried to rid the body of fevers. A legendary cure is to cut the ear of a cat, mix three drops of blood in brandy, add pepper, and administer this concoction to the patient. I was not able to find a willing cat and was not about to insist on a donation from our cat, Mrs. Norris. Even now she only likes me when she pleases.

The first thing I did was cleanse my patient's stomach and bowels to rid phlegm and bile by vomits. Other medicines are more effective when the stomach and bowels are evacuated first. I found that Epsom salts and ipecac worked well, though my patient was none too happy about this treatment.

When his pulse was strong, I bled him with leeches, provided sweet wormwood and a diet of water-gruel, weak chamomile tea, veal broth, and later light pudding.

. . . He was on the road to recovery in six days, and I hope he will be on the road out of the Village soon.

July 24

He may have been reluctant to command the army. He may not have distinguished himself in the French and Indian Wars. He may be unable to successfully demand from Congress what supplies and funds are needed. He may not win many battles. And yet, his Excellency George Washington is held in the highest regard.

Dr. James Thacher's report from Dorchester Heights is typical testimony of how General Washington is admired. He was seen out in front with the troops, encouraging them and rallying them when the tide turned against them. Resolute in his own duty, he inspires others.

He refused the letter sent by Colonel Patterson, adjutant-general of the British Army, and written by Admiral Lord Howe and General Howe because they failed to recognize his title. He was polite but unwavering. He would not permit the insult to himself nor allow the belittling of the spirit and temper of the American people.

Congress reviewed the matter and resolved "that he

had acted with a dignity becoming his character."

I fume with rage at those among us who lack the courage to do their meager share. I sicken when I discover immoral and reprehensible behavior such as seen exhibited by Zuriel Tower—our so-called apothecary.

The King's commissioners must be dismayed that offers of pardon and peace are not being readily accepted. We may not have the power and resources that are at the disposal of the British forces, but we have George Washington. His merit and character provide a moral standard that will not be easily defeated.

To win this war we must be favored with untainted consciences, ethical strength, and power derived from basic truth. His Excellency provides these to us.

July 26

July 1776 will long be remembered. The Continental Congress has declared independence. Our delegates, Hopkins and Ellery, firmly backed the resolution. Our General Assembly voted to remove from our name "colony" and insert "state" and then endorsed the Declaration.

The Declaration was read at the statehouse in Providence with hundreds of us in attendance. Although the sky was dark, a storm threatening, no one made a move to leave. The clerk's voice resonated from the balcony, "When in the course of human events it becomes necessary for one people to dissolve the political bands which have connected them with another . . . We hold these truths to be self-evident, that all men are created equal, that they are endowed by their Creator with certain unalienable Rights, that among these are Life, Liberty, and the pursuit of Happiness." When the clerk reached the end of the document, as if on cue, the sun broke through the clouds and a tremendous "Huzzah!" rose from the crowd.

The union of thirteen former colonies was celebrated by the light infantry firing thirteen volleys, by the canons of the Artillery Company, and by the *Alfred* and *Columbus* in the Bay that fired thirteen salvos each.

In keeping with the theme of the day, we drank thirteen patriotic toasts, at least, back at the tavern.

August 3

An official looking letter addressed to me arrived yesterday by coach at the tavern. Speculation was that I was being enlisted into the army with some exalted rank. When I opened it in private, General Greene was asking for advice on treating dysentery. His veiled suggestion was that he had lost confidence in the advice of doctors assigned to his headquarters who did not prevent the death from dysentery of ten soldiers per week while they occupied Prospect Hill trying to panic the British into abandoning Boston. Now, he lamented, that dysentery was rampant in the New York camps. I responded immediately:

My Dearest General Greene:

Your letter of August 20 arrived by post, creating much speculation at the tavern and instantly raising my fame in the Village. Of course, I did my best to play into the many theories that were proffered: I was being asked to propose military strategy, how best to negotiate with the British, or that I was being offered a commission as a senior officer. No one was taken in by my nods or refusal to provide any confirmation one way or another. All that I would tell them in the end was that I was being asked for advice.

While your letter was about a most serious matter, please accept my apology for using it to indulge in humor with my friends. Dysentery has long debilitated the armies of the world. There are treatments that have been used advantageously, but prevention is far better. Before a soldier will recover sufficient strength to be of real service, weeks, perhaps longer, will intervene. Because you will soon enough be on the march, stock up on soap and insist that soldiers use it. Special effort should be made to provide vegetables. Another critical preventive measure is to make digging and using latrines standard procedure in every camp you establish.

If I may paraphrase your comment to me when we met last: receiving advice is easier than implementing it. Once a soldier has experienced dysentery, either himself or observes it in a comrade, the fear of the disease can act as an incentive for preventive measures.

Your confidence in my advice—despite how little use my recommendations on small pox prevention turned out to be—is greatly appreciated.

Your humble surgeon and fellow Rhode Islander, Lukus Carr

August 7

The German bastards are coming to fight us. Those foreigners don't care who they fight for or who they fight against. Those Hessians will show no restraint. They will pillage wherever they go. They will kill men, women, and children indiscriminately. This is the last straw. Now it is clear. King George will do anything to force us into submission. If he wins all signers of the Declaration will be tried in England. Property of those who are leading us will be confiscated. We will all face charges of treason. We cannot permit him to win.

I told Hope that I was enlisting and would find General Greene in New York. He might find a way to make me an officer. Knowing of his steadfast concern for the health of the troops, I was certain I could advise him on ways to make soldiers fit to fight. I was also ready to do my share of the fighting.

Hope was less enthused now that I had decided to leave, but she said she was proud of me and wrung from me a promise to write frequently.

Colonel Arnold had to be informed of my departure, but I never said a word to my friends at the tavern. They would hear soon enough and learn of my heroic actions.

August 14

This is the time when I can justly be proud to be a doctor. While we often place others above our own welfare and promote higher causes, the five physicians who signed the Declaration of Independence have honored my profession. They composed nearly 10 percent of the fifty-six courageous men who committed to the signing. Benjamin Rush of Philadelphia summed up the tone of the occasion:

> "The pensive and awful silence pervaded the [signing ceremony] when we were called up, one after another, to the table of the President of the Congress [John Hancock] to subscribe to what was believed by many at the time to be our death warrants."

The five physicians were: Josiah Bartlett of New Hampshire; Lyman Hall, Georgia; Benjamin Rush, Pennsylvania; Matthew Thorton, New Hampshire; and Oliver Wolcott, Connecticut. These men will certainly continue to serve liberty as patriots in the militia and political leaders in their states, as well as continue to be distinguished practitioners in the profession of medicine.

Rhode Island was represented by William Ellery, a lawyer/merchant from Newport, and Stephen Hopkins, merchant from Providence. While not from my noble profession, they were worthy representatives. My hat is off to all of these fine men.

August 16

With much effort I found General Greene on Long Island. Sickness in the army was rampant. A third of the army was unfit to fight. "We cannot prevail, Luke, if every one of our soldiers cannot fight. We are outnumbered at full strength."

"The health of the soldiers in the field," I told him, "depends on discipline."

"What do you mean?" he said without accusing me of making an impudent remark to a senior commander.

"Sir, may I respectfully suggest that soldiers eat more fruits and vegetables. They would be doing that if they were at home. Also supply every company with ample soap and order that they wash frequently. Sergeants should supervise a routine. New latrines must be dug every three days. Anyone voiding near their tents or in the trenches dug for defense must be punished."

He looked at me with some disbelief. "Your job, lieutenant, is to see that these steps are implemented. I will announce to the staff, today, that this will be our plan. You have my full authority."

Snapping to attention, I responded heartedly, "Yes. Sir!" and made a sharp soldierly exit.

As I strode back to my own tent I thought, *Now I have a real mission.* And, he called me lieutenant. That was how I learned of my promotion.

As I began to more fully understand the situation, I was embarrassed by my simplistic solution. The regimental surgeons did what they could to combat typhus and dysentery. These had not been big problems in Boston. The term "hospital" was being used to refer to any collection of the sick. There were no beds. Men used their own blankets. The only food was hard bread, salt beef, and a little rum. Typhus was worse in the hospitals and we suspected that soldiers who were able to join their units brought the disease with them. Before the purplish spots, peeling skin, and falling hair, soldiers exhibited chills, fever, trembling hands, and listlessness. The few of us who had any medical responsibilities did what we could to keep men from the squalor of the hospitals. We separated those who were sick from the others. Those with the bloody flux just suffered through it with cramps and frequent stools with blood. We urged the burial of excrements.

There was little time to attend to my new responsibilities. Fruits and vegetables could be found, if at all, only by foraging nearby farms that were soon exhausted of any useful food. There was no soap and not much time to dig latrines. Hungry soldiers will eat whatever they find—unripened corn, green fruit. One scavenging party found a stash of molasses hidden in a barn, which they immediately consumed. My warnings went unheeded and they spent the night squatting in the bushes. I think some of them would have preferred to have been shot.

Despite the sickness, morale was high. The fighting at Fort Sullivan bolstered our belief that we could repulse the enemy on Long Island. General Greene had been scrupulously studying the terrain to provide us with maximum advantage. On June 29th General Howe sailed into New York with 8,000 well-rested and well-fed soldiers and another fleet with 7,000 Hessians arrived on August 12th. Rumors spread that the Hessians had been promised $34.50 for every rebel they killed. Three wounded counted for one killed.

Scouts came with reports that a huge force under generals Howe, Clinton, and Cornwallis were staging for attack. Just before the assault General Greene was confined to bed with a terrible fever. Greene always leads out front and has a definitive plan based on his terrain analysis. General Washington put General Sullivan in command and then General Putnam; neither knew the

terrain nor General Greene's plan. In short order, the
Hessians' main thrust enveloped the forces under General Putnam with devastating effect.

General Washington, without further hesitation,
ordered a withdrawal. Our escape was only made possible by a heavy fog, rain, and wind sent by Providence to
spare us. Our loss was horrific—300 killed, 650 wounded, 1,100 captured. It was a terrible defeat. Our morale
plummeted. Gone was any optimism that we could prevent a siege of New York. Our only consolation was that
we had been saved from annihilation.

August 20
My introduction to the realities of war made me come
to terms with my own vulnerability, my own inexperi-
ence, and my ignorance of how to even protect myself.
I was going to have little opportunity to perform heroic
medicine. My focus had to shift to my own survival. I
had nothing to report to Hope except bad news. And we
would be on the march soon.

Luckily one of my messmates, Blake, took notice. "I
have been with this army for sixteen months and I can
tell you, Doc, that you are not much of a soldier. Our
strategy these days is to hit and run. You are not going
to get to spend much time hanging around headquarters
expecting to take care of the injured. Who knows when
General Greene will be well enough to resume command. If you want, I will show you what I have learned

the hard way—how to fire from protected areas, how to keep your powder dry, how to aim your musket so that what you hit does some damage. . . . More important, you have to ration what little grub they give you so you will not starve. You need to learn to trick yourself into believing that you can march five more miles when you think you are totally exhausted."

True to his word, Blake began to make a soldier out of me.

September 10

We got orders to form up. They never tell us where we are going but rumor had it that we were headed toward Harlem Heights. It had rained all night and was still raining. The mud made slow going. Our soaked clothing made everything twice as heavy. The wagons got stuck or broke down.

Several miles into the march my musket wore a sore place on my shoulder. The further we went the musket began to bore into the bone.

I was already weary, but I was determined to stay close to Blake. My greatest fear was being left behind—alone. Blake kept me distracted with talk.

By sundown a deep fatigue had set in. Our tents were miles behind us. We slept in the mud at the side of the road. Our only food was what we had carried in our sacks. Morning arrived all too soon; we were on our feet and marching, trudging actually. No fifes and drums were with us to lift our spirits. We stumbled on. I lost track of time. The senior officers told us that the wagons would catch up with us by nightfall. But we saw no wagons that night or the next either.

Finally, we reached Harlem Heights and made camp. The army is melting away. Enlistments expire. Others desert. It is no wonder. We have seen little success. No one is paid. We have few blankets and no replacement uniforms. Our shoes are worn through. The holes in our stockings invite grit that rips between our toes and turns our feet into bleeding pieces of meat. What little food we get barely keeps us alive. When the next battle comes, we will have to face it with little powder.

September 16

We established our defensive positions. We saw them coming. They came in wave after wave as far as the eye could see. "Hold your fire," Captain Ahearn shouted, "until I give the command."

In perfect order, they came at us. The sight was awesome. The fields were ignited with row after row of roses bobbling in the breeze. The rows blended into a blanket of red. But there was no breeze and there were no roses—only certain death facing us. And still they came.

Blake looked over at me to quell my terror, but even he looked frightened. Then the commands, "Make ready, take aim, fire!"

The British fell like wooden sticks, as in our childhood

game of ninepins. Others stepped over them, firing as they got closer.

In seconds the battle was a confusion of drums, wild shouts of men on the attack, and deafening explosions. The front line of the British fell back but not far. We had time only to reload before they came at us again. We held our ground and they fell back. They brought their field cannons forward and began their bombardment. Smoke filled the trenches in front of us. No longer could we see where they were or the effect of our muskets. The taste of powder choked my breathing. Someone yelled, "Move left." We moved, tripping over our dead, running past those strangling in their own blood. Men coughed on the dense smoke or, perhaps, on impending death. I ran with the others.

As we broke into a small clearing, there they stood. A squad of Hessians charged at us, bayonets thrusting with menacing force. I saw our captain go down. A Hessian was charging at his wounded body to finish him. I threw myself over his body as others fell around me. Looking furtively out of a corner of my eye I saw one of my comrades take a bayonet in the side. Outraged, I sprang to my feet and went on the attack. I hadn't gone ten yards when a searing pain tore my right leg. Before I could take another step, I collapsed. I lost consciousness. My last thought was "I am undone—."

When I stirred awake, Blake was standing over me. "I think you are a soldier after all," he smiled as he wrapped a torn piece of shirt over my bleeding wound.

The next time I was alert enough to notice, I was in some kind of makeshift camp. My pain was nauseating. The wounded were everywhere. The air was filled with the stench of men belching.

I remember nothing of the next two days. Fortunately, Blake stayed at my side as those around me died or were provided with whatever care was possible. Blake told me that the surgeon had fished out the musket ball embedded in the calf of my leg. My overwhelming thought was that if the wound looked infected, they would amputate. My fear of battle or of dying from a bayonet wound to the chest paled at the thought of living with an amputated leg. I begged Blake to drag me off so they could not find me.

September 20

I had experienced my own corner of hell. The wound festered but I treated it myself with a little yarrow that I had in the medical kit that I had carried under my shirt. Blake kept me alive with water from his canteen and with food he scavenged or stole from somewhere. I shall be forever indebted to him.

Captain Ahearn found me trying to stand long enough to put some pressure on my right leg. He told me I was a hero. I had saved his life by throwing myself over his body. I didn't feel like a hero nor did I look like one. Yet weak from the ordeal, I was still alive.

What was left of my unit got transported to Fort Washington in New Jersey, where I was united again with General Greene. While New York burned, Greene fortified Fort Washington and Fort Lee across the river in a determination to block the British path to Philadelphia. The Congress had already moved to Baltimore.

I still could barely stand and, at best, could only hobble a few yards. General Greene noticed my pathetic attempts at walking and suggested that I go home to Rhode Island to recuperate. "We will need you, Luke, for the battles that lie ahead. Get strong and return to us."

My enlistment was up, but I never would have asked him for leave to return home. Nevertheless, as soon as a wagon was going north, I got added to the baggage.

November 22

The news much alarmed us when we learned that the British had taken Fort Washington and Fort Lee. Nearly our entire army defending these was taken prisoner; some say as many as 2,800. I surely would have been among them.

The suffering of prisoners of war is unimaginable. The British believe that rebels should be punished as well as imprisoned. The *New Hampshire Gazette* reported:

"The enemy in New York continues to treat the American prisoners with great barbarity. The meat they are obliged to eat raw. In the small space of three weeks no less than 1,700 men perished."

The prisoners taken to prison ships such as the *Jersey* have little chance of surviving.

November 25

The whole Village seemed to celebrate my return. When I was feeling stronger, the neighbors held a collation in my honor. Everyone wanted to shake my hand and thank me, as if I had done something to win the war. Victory was still uncertain from my perspective. When I returned to the tavern, the boys wanted to hear my war stories and how I had saved Captain Ahearn's life. Apparently, he had written a letter to the Providence paper extolling my courage and calling me a hero.

I do not know why I did not bask in all of this glory. To me, Blake was the real hero . . . and so many others. I know I have done right and I am on better terms with myself, but there must be something more.

November 28

I fear that if the destruction continues there will be no cities left in America. Boston is in ruins from its occupation. Now New York has been burned. From the accounts, it is not clear how much of the danger was done by a simple fire that an ill wind spread, how much was due to British intent, and how much was deliberately set by fleeing

citizens determined to deny Tories any comfort in occu-
pying the city. A published account, which has fallen
into our hands, has been circulated:

> "It is almost impossible to conceive a scene of
> more horror and distress. The sick, the aged,
> women and children, half naked were seen going
> they knew not where, and taking refuge in houses
> which were at a distance from the fire, but from
> whence they were in several instances driven a
> second or even a third time by the devouring
> element, and at last in a state of despair laying
> themselves down on the Common. The terror
> was increased by the horrid noise of the burn-
> ing and falling houses, the pulling down of
> such wooden buildings as served to conduct the
> fire. The confused voices of so many men, the
> shrieks and cries of the women and children, the
> seeing of the fire breaking out unexpectedly in
> places at a distance which manifested a design
> of totally destroying the city made this one of
> the most tremendous and affecting scenes I ever
> beheld."

Burned were about 600 houses and several churches. This is not war waged by opposing soldiers in open
fields. This is misery—horrible and terrible—visited
upon citizens in our population centers.

November 30

Once again, we have evidence that we will prevail in this just cause. While He tests our fortitude and depletes our spirit with military defeats, He provides us signs of hope.

Dr. Thacher sent us word by the New York stage that stopped at Aborn's Tavern. His report explained that we were outnumbered two to one on Long Island and that the enemy possessed every advantage. Thacher believed we had lost twelve hundred killed and wounded in the battle. Our remaining forces, fatigued and discouraged by defeat, were about to be surrounded and totally destroyed.

General Washington resolved to withdraw what remained and personally conducted the retreat. But Divine Providence interceded. A thick fog enveloped the whole of Long Island during the early morning hours. On the enemy side in New York the sky was clear. On our side, an unusual fog interposed. The fog permitted nine thousand of our men, their baggage, provisions, stores, horses, and munitions to cross the river, which was a mile or more wide.

The enemy saw nothing.

The Americans miraculously escaped.

December 2

Long orations are being recited in an attempt to make clear why independence from Great Britain had been declared. *Common Sense* put it simply:

> "Britain was too jealous of America
> to govern it justly; too ignorant of it
> to govern it well; and too distant from
> it to govern it at all."

Nothing more needs to be said.

December 18

A large flock of wild geese were observed today flying southeast. The old timers hail this as an unwelcome sight—a forerunner of bad weather. The soreness in the scar on my thigh is another sure sign.

December 19

Joining the Pawtuxet Baptist Church was a trying experience. Had I known all that it entailed, I might not have put myself through the ordeal. I did not have much choice.

Reverend John Graves has fallen out of favor at King's Church. He believed he was obligated by this ordination and appointment to the ministry here to pray for the King and the Royal Family. For the most part, those of us in his congregation thought otherwise; we invited him to leave. This left King's Church without a minister; no prospects were in sight. Suddenly, being an Anglican colored you as a Tory or raised suspicion about your support for the war. Many had already left King's Church. With diminished financial support, the church had to close.

My own conviction is that regular worship is necessary and desirable. I think it is important to join with neighbors in common belief and concern for one another. Few choices were available to me. There was a growing Jewish population in Newport. For me becoming Jewish was not viable. Trinity Episcopal, though stronger than King's Church, was suffering similar problems with its ties to the King. Nor was I about to become a Quaker.

From its founding, Rhode Island has not embraced organized religion despite a commitment to spiritual principles. The Baptists in Providence have long been established and are strong. A group of them have decided that travel to Providence is unnecessary and have begun to meet at various homes in the Village. There is much talk of building their own meeting house.

When I inquired of neighbors and some of my Masonic friends who were Baptists, they spoke highly of the theology, the sound Biblical foundation for their faith, and the range of freedom that the church permitted.

To my chagrin when I asked if I could join, I discovered that membership required the "scrutiny of the congregation." Each prospective member had to "give satisfaction" that he was at peace with his neighbors. This seemed reasonable to me, but was reminiscent of the process I had been through when I joined St. John's

Lodge. "Well," I thought, "the Masons thought I was acceptable. The Baptists might also approve."

Apparently, I have not made enemies among the Baptists, or they thought that adding another surgeon to their membership list would be useful. Neither Hope nor I had to answer objections from critics. We did, however, have to stand before the congregation and affirm our faith. I was trembling so much that the perspiration soaked through my shirt. Hope carried herself with confidence. In the end, there should be no objections in declaring one's faith publicly by either word or deed, but I was glad when the verbal part was over and we were elected.

Members of the congregation warmly congratulated and welcomed us.

December 21

The pulpit may be the most influential voice in rallying citizenry to the Revolution. Newspapers are widely read, but most of us have learned that the rhetoric is typically inflammatory; the facts, as presented, are questionable and contradictory. Within weeks, a "correction" must be published.

Pamphlets and broadsides are somewhat more reliable, but most are written under pseudonyms. Veracity is difficult to evaluate when the author is unknown.

However, we all know and trust the word of our ministers. Why would any of us consistently attend meetings if we did not believe that we are being presented with well-reasoned, intelligent messages from the pulpit? I listen intently to the hour or hour-and-a-half sermons, believing that the lesson presented is grounded on a foundation of ethics and sound values.

Old man Potter, who must be seventy now and who has been a churchgoer for all of his life, told me that he calculated that he has heard 7,000 sermons, totaling 10,000 hours. None of us spends more time attending anything that shapes our thinking as much as sermons do.

For instance, last Sunday Pastor Grew used as his text 2 Chronicles 13:12: "And behold, God himself is with us for our captain." Ministers and military chaplains often claim that "God is on our side" and, therefore, we must surely be victorious. This belief is comforting.

Pastor Grew was particularly inspiring in this sermon. He built his theme beginning with the idea that all events are preordained, and we in Rhode Island and the colonies as a whole are chosen to be the vanguard of a new world order. He speculated that we are meant to become the new Jerusalem, and each of us has a portentous role to play. It is hard to deny that this idea is both inspirational and frightening in its implications. . . .

Pastor Grew went on with great flourish to exhort us, "We have in our power to begin over again. A situation similar to the present hath not happened since the days of Noah."

In persuading us that we are God's special people who have been planted in the American wilderness to restore the Devine as the supreme authority, Pastor Grew made it clear that we must be prepared for "real service." He warned that military skill and weapons would not be enough. "We must," he explained, "have moral and spiritual resolve. We must believe in what we are fighting for, and we must trust in God's power to cover our heads in the day of battle and carry us from victory to victory."

I felt like standing up and cheering. I wished that every soldier and all those working at home to support them could have heard him. He is a thoughtful, lucid preacher. While he is quiet in action (I like that), he holds the attention of his congregation. He is mostly responsible for the growing membership in the church.

Only a few months ago, sermons had been exclusively devoted to local concerns and more especially to individual salvation. Not any longer.

I am beginning to see the unifying power of inspirational messages such as the one offered by Pastor Grew. If such a message can eliminate political doubt or lack of commitment, remembered messages potentially could enable acts of renewed hope and courage on the battlefield.

Might something similar have healing power over disease?

December 24

The second child seemed to cause Hope less distress. Perhaps, we knew more of what to expect. Perhaps, Daniel distracted us. Hope's transformation was just as exiting as it had been the first time. I worried less but prayed just as hard. She asked but I tried to be more helpful with domestic tasks and with caring for Daniel, but my patients kept me occupied more than she might have liked. She did suffer from leg cramps but taking short walks together helped and she found my gentle massage of her back — soothing.

There was no doubt in her mind when she went into labor. Hope had made all of the preparations: selected the midwife and discussed what needed to be done, talked with her mother and with selected neighbors who promised to attend her, even prepared towels and rags. The new one's clothing and blankets had been set aside in a special chest near the bed.

My job was to build a cradle which I lovingly accomplished and my duties were to make the notifications when the time had come.

Hope was in obvious pain when she instructed me to be off on my notification duties.

We all gathered around her, taking turns wiping her forehead and muttering encouragements. I held her hand but she hardly seemed to notice. The labor continued for long hours. Occasionally, Hope would drop off to sleep but the labor pains would force her awake.

The birth was taking too long. I began to get worried that something was amiss. My concern must have been reflected in my face or in my voice. I don't really remember what I said.

Finally, the midwife whispered in my ear that I should leave the room, heat some water and stay away until she called. I shook my head in disagreement; I was, after all, a doctor. She insisted. I baulked. Her tone changed from invitational to a sergeant's bark. The scowl on here face, now filled with impatience, left little doubt. She looked pleadingly in the general direction of Hope's mother who immediately guided me out of the room.

Time dragged on. I was sick with worry. Every moan, every cry rushed down to me sitting in the kitchen where I, inconsequently, kept the water from getting too hot.

After what seemed like days — must have felt like months to Hope — I heard her first cries. I hesitated but a moment and rushed upstairs to welcome our new daughter, Eliza. No time in my life have I ever been so ecstatic or so thankful. I gave the beaming new mother a gentle hug and acknowledged the help of the women in the room who now sprang into action doing I know not what.

Eliza was pink, wrinkled but, oh, so beautiful. I could hardly wait to spread the word and I didn't wait for long.

December 30
General Greene has come back to Rhode Island for the

holidays and honored me with a visit to my home.

"Thomas Paine has summarized the situation accurately: 'These are the times that try men's souls.'" General Greene initiated our conversation with uncharacteristic foreboding. "Since we first met," he continued, "I have been despondent. The war, as you know, has not been going well. The human costs of our defeats haunt me. I do not mean to minimize the loss you must feel when a patient fails to respond to your treatment and dies. Yet, when I fail to plan properly to prepare our troops or when I make an incorrect assessment of enemy capability as I did at Fort Washington, the results can cost the lives or hundreds, sometimes thousands."

"The difference, General Greene, is not in the number of lives. My patients come to me with an absolute expectation that I will cure them. Your soldiers expect you to lead them well, but they know the risk of combat. Some know that their service may mean that they will never return home."

"The other cause of my despondency, Luke, has been my poor health. I have missed critical meetings and even key engagements."

"From what I hear, General, you have General Washington's confidence. Because of your leadership, the Rhode Island troops are the best in the Continental Army."

"My experience has been hard earned. My lack of combat experience has forced me to study historical leaders and to learn by doing. I am learning, but that is not sufficient."

"General, I will remind you of your own advice to me. We do not know what fate has in store. You received the appointment to brigadier general, somewhat to your own astonishment since your friends in the Kentish Guards did not elect you to command the Rhode Island Army of Observation. Now Congress honors you with an appointment under General Washington. You told me of the importance of trusting instincts and of the need for patience. You have both. Pardon my bluntness, General. You have been called to serve."

"Luke, it is easier for me to give advice than to follow it myself. As I think about it, many events demonstrate a remarkable intervention of our Creator. The Greene family forge, to which I had been entrusted, burned to the ground in 1772. We were back in operation within a year. To have General Washington as our commander is another miracle. During the French and Indian Wars, he had two horses shot out from under him and four musket balls whiz through his coat. We do need to accept what God has set before us and walk in his ways.

"Before we part tonight, I want you to know that there may be more support for inoculation. Mrs. Greene and I have both been inoculated. General Washington is considering ordering the inoculation of the entire army. We cannot afford to diminish our numbers because of a disease like small pox.

"Thank you for your patience in listening to me. My separation from Caty means I have no one I can comfortably confide in. Next time we meet, let us explore less gloomy topics. Let us discuss our favorite books."

December 31
It was a year of jubilant joy; it was a year of dark depression. It was a time of anticipation; it was a time with few prospects. It was a season to give thanks for new discovery; it was a season when no insight emerged. We know exactly what lies ahead; we have no idea where the road will lead.

We thought we were independent and free—we are not.

1777

January 9

Mrs. Butler asked me to attend to her ten-year old daughter, Amity. Her face and chest were covered by small spots, resembling flea bites. She was most uncomfortable with the itch, a sore throat, and swollen eyelids, which hampered her vision. Mrs. Butler was pleased to learn that the problem was only measles but that was of no comfort to Amity.

She started to cry as soon as she saw me. I evoke fear in children by just walking into the room. I tried to joke with Amity about how colorful her face had become, but she saw no humor in my remarks.

Her sister Lydia and two brothers had been making fun of her to their amusement until their mother scolded them into silence. Actually, I think their tormenting of Amity came from nervousness that they might get whatever she had, which in all likelihood they will. They fidgeted all of the time I was present, almost as if each was beginning to itch.

Her fever seemed mild . . . and I dislike bleeding children—seeing their own blood leaking out strikes terror into many of them, especially the girls—but I do it anyway if it is in the patient's best interest. I try to distract children when I bleed them, usually with little success; so this time I prescribed other treatments.

"Mrs. Butler, make a decoction of liquorice and marsh mallow roots with sarsaparilla and, to induce a vomit, calomel tea." This treatment would not endear me to Amity, either. If her throat continued to be troubling, I suggested using oil of almonds. She should be kept on limited, light food, drink buttermilk and be kept out of cold air.

I warned Mrs. Butler that the other children would likely get the measles as well. Unfortunately, each might come down with the disease just as the previous child was feeling well. Mrs. Butler might be dealing with measles for a full month or more.

January 15

Few ailments are more painful and debilitating than earaches. Mrs. Boucher had anguished for over a week with hers before seeking my assistance. Her drawn complexion and listlessness attested to her suffering.

Nelly had placed warm milk in her ear for three days. No relief. She wondered if placing leeches on her ear might be what was needed. I cautioned that placing leeches on the ear ran the risk of a leech or two crawling into her ear, compounding the problem.

Instead, I ignited a strand of hemp. I extinguished the flame and blew the smoke directly into her ear. This treatment has often proven therapeutic. I also instructed that she fill a hog's bladder with milk and mallows, mull in cider, chamomile, linseed, and saffron and apply this to the ear.

"If you do not feel better in two days," I told her, "take the juice that remains in the pot after boiling lean mutton. Make this ointment as hot as you can tolerate and place it in your ear. You have suffered long enough."

January 16

There are rumblings now and then from the Quakers—but from hardly anyone else—to halt Rhode Island's participation in the slave trade.

This is not likely.

Our economy is highly dependent on slaves, and they are treated decently here compared to serving on sugar plantations in the West Indies. I am told the percentage of our slave population is almost twice as high as any other New England colony.

The loss of slaves or, God forbid, their abolishment would be devastating to the large-scale farms in South County. I hear that William Robinson has forty slaves to run his estate in Narragansett as have the Stantons. Our wealthiest merchants have built their fortunes on the slave trade: James, Obadiah, Nicholas, John, Joseph, and

Moses Brown, for instance. Thousands of hogsheads of rum sent to Africa to trade for slaves is extremely profitable. Our command of this market is increasing. Rhode Island merchant ships are highly dependent on slaves to fill out the crews.

Even here in Pawtuxet, Captain Thomas Remington on Post Road has made ample profits from shrewd dealings in the triangle trade. He has kept slaves chained in a building behind his house and held auctions in his barn.

Slaves are property. They are vital to the growth and prosperity of this colony. The Quakers, as usual, are out of step and out of touch with our laws that have been popularly enacted.

January 17

Hope is an angel, a reincarnation of Hygeia between her loving care, insistence that I exercise, nourishing soups, and spirit-lifting pies. Pain persists, but I am moving better and have more stamina. I am much mended.

January 20

A blessing?

An unexpected opportunity?

A curse?

With the unexpected passing of her father, Hope has inherited a large sum of money. She had always been his favorite. He had encouraged her education, not only in domestic arts but also in mathematics. In a most generous act, he provided her with funds and a sizeable piece of land in East Greenwich.

Hope's father had offered several times to give her a loan to expand the family business in the Providence area or to invest in some other endeavor. He reserved the right to approve of and monitor any decision. Characteristically, Hope refused; she would not condescend to his control.

I have not thought about my own father for some time, but the inheritance from Father Tucker brought the memories back. Had I made a grievous mistake years ago when I rejected my father's offer to join him in business in our hometown of Kingswood? I wouldn't want him to know I was even considering a typical business venture now. He had cast me off and I had no inclination of thinking about what he might advise.

Was Mr. Tucker, who never really liked me, reaching out beyond the grave to lure me into a commercial enterprise with Hope in which I had little interest? Even now I also did not want to be in debt to Hope's father and had never had an interest in creating or managing a commercial enterprise. My rejection of my own father seems like a long time ago.

Hope and I have discussed, over many meals and glasses of claret, what options we might exercise. We have considered donating the funds to the church to use in assisting widows and orphans or others left impoverished by the war.

In truth, we have had to admit, we are barely making do and are often dependent on payment of some kind from my next patient to supplement our garden. Villagers have little money. My patients rarely pay in hard currency. Even those who pay in specie do so with Continental dollars, which can buy very little. Many weeks we have nothing other than what we grow. Desired goods we make ourselves or we trade with neighbors. We do not complain.

As we weighed our options, I made suggestions and Hope did the analysis. She has often amazed me with her knowledge of the market place and the potential for our investment success.

"We could substantially expand our concoction and market of the Carr tonics and elixirs." As a practical matter, I am still in the early stages of developing my own nostrum. I knew, of course, that she would not simply dismiss this out of respect for me. But, I already knew this idea did not hold great financial promise, at least until after the war.

"We could invest in one of our local distilleries. Surely there is ongoing demand and profit to be acquired."

"Aye, we could," Hope responded, "but there are already over twenty distilleries in this area, six right here. Competition is fierce and the supply of sugar and molasses is uncertain with blockades and the interception or our ships by the British."

"There must be opportunity in one of the mills," I suggested.

"Now, that idea is better than joining those making rum," she offered, "but . . ."

"But, what?"

"The Browns appear to have an advanced start on that industry with their development of the mill in Paw-tucket. They do not know much about finished cloth and they do not yet have the looms necessary, but they have the resources. We should leave that 'opportunity' like the iron works to them."

I had to agree; I did not want to join the Browns in any enterprise or to compete with them.

"One business we might invest in is chocolate. Invest-ing in grinding beans and making chocolate would, at least, give us easy access to something we enjoy."

Hope was not sure if I was joking or not. She just asked me for my next idea.

I was not out of ideas. So far Hope has not, on her own, offered a product. I know her strategy well enough to recognize that she wants to discover what I am thinking.

"I have heard a lot of discussion about the new Salt Works Company. Salt is a common essential for preserv-ing food and for flavoring. The war has created a huge demand and a short supply. There is heated discontent over the current shortage. I know several of the men—William West and Abraham Windsor—who are building the Salt Works on Post Road on the Rhodes Arnold's former property."

"Those men have identified a legitimate need, and the sea positions Pawtuxet well to meet this requirement. I fear, however, that the expanded need will fade once the war is concluded."

I was down to only two more ideas: ship building and candle making.

"Rhode Island, Pawtuxet very much included, is already well known for ship building. We have plentiful timber, excellent harbors for launching, and skilled artisans to support this industry. The British had purchased Rhode Island ships before the war and might do so again. The Continental Congress has started a navy under the command of our own John Paul Jones. Certainly, ship building has potential for solid investment."

Hope agreed but thought that investment in the short term was too speculative.

I was down to my final suggestion: "Invest in candle making. Everyone needs and will always need candles. Spermaceti candles have become very popular and the candle factory is making candles from tallow, bees' wax, and bayberries. We have an abundance of all of these. We could advertise—*Carr's Candles Will Banish the Darkness.*"

Hope's eyes brightened. "What a wonderful idea. I've been thinking about candles myself! I will investigate," she promised, "and I will determine if the current factory owners are interested in expansion."

I predict that she will have a plan and full financial analysis in a few weeks.

February 18

Jason Sheldon came to me today in a terrible state. He could not control the saliva dripping from his mouth. Upon examination, Jason had bleeding gums, mouth sores, and he admitted to bloody bowels. He told me, "I am being treated for an exceedingly sore throat and a deteriorating capacity to breathe. I can scarcely climb the steps to my bed chamber."

"By whom are you being treated?" I inquired.

He claimed to be treating himself. "What medication are you taking?"

Jason hesitated and told me that he had been taking Dover's Powder and calomel. "At first, I was feeling much improved and then I got worse."

"How much are you taking?"

The amount he had been taking was way beyond a safe proportion.

"Who gave you the calomel?"

His hesitancy to answer was more prolonged than it had been before. I asked again with greater impatience and authority.

"Zuriel, the apothecary, sold it to me and said I should take it as rapidly as possible until it was all gone. 'More might be needed,' he told me."

I was furious. That charlatan is endangering lives. I tried to maintain my composure but could not hide the anger in my voice and the redness in my face.

"Stop taking the calomel immediately. Come back to see me in three days. I will adjust the amount of your medications if you are doing better. For now, I want you to rest, fast from eating meat, and drink warm tea made from pouring hot water over new apples.

I will speak with Zuriel about this. But, he dislikes me—perhaps all surgeons—and is not likely to acknowledge my concerns.

February 26

My Dearest Luke:

Your letter of 23 January has weighed heavily on my thoughts. Like many of our countrymen, who had hoped for a speedy resolution to our conflict with England, you are disappointed with the results achieved over the past eight months.

I had also expected that you were committed to our victory. However, your most recent letter raises doubts about where you stand. This is not a time for lack of resolution. It is not a time for weakness. It is not a time to give up, give in, or succumb.

Such behavior, even such thoughts, does not become you. I pray that the sentiments you have expressed have only been shared with me—your good friend. Any public declaration of your discouragement will only bring you harm, even retribution like that increasingly being visited upon Tories.

Such thought is unworthy of the man and friend that I know so well. Consistently, you have shown anger against those who would impose their power and sentiments upon you in your life. You have not tolerated those who would do so when you were on board ship, in your first apprenticeship, or with your medical colleagues who refuse to think for themselves and insist that others follow the old practices. Why should you now feel any differently toward those in politics who would enslave us with their single-minded concept of how we should be governed?

In all of your work, especially in medicine, you have demonstrated such clear thinking, such pragmatic and systematic thinking, that I cannot imagine the befuddled thinking that you recently exhibit about the war.

You have always shown such persistence, courage, and fortitude that I cannot conceive of your backing down from fighting on in this glorious cause for independence and liberty.

Your comrades in the Pawtuxet Rangers need to sit you down for some serious discussions.

While the preceding sentence intends some light humor, I think the time calls for great seriousness and renewed commitment. Since I know of your respect for Tom Paine, I wish to remind you of what he argued in "American Crisis." I have read and reread it. You should do the same.

"What we obtain too cheap, we esteem too lightly," he warns "Because tyranny, like hell, is not easily conquered, we must expect to be tested. We must understand that our very souls will be tried."

Paine, as you know, had practical military experience. He was with our troops at Fort Lee and marched with them to Pennsylvania. He saw and felt firsthand the dangers inherent when faced with little ammunition, few supplies, and temporary forts. He faced Howe's superior forces and knows that we had to retreat in order to fight another day.

Yet, Paine celebrates the manly spirit of those who stood and fought and gave thanks for Washington's fortitude and wise decisions.

He calls upon us, Luke, knowing to the last man in the colonies that we must, in time, separate from England. He urges us like a "generous parent" to accept our responsibility in this time and place that our children "may have peace."

It has not been a good summer, Paine admits. But we held. He calls upon us all to "gather strength from distress" and to come forth from the depth of winter with hope and virtue.

Because the war has shifted south to the middle colonies, do not be smug in the relative security of Pawtuxet Village. Do not rely on some unwarranted dream that the enemy will be merciful after all that they have, so far, suffered. You have related in previous letters the brutality inflicted on prisoners who have been left to rot on board British prison ships. You have heard about the devastation suffered in Boston. In the end, do you expect anything less?

In any way that your conscience and talents permit, join us in this historical moment.

I remain your humble and devoted friend,
Benjamin Tillinghast

February 27
Why must everyone, as Benjamin suggests and T. Paine advocates, be absorbed by this war? I understand the social implications of choosing sides. Indeed, our souls will be tried by this conflict, just as our energies and fortunes will be taxed. Some will sacrifice their family unity, even their very lives. Perhaps, I have become smug about the war. I long for it to be over. But, I fear, it has only changed location and may be prolonged. If Benjamin Tillinghast sees my lack of commitment, others might also question my resolve. I do not want to be labeled as a sunshine patriot. But, we all do not need to be consumed by it. I can declare my allegiance to the cause. But we have already seen the horrors of war in Massachusetts Bay.

March 1

After the storm last year that washed away the bridge—the third time some older Villagers say—they built yet another. This one was designed to outrival any of our neighbors. It was covered, which gives us temporary protection from the elements: wind and cold in winter, drenching rains in spring, blazing heat in summer.

If their timing is right, the young people can steal a romantic moment, temporarily secreted by the bridge. I have caught them a couple of times!

But, the covered bridge can be a nuisance. If your cart is carrying a wide load, part of it must be reduced to navigate across the bridge. Then you have to carry the unloaded items across. Aggravating.

March 3

A young soldier on his way home to Maine spent the night at the tavern relating his trials and tribulations. The usual frivolity of the tavern soon dissipated as we became absorbed in his stories.

More than anything the British inflicted on him, he said, hunger was the constant enemy. He had served for two years and rarely had three meals in one day. Often he went one, two, three, even four days with nothing to eat. When he could sneak off, he and his messmates would forage the countryside for whatever they could find. Sometimes, a farmer would give them a handful of crops from the field in exchange for help in harvesting.

Otherwise, they stole what they could find. Fatigue, hunger, and cold were constant companions.

We kept his tankard full and the tavern keeper brought him food. He was grateful, but we knew we could not make up for what he had suffered.

He seemed eager to get some rest. Fascinated and horrified by his tales of deprivation, we kept him talking as if he were Odysseus relating his adventures in the Court of King Alcinous. As the evening progressed he recited this poem:

> "You may think what you please, sir. I too can think-
> I think I can't live without victuals and drink;
> Your oxen can't plough, nor your horses can't draw,
> Unless they have something more hearty than straw.
> If that is their food, sir, their spirits must fall,
> How can I labour with—nothing at all?"

Here was a young man faithfully serving his country far from home and family, suffering everything short of death. The misery he had seen and experienced was far greater than I had suffered in the New York campaign. His story had a sobering effect on everyone at the tavern. We, in the meantime, lived in relative comfort. To a man, we were embarrassed.

He lamented that they had hardships enough: soaked to the skin with torrents of rain, so few clothes they were half naked, fatigue from constant marching (up to forty miles in a single day), constantly digging trenches, and bone-weary fatigue from lack of sleep. But the worm of hunger was the worst. Many times, he said, they would have preferred to die in a battle than to starve to death in camp.

The young man amazed us. He and his fellow soldiers had grappled as best they could. On occasion, a house by the side of the road would open its door so they could get a meal, warm themselves by the fire, and rest. These kind souls saved his life more than once he told us. Often the officers had no remedy. The men learned to make a virtue of necessity and went on, despite the gnawing pains of hunger. Justifiably, he took pride in still being alive and in having done his duty. He was strengthened by the thought that he would soon be in Maine and home.

None of us will ever forget this young soldier.

March 15

Now I know why I attend so few medical lectures. Dr. Nathan Follett, visiting the colony from New Jersey, delivered several lectures in a rented room in Bristol. His topic was smallpox—a disease I have been interested in for some time.

Recognizing no one in the room, I wondered who the attendees might be; I took a seat near the back.

Dr. Follet's lecture began reasonably enough with the symptoms of the disease. Immediately following these introductory comments, he launched into a strongly worded denial that smallpox even existed. His belief was that it was a common variant of chickenpox. Then, he proposed that concern over the so-called smallpox was overblown, that the disease had an extremely low mortality rate, and that there was no treatment for it.

I fidgeted through all of this, but could no longer remain silent. "Dr. Follet," I asked, "have not whole tribes of Indians on this continent been eliminated as a result of the introduction of this disease by Europeans?"

"That is a preposterous myth," he shot back. "Europeans get blamed for a disease that was indigenous to the Indians long before. Some say the Aztecs were destroyed by a European disease, but their civilization had long been in decline. Both primitive savages here and the Aztecs invented some supernatural power which they attributed to their conquerors as the reason they were defeated. Whatever diseases that appeared, I can assure you it was not smallpox."

"What is the disease, if not smallpox?" I asked.

"It looks like and behaves like chickenpox," he insisted. "A rash appears, raised spots form on the body, fever develops, dry scabs eventually form and drop off. The patient recovers. It is a variant, nothing more."

"And the cause?"

"Problems of the blood, perhaps too much contact with infected cows."

I was having a good time with my questioning. Others

in the audience remained silent, either entertained by our exchanges or still too intimidated. Dr. Follet looked plaintively around the room hoping to see the hand of someone else. I continued.

"Smallpox, I understand, covers the palms and soles of the feet with dense pocks and develops slowly—much in contrast to what we see in chickenpox."

My challenge was more than Dr. Follet was willing to tolerate. He did not want a public discussion with me on a topic on which he felt he had expert knowledge.

"My dear, Sir," he began. I could hear the derision in his voice. "I do not have the honor to know your name."

I told him.

"And, at what university did you earn your medical degree?"

I knew I was in trouble. Confidently, I told him that I had been trained by an outstanding physician, Dr. Benjamin Randall.

"How many cases of smallpox have you treated, doctor?"

I told him that I had treated many cases of chickenpox and neither the symptoms nor the mortality rate resembled the smallpox cases that I had heard about.

"Well, then, Sir," he pronounced, "since you have never treated a smallpox patient—never even seen one—I suspect you have no credential for challenging me or for raising uninformed conjecture in the minds of the sound reasoning gentlemen who sit in this audience."

He had shifted the discussion from an examination of the disease to me. It was an embarrassing moment. I sat down and formulated a series of questions that I wished I had presented. Further discussion, however, would not have been possible.

That is why I do not go to many of these lectures by itinerant physicians. Dr. Follet has, nevertheless, increased my determination to make a contribution to the elimination of this disease.

March 22

Hope has not found much interest in having new partners from the factory here that makes candles. But she is undeterred, thinking that we could open our own shop and specialize in holiday candles. This is not a good time to start a new business.

March 28

While sitting out on Pawtuxet Neck, watching hundreds of hogsheads of molasses being unloaded from the East Indies, I began thinking that there might be another use for molasses besides turning it into rum. Not that making rum isn't good for our economy. The Still House on the cove has been doing extraordinarily well. There are now thirty distilleries in Rhode Island that demand the 14,000 hogsheads of molasses that come ashore each year.

Yet, I am considering that molasses might have some special properties that, in combination with other ingredients, might produce a powerful spring tonic. If molasses converted to rum can bring out such euphoria, why not a tonic based on molasses?

Certainly, I can create something with greater therapeutic effect than dandelion wine.

April 10

Began experimenting with the creation of what I have already named Luke's Spring Tonic. Daffy, Godfrey, James, even Mrs. Winslow have become famous and wealthy by formulating tonics and elixirs. I could as well. Why restrict myself to treating the few in Pawtuxet when I could take my rightful place in the history of medicine by inventing a cure that helps hundreds, thousands. I just need the right combination of ingredients.

Formula #1
Uses straight molasses combined with saffron and parsley.

Formula #2
Uses straight molasses combined with senna, aniseed, jalop, fennel, and a dram of gin and cider.

Formula #3

Boil the molasses as they do in distilling rum, but I stop the process before full fermentation.

Unlike most tonics that I have sampled, Geoffrey's Cordial, Dr. James Powders, and Wickets' Remedy, for instance, that have an unpleasant odor and a terrible taste, all three of my formulas have a terrific taste due to the molasses, which everyone loves. Some believe that the fouler the taste the more effective the tonic. I do not believe this. If I can make a better tasting tonic, I can outsell all of the others combined.

Hope, by the way, totally disagrees with this venture into capitalism. I have argued that tonics are a far better way to increase our income than pulling more teeth, reducing fevers, or creating poultices for colds. She hates having me puttering in the kitchen, mixing various formulas and getting in her way.

I do make a mess. She thinks the whole idea is folly but she would be outstanding in marketing our elixir. I have some ideas for the design of the label and to promote the elixir in the shops and taverns. We will call it Carr's Springtime Tonic:

> "Get a New Release on Life
> The Taste You Will Come Back To"

I need to test these formulas out on neighbors to

determine which would be most popular. Possibly, Nel would be willing to try it.

April 13

I become furious when I discover an advertisement in the newspaper that promises cures for all sorts of conditions from the same tonic. Godfrey's Cordial claims to cure:

> "The Colic and all Manners of Pains in the Bowels. Fluxes, Fevers, Small-Pox, Measles, Rheumatism, Coughs, Chills, and Restlessness in Men, Women, and Children; and Particularly for Several Ailments incident to Childbearing Women; and Relief of young Children in forming their teeth."

I do not know what miracle medicines could be packaged in this ready-made mixture, yet I am certain that the bottle could not be large enough to contain all of the ingredients needed to treat half of the listed problems. Hopefully, few thinking citizens will be taken in by these ridiculous assertions.

April 29

My approach to creating the perfect elixir or tonic that would become famous has been wrong. Many tonics and elixirs will address multiple problems, but now, I am convinced that curative claims for many of them are false. Certain mixtures will address only specific complaints. I have also been amiss in believing that my tonic must be liquid and bottled.

Best-selling tonics with which I am familiar—Mrs. Winslow's Soothing Syrup or Wicket's Remedy, for instance—offer vague claims:

> "Two spoonfuls will lift your spirits,
> purge your blood of impurities."

These, I am now convinced, work as much on the power of suggestion as they do on any physic of medicine. They also provide only temporary relief, perhaps for only a few hours. A couple of good shots of rum might do as well!

I am testing a soup that shows considerable promise. I have been observing migrating birds as they return to our cove after wintering far from here. Having flown long distances, they arrive just in time to be strengthened for breeding by young green plants. They are fond of young spinach leaves and parsley. I have created a soup with these tender, green plants, which combined with onion, carrots, garlic, potato, and pieces of cooked chicken in a broth produces a delicious mixture. It cleanses, strengthens, and renews energy after the sedentary effects of winter, while restoring the natural balances of the body. Even Hope applauds this tonic.

By the end of winter, the reserves in our bodies are

running low. As in migrating birds, these reserves need to be restored. Yet, unlike the birds, we wait for the later growth of green plants.

Our bodies are like the tides that ebb and flow in the Bay. At very low tide, there is little observable sea life—sandbars emerge, water is motionless and murky. When the tide comes in, it shows renewed energy—the plant life and fish flow back to our shores—the water is clear and sparkling.

Or, we might think of our bodies as oil lamps. As the oil is consumed by long nights, the flame diminishes and flickers. When we fill the lamp with new oil, the flame leaps to new heights, burning steady and bright.

Carr's Springtime Soup . . .
This may revolutionize the whole concept of tonics.

May 14
I think Carr's Springtime Soup is going to be the break-through. The apple cider tonic, the molasses-based elixir, the sage and rum mixtures were all short-lived. They did not capture the imagination or an audience of buyers. But, Carr's Springtime Soup is going to be different. I can see myself up on the platform at the Fair now, hand-ing out spoonfuls to sample and jars to sell. The crowds will gather in fascination to hear of its miraculous pow-ers to restore the body—and soul.

I shall fill my pockets with coins until I can hardly

walk. My face will be recognized wherever I go. My fame will be celebrated throughout the Village and across America.

I will never have to buy a drink at the tavern. I shall be wellcontented.

May 23

Our turn has come to garrison Fort Independence on the Neck. I dislike leaving Hope and the comforts of home even for only a few weeks. The Rangers are not hardened soldiers, myself included. Since we cannot leave the fort, we must do everything ourselves: cook, clean, repair. Sleeping is uncomfortable. When it rains, as it did frequently during our first two weeks, we are wet most of the time. Our food is basic—stew.

There is little to do. We posted a watch for ships coming up the River—none came. The day is occupied with the routine tasks of living in the fort and with endless cleaning of our flintlocks and cannons.

While I have my musket with me, the bruises from carrying my brown Bess on the long marches in New York will not soon be forgotten. When I can avoid it, I no longer fire the musket.

Col. B. Arnold, who commanded the first division for our initial two weeks, and his brother Lt. Col O. Arnold, who commanded the second two weeks, tried to keep everyone busy with improvements to the fort and with mock "engagements." The days, however, were tedious.

At night we would tell stories and play cards. Even this got boring after the first few nights.

My misfortune is that I am the only surgeon who is a member of the Rangers, so I must perform duty for four consecutive weeks. What an aggravation. When my fellow Rangers were relieved by the next seventeen members, no one relieved me!

Had there been a greater need for my medical skills I would have found some purpose and satisfaction in this duty. No one was being fired upon so there were no wounds. My contribution was in treatments for common complaints:

P. Rhodes—earache
Boiled rosemary and let it steam into the ear through a funnel.

C. Thornton—headache of two days duration
Brewed a tea from willow bark.

B. Babcok—itching on arms and back.
Probable cause: clearing the area of poison ivy.
Prepared poultices of moist flour and meal with comfrey. When the itching failed to yield in four days, applied salve of flour, sulfur, and hog's lard. Itching corrected within six hours.

J. Harris

B. Waterman

O. Payne

Colds. Probably spread from one to another.
Prepared paste: one part mustard, eight parts flour
in lukewarm water; spread between two pieces of
muslin and placed on chest until well reddened.

J. Randall

Initially believed to be camp colic. Assumption
incorrect. Patient needed a purgative—castor oil.
Problem resolved.

My other major "glorious" responsibility was sanita-
tion. I inspected latrines daily and ordered them cleaned
as necessary; insisted that each soldier bathe once in the
two-week period of occupation, shave or trim beards
to maintain a soldierly appearance, and cut long hair
to prevent the infection of lice. Placed anise in various
locations as bait for mice, which were attracted by our
food supply.

June 2

Charles Ward rarely comes to seek medical attention.
Even yesterday, he was reluctant but was clearly worried
about his capacity to continue to work. His eyes were
red and tearing. His feet were so swollen he hobbled
when he walked. The toenails on both feet were dark

with infection. He told me these problems had started to appear in April and had gotten worse. Now, his work was painful. He was in terror of having to stop. He could not recall having had these problems before.

"Are you doing something different?" I inquired

"Nay," he insisted. "I always return to my brickyard in the spring, after working in the barn over the winter. I am worried; making bricks is my livelihood, and the only skill I have."

I wondered if this patient might offer me an opportunity to prescribe a tonic—perhaps I could test my latest concoction. Confident that a tonic or my soup would be helpful, I told him I would mix up a batch and bring it to his brickyard in the morning.

When I got there his seasonal work already showed evidence of considerable effort. There were thousands of bricks stacked up in the yard and hundreds more in various shades of gray set out in the sand, drying in the warmth of the June sun. I examined the bricks, which he was preparing for several chimneys in town, and sniffed the clay on these bricks—still wet from their wooden molds. There were mounds of oyster shells that emitted a terrible stench and piles of fine sand nearby. I found him shoving split lengths of wood into a blazing kiln. The heat was so intense that I could not approach closer than ten feet. Without saying a word, I watched him for several minutes until he had finished loading the kiln with wood and looked up to note my arrival.

He hobbled over to where I stood, his face flaming red from the heat of the fire, and greeted me with gratitude that I had come, as promised.

"Dr Carr, I do not have the strength to prepare the molds over there. To prepare the clay, I must mix it for over an hour by stomping through the mud pit."

His boots clearly showed the evidence of this process. I learned that the boots wore out quickly. "Mr. Ward, please remove one of those boots." He struggled, since his feet were considerably swollen, but finally managed with much pain to get one off. Despite his having stood near the kiln, the boots were very damp.

It was clear to me what was causing his problems. "Find an apprentice or assistant to mix the clay in the pit," I warned. "Wear only dry boots for at least the next month. Take your boots off as soon as possible when you go home and sit with your feet outstretched toward the hearth. Keep, as much as possible, from looking directly into the kiln. You are to eat a bowl of a special soup that I had prepared for you—a concoction of white fish bones, onion, carrots, celery stalks, olive oil, white wine, cloves, parsley, and salt."

"Could you just give me a tonic?"

"If you follow this plan for the next month you will see improvement. Report your progress to me."

"Doc, I cannot pay for the soup or your advice until the chimney bricks have been sold." His voice shook with apology and embarrassment.

"Instead of cash money, Mr. Ward, you could replaster, as your time permits, one of my rooms with your mixture of lime, sand, and animal hair."

June 20

As General Greene warned, there is a great danger that any one of the states could be pressured by the British Army or by negotiations with the commissioners appointed by the King to enter into a special arrangement to fight on the side of the Crown. There are citizens who do not support this war. Certainly there are those who desire to return to a previous state of ample food, safety, ease, and profitable commerce. All geographic areas among the thirteen states have not equally suffered the burden of depravation, destruction, and loss of life.

The congress has no way to prevent a splintering and must depend on good will. In a curious way, the weakness of the congress is also a strength. Their ineffectiveness poses no threat of usurping power from the states. Our own representatives excepted, the congress is held in such disregard that we are united in this criticism.

I do not envy General Washington's task of trying to get direction and material support. Contempt for the King, Parliament, the British Army, their mercenary dogs (the Hessians), and the outrageous policies and barbarous acts inflicted on us is what has, so far, blended us in this common cause.

June 25

"You want me to do what?"

"I want you to dig up the roses that can be seen from the road," Hope demanded.

"Whatever for?"

"Mrs. Sprague, down the street, reminded me that the rose is a symbol of England. It is its national flower. Our having roses in our yard makes us appear to be Loyalists."

"That is preposterous," I scoffed. "I will not destroy the beautiful roses that have taken years to grow just so Mrs. Sprague, that ole busybody, can have the satisfaction of dictating what we can and can not grow in our own yard."

"Husband, it is not just Mrs. Sprague. Many Villagers are removing roses from their gardens as a protest against the Crown."

"Practicing non-importation of English goods and substituting products made here such as tea and fabric in order to pressure English merchants is one thing. Removing roses from our garden is quite another."

"We talked this over in our quilting circle, Luke. We cannot all go off to war or even participate in public debate. We are determined to do what we can to support the Cause."

"Hope. We will not win this war by destroying roses. The next step will be to stop speaking English."

Hope saw no humor in my quip. She gave that look

that said, unmistakably, that she felt the roses had to go.

"I am not going to destroy those roses," I protested. "I will move them to the back garden out of sight, to please you. I intend to continue to use rosehips for medicinal purposes," I grumbled, "but I'll move the roses."

At one time in history, the rose was a symbol of secrecy and silence. The practice was to hang a rose from the ceiling of a council room to remind the participants that their business was private. Deliberations and decisions were to remain within the room. History is repeated again as we create our own *sub-rosa* by hiding the English rose that we have grown for years in our gardens.

July 10

The Rhode Island militia proudly serves the Cause. A gill of rum for all tonight at the tavern.

William Barton, with a group of militia, captured Gen. Richard Prescott on Aquidneck Island. What a bold move! Imagine the audacity of Lieutenant Colonel Barton daring to take prisoner the garrison commander of Newport with thirty-eight of his fellow militiamen. Newport is occupied by 4,000 British regulars and is fortified with a fleet of ships of the line that are large and powerful and designed to take part in the line of battle.

Details traveled quickly. Under the cover of night and with undressed sheepskins to muffle the oars, this group rowed beneath the cannons of the warships *Chatham* and *The Diamond*, through the passage between Prudence and Patience Islands, landing at the cove below the Overing house.

Having reconnoitered the area well and armed with intelligence regarding Prescott's sleeping habits, Barton maneuvered his men to avoid the sentry. If an alarm had been given, it would have been certain death for this band of patriots.

Prescott was captured in his nightshirt and taken barefoot to Warwick Neck. The capture went undetected for hours.

What a brilliant plan! What a daring execution. The Congress should promote Barton and recommend him to General Washington, who needs men of Barton's genius and bravery.

Imagine the embarrassment to the British, especially General Clinton, who is in command at New York, over the capture of a major general in the middle of a well-fortified stronghold. The repulsion of having to admit that a hatter—a hatter no less from Providence—and an untrained group of thirty-eight Rhode Island militiamen could be responsible for such a demeaning accomplishment.

This will dampen the incessant, disparaging remarks about the worth of the militia. Barton's achievement should prove useful in negotiations for an exchange. Surely, we shall salute Barton—a fellow Rhode Islander from Warren—and the militiamen with more than one gill of rum.

July 28

There is no freethinking among Quakers—not if you disagree. Hypocrisy is rampant. Many accumulate huge wealth, like Moses Brown has done in textiles and William Rotchin has done in the Nantucket whale industry. In England the living standards of the best-known Quaker families in banking and commerce (Barclays, Lloyds, Dimsdales, Christy's) are anything but plain and simple.

Quakers claim exemption from military duty under the Test Act and refuse to serve in any capacity. Yet, William Penn had no problem during his "Holy Experiment" in Pennsylvania under the charter from Charles II in exercising full military authority as Captain General of the army.

Quakers demand toleration for their own denomination while having no indulgence for Indians. Penn raised funds for war with the Delaware and Shawnee Indians. Quakers campaign against slavery while many Quakers refuse to free their own slaves.

If they must be in this colony, let them huddle in Newport.

August 5

We were playing a rather uninspired game of checkers at the tavern when Nehemizh Knight challenged me to a game of darts. Although not my favorite game, I agreed. "Let's make this interesting," he suggested. "Whoever wins can ask the other an important question which must be answered honestly." Not knowing what I was getting myself into, I consented.

Nehemizh beat me handily.

We ordered a couple of tankards. "My question, Luke, is what would you really want to be known for when your working days are done?"

I felt vaguely confronted and uncertain how honest I wanted to be. He had advanced his question straight at me like a charging goat, horns intent on a forceful butt should I try to renege on the agreement.

I took a long swallow of the ale. I was, however, obliged to pay the wager. "If you want the truth, I would like to be known for having invented a powerful elixir that would bring me fame and fortune."

The sides of his mouth turned up in a slight grin and his eyes gleamed.

"If we are going to benefit from this conversation, we need to be totally honest. Agreed?"

I nodded, shifting in my chair.

"If you want to make some great discovery, what are you still doing in this one-blacksmith Village? No one is going to become famous by living in Pawtuxet. This place is only known for potash, salt, and ice."

"Pawtuxet is a perfect place to work—as good a place as anywhere to make discoveries," I shot back.

"Your problem, Luke, is that you won't take any risks. You have no creative ideas. You have got to get away from here, find some stimulation."

"I have all the stimulation I need."

"Exactly the point. You want fame, but you would rather just go it alone until a lightening bolt comes out of a clear sky and strikes you with inspiration."

"What makes you the expert philosopher?" I protested with considerable sarcasm.

"Luke, you keep thinking there is some huge fish out there waiting to swim up the cove so you can scoop him up in a great net. Success is not that easy."

I was not enjoying this. I began to think of how I could change the focus. "You are still living here. What is going to make you famous?

"Holla, my friend. Do not get so irritated. This little exercise is because you lost at darts. You did not win the opportunity to ask me a question." He paused. "But, if you want to know, I will make my mark in politics."

"That figures. You would choose to weasel your ideas into others' heads, pretending they were in the public good and that you alone had the only concept of the perfect world."

I was relieved to have started to shift the burden.

"We could play another game of darts, or maybe you would prefer another game of checkers."

"Checkers," I quickly offered.

"Now, how did I just know that is what you would choose?"

Instead, we ordered another round.

August 9

Nehemizh's remarks during the dart game have bothered me for several days and interrupted my sleep. But, I am who I am. His caustic comments kept bothering me until today. Mrs. Howard brought me a jar of her famous rhubarb jam . . . for no special reason. In large part her gift eased Knight's insults.

August 11

Although we don't have as much food these days, we still get treated to Hope's delicious cooking. She made us jonnycakes from our fresh supply of cornmeal. Mrs. Bowen, our neighbor, told us that we learned about jonnycakes from the Algonquian Indians who ate them when they traveled. They called them "journey cakes." With a little raspberry jam on them, Eliza, Daniel, and I can pretend we are at a banquet.

August 16

Smallpox is a horror, as much to be feared as any British musket ball. The epidemic in Boston during the occupation served our Cause with as much consequence as our militias stationed on Dorchester Heights. The repugnant look of those afflicted and the high mortality rate create dread of this unseen killer.

What can be done?

So far, we in Pawtuxet have been spared. Yet, with so many colonists fleeing from Newport, sailors arriving

here on merchant ships, and many military units passing through, we most assuredly cannot isolate ourselves
from the ravenous devastation. It confounds us.

September 12

At first I did not see him and I did not expect he would
be at the meeting where I was encouraging inoculation.
But, there he was in the third row. I suppose he came
just to taunt me. I stared at him in disbelief. He gave
me a contemptuous grin, knowing that I would begin
to squirm.

He said nothing during the presentation. When I
looked in his direction, pretending to be looking at
someone else, he had maintained that insulting grin. As
I continued to argue that preventive measures for the
ravages of smallpox were in everyone's interests, he surprisingly said nothing but kept shaking his head from
side to side in disagreement.

He had infuriated me without saying a word.

As soon as the presentation ended, he was out of his
seat, standing as close as he dared in front of me.

"Well, I suppose you are trying to build your medical practice by encouraging needless inoculations." His
voice was much louder than it needed to be.

Squeezing my fingers into a tight fist at my side, digging my nails into my flesh to distract myself, I calmly
stated that I hoped he would support the members of the
medical profession to encourage this well-documented

prevention.

"I certainly will not," he retorted, raising his voice even more. He was drawing attention.

Stepping back and shifting my weight from one leg to the other, struggling for self-control, I told him he would be most welcome to join with the rest of us to keep the disease at bay and to lessen its impact. (I lied; he was not at all welcome, and he knew it).

"I'll have nothing to do with you and that pack of do-gooders you are in league with, who are determined to serve nothing but their own interests."

"If you want to discuss this further," the volume of my own voice nearly equal to his, "I would be pleased, good Sir, to arrange a more appropriate time to do so." (If I had dared, I would rather have smashed him). I grabbed my pocket watch to check it, as if I had somewhere important to go, and then stuffed it back into my coat.

He sneered, deliberately turned his back to me, and sauntered off, delighting in the spectacle he had created and, perhaps, in the confusion now in the minds of those who overheard him.

September 17

The snake is full of venom. He strikes out with forked tongue to poison without provocation. Zuriel Tower, the area's sham apothecary, has decided to oppose the joint effort of several respectable surgeons to inoculate against smallpox.

He spreads fear. He warns those who would be protected that they will get the disease. He insinuates that children and the old are at great risk of dying from the inoculation.

He slithers around looking for victims. As always, he deceives. Besides the damage he personally does as an apothecary, he attacks the rest of us. Without any hint of his usual humor, Peleg tells me he heard that Zuriel had maligned me. He tells people, who do not know me, that I know nothing about smallpox, and that I am so incompetent that I will poison people trying to inoculate them.

Snakes are surreptitious. They appear when you least expect them. The only way to be rid of these menaces is to trample them underfoot. Unfortunately, they are hard to capture.

At the very least, this area would benefit from one fewer apothecaries.

October 10

When Villagers come to me frightened for themselves and for their families of the pox, I have little to offer them: stay away from sailors arriving at our piers, do not engage strangers who suddenly appear in the Village, do not visit nearby military encampments. The only token preventive agent is a bland diet. Few are willing to live on gruel.

His Excellency George Washington is apparently convinced that protection is possible. He has the letters he receives dipped in vinegar before reading them. We hear this from those who have worked as his aides. He has ordered that the whole army be inoculated. He even had Mrs. Washington inoculated.

Fear of inoculation is as strong as the fear of the disease itself. I am having a challenging time convincing Villagers to accept this procedure.

October 16

Pawtuxet has seen its first case of smallpox. A sailor, recently returning from a long voyage, got off the ship with a fever, which had bothered him for some days, and a mild rash had recently developed. He was not concerned.

However, the rash got worse, spreading to his hands, face, and the soles of his feet. His fever rose. Doctors C. Carpenter, E. David, and S. Bowen, and I each examined him. This was not a case of chickenpox in an adult, as Follet would have asserted. All of us agreed that this was smallpox.

We isolated him immediately in a small vacant house on the edge of Horatio Slocum's farm. Within a fortnight he was dead.

Word spread rapidly. . . and panic. Drs. Carpenter, David, Bowen, and I agreed that we would use this opportunity to promote inoculation. In an unusual effort of focusing attention on a single medical problem, we divided up tasks:

- Write and post broadsides.
- Address the threat at churches and at meetings of community organizations (I agreed to talk to the Baptists and the Freemasons).
- Visit women's sewing groups (Hope helped me identify these. We agreed that wives and mothers could be instrumental in the family decision to inoculate).
- Lead discussions at the taverns (We all agreed to do this!).

Initially, we met with very limited success. Inoculation was greeted with misgivings, mistrust, doubt, downright denial, and anger:

"Why would any sane man purposefully permit this disease to be injected into him?"

"Some people have died because they were inoculated."

. . . Some accused us of spreading the disease.
"I could not permit a member of my family to be subjected to this."

"I have no time to be bothered with this. (Variola inoculation requires being quarantined for up to two weeks and experiencing a slight fever)."

"The problem is in big cities. We have little to worry about here."

We were discouraged with the meager results of our efforts. Even our own friends and families were difficult to persuade.

And then the second case of smallpox appeared in the Village. A long-time resident contracted the disease. He had no idea how he might have gotten it. Perhaps, Dr. Follet's theory about being in contact with cows was possible. George Sheldon had a milder case than the sailor. He had symptoms for a week, so the disease was probably already at work on his family. We isolated him at home, applied blistering cups to his limbs, gave him a decoction of mustard seed, and encouraged his exposure to cool air. We hoped he would survive with only pock marks to bear witness to his suffering.

The Sheldon case turned the tide. Villagers started to come to us for inoculation. We had to expand the number of houses we put in use for quarantine. A hospital was put to this use at Tockwotton. If anyone appeared sick when a ship came into the harbor, he would be sent to a pest house and the ship would be washed and smoked. I have been asked to certify that this cleansing has taken place. Ferries are prohibited from bringing people from an infected area. Guards have been placed on bridges between Pawtuxet and Cumberland and troops have been asked not to march through town.

While our success will only be revealed over time, there is considerable satisfaction in believing that we may have blocked an epidemic. For once, we have found a way to prevent the ravages of a disease rather than battle it once it has already taken hold.

October 20
Last night our sham apothecary appeared in my dream. He pesters me even while I sleep.

While I cannot remember the whole dream, Zuriel was advising me, as if he were a respected colleague. He suggested that he had concocted a miraculous powder that promoted sweating—just what Abby Osborne needed. I have been struggling—so far unsuccessfully—to find some drug that would soothe her rheumatism and fever. Zuriel whispered that the secret ingredient was antimony.

The man is an agent of the devil and just as proud as Lucifer. What am I to make of that dream?

November 4
I now have evidence that the amount of disease increases in the Village during the winter months. Because I have always found myself busier between October and

March, I decided to examine my treatment records for several years. There is no doubt that the number of cases that I treat precipitously climbs in the winter. The pattern shows a steady increase beginning in October, reaching a peak in December and January, and then slowly decreasing. The prevalence is with chest problems, breathing difficulties, coughs, and head pain due to congestion. I treat more injuries to limbs during the rest of the year, but the overall volume of disease is much lower during the rest of the year.

Logical reasoning suggests that this winter pattern could not be true. Heat and moisture create heavier air and the miasmas that cause disease. This is why malaria and yellow fever are more common in the warmer climates, such as those found in the West Indies.

Why, then, do I see more patients in the winter? I wonder if this pattern is unique to Pawtuxet?

I have several theories:

1. The temperature of the water in the Bay, somehow, contributes to this phenomenon. I cannot explain why this annual change would cause disease because some years the Bay is frozen over for weeks.

2. Or, the reduced amount of sunshine during the winter has an adverse effect on how people feel.

3. Or, maybe birds and ducks remove harmful elements from the air by eating insects during the warm months. Many of them are migratory and are not seen in winter.

I do not see how I can substantiate any of these theories. I will write to several surgeons that I met in Newport who live in southern colonies. I also know a couple of surgeons who practice onboard ships that frequent hot climates and are often in port here. Dr. Benjamin Rush, who graduated from the College of New Jersey and the University of Edinburgh and serves as surgeon general of the Middle Department of the Continental Army, may offer a useful opinion. He seems to know something about everything medical. I will write to him also.

November 30
The responses I got from fellow surgeons about increases in disease during the winter months proved inconclusive:

Dr. James Huston from North Carolina explained that he does not keep any records, but did not think the number of patients seeking his services fluctuated in any seasonal pattern.

Dr. George Draher from Virginia said he saw more patients in the summer and congestion was not a major complaint any time of the year.

Dr. James Craik from Virginia thought I might be on to something based on his recollections, but he had no idea what the cause could be of a seasonal increase.

Dr. Benjamin Rush never responded.

The two naval surgeons I spoke with were convinced that the risk of disease increased with heat and humidity and had something to do with sweating.

Dr. Zuriel Waterman, another Pawtuxet doctor, told me that I was wasting my time on even considering such a useless investigation. (I would not have bothered to ask the opinion of this narrow-minded, arrogant excuse for a doctor, but I just happened to encounter him at Thomas Howard's store.)

However, the data I have from my own practice is irrefutable. My latest theory to explain this increase of illness in winter has to do with people making more contact with one another.

Winter keeps most of us inside. We spend more time entertaining friends and family at home and more time in the taverns and visiting in the shops. With no reason to be in the garden or to be out walking, more people attend church and sit huddled together for long hours. There are more winter holidays that bring us into contact with one another.

With less time to breathe fresh air and to be about outdoor work, we are susceptible to any contagion that is in the winter air.

That is the answer. But there is not much useful advice I can give to deal with it. Maybe it is a good time to promote my elixir.

December 4

Zuriel Tower was right; I hate to admit that an apothecary of his limited knowledge could be. I inoculated Arnold and now he has a severe case of smallpox. This was not supposed to happen. He had been reluctant to be inoculated from the start. "I will not poison my own body," he insisted.

Peleg supported my argument, "That good luck hat of yours, Arnold, might not be sufficient to protect you. The Doc knows best."

I talked him into it. He decided to let me inoculate. We had joked about his paper-thin courage. Now, I think he should have followed his premonition, and I should have backed off.

I visit him every day in the isolation house where he is being held. He looks worse each day. He grows thin.

Eats little. Arnold's vacant stare haunts me. He is not strong enough to talk, but his eyes accuse me. The postulates are multiplying. He is feverish. He is miserable and so am I. Tormented by my leading role in this, I am tortured by Zuriel's prediction. He had campaigned against inoculation and me specifically, boldly warning that those being inoculated would suffer the disease and might die. He cautioned, "Don't trust that homegrown doctor." I cannot stomach Zuriel being right—about anything. I can see his indicting eyes starring at me, accusing me of "killing" my friend. He will claim that I am receiving just retribution for playing God, for using my insufficient knowledge to interfere with the natural order and real medicine. He will denounce me at every opportunity.

I could argue that so far few have really gotten sick from the many we have inoculated, but my heart is not in the debate.

December 9

Arnold died today.

The sky was grim with menace—the darkness closing in. There is a smell when death is near. I knew as soon as I went to his bedside. The realization that he was gone left me strangely detached. There could be no pretensions. His limbs were already stiff, his features frozen. I thought—a corpse does not look as if it were sleeping. His mouth was agape, his eyes bulged. This is not the image of God.

Perhaps, others had also died that day in this isolation house. Death and the ravages of the pox filled the room—a pungent smell like seaweed rotting at low tide on an excessively hot August day. But, it was December. I closed his eyes, covered him over with a blanket.

Whenever I face death, I try to console myself by thinking, "Death is but the next great adventure." I kept saying this over and over and over. "Death is but the next great adventure."

When I face a crisis such as this I think of Blake and his advice about the need to convince yourself that you can go on, that you can go another five miles.

December 12

He has not been to the tavern. I have not seen Peleg—actually since Arnold's funeral. We had not spoken then or since.

Perhaps, he is not well.

1778

January 10

Cotton Mather, minister of the Old North Church and author of many medical treatises, once said about headaches, "to know the cause is half the cure." He believed that the fibers in the head get irritated by sharp particles in the blood. Animal spirits, he concluded, carried these particles to the nervous parts of the head and caused the headaches.

Ever since the British occupied Newport, I have seen many more patients who complain of severe headaches. Whether their headaches are caused by sharp particles in the blood, I cannot venture to know, but the closeness of the war, the daily worry about the British sailing in force up the Bay, and concern about the increasing shortage of food and other essential goods have had a physical impact on a number of Villagers.

Mrs. Lyman is one of them. With the British occupation and as a result of the stories that have reached us about wanton disregard for the property rights and mistreatment of anyone suspected of being a patriot, Mrs. Lyman has not had a tranquil day. She had always lived by the rules. Now she does not know what the rules are. She has always been compliant, believing that whatever is—is best. Now she is nervous all of the time, uncertain of what to do—what to believe. She dislikes change, and she has terrible headaches all of the time.

Whatever I have done for her brings only short-term relief. After several of these attempts, I told her that the headaches would not go away until she stopped her constant worrying.

Her retort, "Do not tell me that worrying does no good. I know better. The things I worry about do not happen."

No surgeon or minister can help much with that line of reasoning. She imagines the worse thing that might happen. She asks for help but will not follow advice. She wants relief from powders that I might provide to her, some change in diet (which she will not follow), or some other treatment. She has visited other surgeons and apothecaries in the area without success.

Mrs. Lyman refuses to face the situation the way her neighbors do. She will not adopt the notion that you should change what you can and accept what you cannot. She wants a simple remedy.

I wish I had an elixir that would resolve her headaches. I do not.

Instead, I advise her to bathe her head in warm water,

to rub oil of nutmegs on her forehead, and to forgo salt and meat. Perhaps, these help her. Nevertheless, she returns to my house every few weeks.

January 14

When I was down on the wharf today I saw Peleg. Our conversation was brief and restrained.

"Pray, Sir, how are you?"

"Well."

"How does your family?"

"Well."

"Are you getting enough carpentry work?"

"Yep, I am busy enough."

And then he limped off. He might be in mourning for Arnold. He might be angry with me. Being so taciturn is uncharacteristic.

January 22

Mrs. Lyman will be pleased. Dr. Throop has shared with me other headache cures in which he has great confidence.

I have been reluctant to bleed or to use purgatives for headaches, but Dr. Throop has used both. He says that leeches placed behind the ears and on the neck are effective. Among his other suggestions is a drink of wood ash in water. This, he cautions, may cause vomiting, but relieves the headache sooner than most cures. To absorb the gasses of undigested foods, which he believes causes headaches (not sharp particles in the blood, which Cotton Mather says is the cause), Dr. Throop creates a drink with powdered charcoal in warm water. His third remedy, which he proclaims is popular with his patients, is to put peeled and sliced raw potatoes on the forehead.

New solutions to old problems are always welcome.

February 4

Why not negotiate a new approach with General Howe to fighting this war?

Assuming that neither side will "win" in the traditional sense, we could use music to battle one another.

A strategy based on the use of music could be just as intense as physical battles. The available weapons are numerous. Victory could be just as sweet.

Howe could start the invasion by promoting the playing of "Rule Britannia." We could counter attack with "March to Boston." Together we could agree that the terms of engagement include the use of wind octets—oboes, clarinets, horns, and bassoons—to replace military trumpets and drums.

The English would have to face our offensive of work music to increase productivity, like the use of sea shanties used aboard ships to coordinate the raising of sails and the weighing of anchors.

Our battle grounds would no longer be fields populated by cannons and muskets. The new "Bunker Hills" would be great halls where competition would rage on the harpsichord and clavichord. Colonial leaders like T. Jefferson could hold contests on the violin with representatives of the Crown—players to be named later by the governors of the colonies.

The playing of "Yankee Doodle" could become the ultimate contest of wills. The redcoats think that playing this tune is a great insult. They think it ridicules the country bumpkins of the colonies whose big outing is to ride into town on a pony. They think the greatest sophistication we can muster is to dress up by placing a feather in our hats and pretending we are as outlandishly fashionable as they are by calling it "macaroni." They think this lampoon angers us. Not so!

We think the tune is humorous. The Pawtuxet Rangers' fifes and drums play "Yankee Doodle" every time we parade. This could be a battle song for both sides— who can play it loudest, longest, with the greatest number of variations.

Composers could become the war heroes. We could convert organizations like the Sons of Liberty into St. Cecilia Societies or clubs patterned after the Tuesday Club in Annapolis. In the end, we could create a truce on common ground: Handel, Vivaldi, and Purcell. How the world would change. No one ever died by being shot with music!

Music hath charms to soothe the savage beast
To soften rocks or bend a knotted oak.

February 9

Peleg came to the tavern last night, but he was not himself. He answered when spoken to but offered nothing on his own. He sat next to me, as he usually does, which I took to be a good sign. However, I noticed that he was not wearing his dark red cap.

February 17

"What is your name, soldier?" I wanted to know.

"Who said I was a soldier?"

"Anyone who wanders into the Village in your desperate condition must be escaping from the army."

"Well, I ain't no soldier."

"You have a wound on your right thigh that looks like it was made by a bayonet."

"It ain't noth'in. I fell on a sharp rock."

"That 'sharp rock' made quite a wound and now it is infected. It should be drained before the swelling gets worse. Does it hurt?"

"Nope."

As I pressed along the edges of the wound, the man grimaced. "I thought you said it doesn't hurt."

"It don't hurt none unless you poke at it."

"How long have you been traveling?"

"About four days."

"Where are you coming from?"

"Savannah."

"I thought you said you had been traveling for four

days. You didn't walk from Georgia in four days."

"I said I had been traveling for about four days. Maybe, I lost track of a few days"

"Did you see any combat in Savannah?"

He could not resist. "I sure seen a lot of redcoats charging in a long line with their bayonets flashing in the sunlight."

"You confuse me. You said you were not a soldier."

"You are easily confused, Doc. I said I aren't no soldier now."

"Whose command were you serving under?"

The man made no reply.

"Did you hear my question?"

"Don't make no difference. I don't belong to no army now. I thought you were a doc—not some official looking for deserters."

"Are you a deserter?"

He made no reply, but grimaced in pain as he nervously shifted his weight.

"I'll treat that wound, but then I want you to move on. You are not welcome in this Village."

"Sure, sure, Doc. Whatever you wants. Just make this damnable pain go away."

February 24

Bad decisions are made in times of desperation. There will be hell to pay for decisions made for expedient, short-term gain.

The Rhode Island Assembly, acting on a proposal by Brigadier General Varnum, has authorized the raising of two battalions from among able-bodied Negro and mulatto slaves. The act specified that they will be entitled to everything that an enlistee would receive.

Although the recruiting of 1,430 men for two regiments from Rhode Island authorized by the General Assembly two years ago for the Continental Army has not gone well, this buying of slaves to fill out the regiments is blatantly wrong. I cannot comprehend how General Washington could permit this.

Worse than buying "soldiers" is that those who enlist (or perhaps are sold into the army by their masters) will be given their immediate freedom. Slave owners might sell some of their slaves who are troublemakers or lazy just to get rid of them at a profit.

The General Assembly has authorized up to £125 as compensation to their masters for each slave who "joins up." If the 3,000 blacks who live here enlist, we would have to pay out £375,000. We would be bankrupt.

What kind of soldiers would these "former" slaves make? They have no patriotic commitment to protect their rights, property, and communities. They do not believe in the Great Cause. They will turn and run when the first shot is fired.

When we win this war, what will these free slaves do? Where will they go? They will be without skills to become tradesmen. They will become a long-term burden on Rhode Island as it struggles to recover from the costs of this war.

This is a foolhardy, desperate act by the Rhode Island Assembly.

March 15

When Ira had Tucker carried into my house, he already looked dead. He was barely conscious.

He was bleeding from his nose, mouth, and the back of his head. It looked as if he had taken several blows with an ax handle.

"Just patch him up, Doc. I can't afford to loose him," Ira instructed.

When I cut away Tucker's shirt, it was clear he had also been repeatedly whipped.

"Why bother?" I retorted. "You obviously wanted to kill him. Why not just let him die? He is nearly dead now."

Ira admitted that he had gotten carried away in his rage. "I just wanted to teach him and my other slaves a lesson that would not soon be forgotten."

"Whatever did he do that warranted this?"

"I caught him stealing vegetables from the garden. He has stolen food from the kitchen and, lord knows, what else. I won't tolerate it! He either starts to show proper respect and gratitude for working for me, or I will sell him off. Just bandage him up and I will have him carried out of here."

Shaking my head, I told Ira that I could bleed him to correct his errant behavior, but it looked as if he had already been bled enough.

As I examined him, his eyes were hard to find; they kept rolling up into his head. I tried to get more information about his injuries by asking Tucker questions to locate problem areas. He either could not talk or would not in the presence of his master. When I tried to move him, it was clear that he had either cracked or broken ribs; I don't know how many.

The bleeding from his nose and mouth had nearly stopped. I bound his chest with heavy strips of cotton to try to stabilize the ribs, put liniment on the deep stripes that cut in multiple directions across his back, and cleaned up the blood as best I could.

"I don't know, Ira, whether he will survive this time. You are not going to get much work out of him for a while. That blow to his head already shows some swelling. I may need to go into his skull with a trephine and drain out the fluid. Bring him back in a couple of days if his speech is garbled or if he wobbles when he tries to walk. And, stop wasting my time and medical supplies. Either find another way to 'correct' him or get rid of him."

March 18

"Did you see the fight? They went at it like cats and dogs."

"Who went at it?" I wanted to know.

"It is just like Alex to stir up a hornet's nest over some trivial matter. They kept going around in circles about who owed who what. Like a loose canon, Alex started using profanity. That was the last straw. 'I've helped you through thick and thin. Now when I am down and out, a bit down on my luck, you turn your coattails. You are a far cry from being a friend. I've walked that extra mile for you without ever being asked.'

"The line had been drawn. The shouting erupted into pushing. As quick as a flash, Alex knocked him aside of his head. As he stumbled, Alex kept at him. They were engaged in full fisticuffs and going at it tooth and nail. They might have stayed at it until the bitter end and done some damage if others had not pulled them apart."

I asked again who was fighting and over what, but Sylvester was gone, swept away in his own excitement.

April 10

Nothing I have suggested has relieved Mrs. Hutchinson of her current state of barrenness. God, in his infinite wisdom, may have intervened to preclude Mrs. Hutchinson from having another child. On the other hand, Mrs. Hutchinson might not have been totally honest with me regarding the circumstances that were precluding her from conceiving. While I am hesitant to admit it, my own knowledge of how to resolve this dilemma might be deficient.

Having exhausted many remedies over many months, Mrs. Hutchinson came to me in desperation. There is no shortage of women in the community who are certain they know of a special formula which "works every time" for this malady. Mrs. Hutchinson has tried them all. Her deep melancholia stems from the untimely and mysterious death of her infant daughter within three months of her birth. For Mrs. Hutchinson the ache remains. She and Mr. Hutchinson wanted to replace this child and were committed to building a large family. But, it was not to be.

The pressure to have a family was compounded by her sisters and brothers whose families had grown rapidly. At family gatherings, the presence of young children, laughing and playing, was at first a delight. She derived pleasure from hugging them and sewing clothes for them. Soon, however, they became reminders of her own failure.

Mr. Hutchinson's relatives were not too subtle in suggesting that she and Mr. Hutchinson were delinquent in "their duty." Her relatives and close neighbors provided unsolicited advice. Eventually, she stopped listening. Irritation led to an utter loss of hope. She was convinced that she must be unworthy. The relationship with Mr. Hutchinson became strained; they spoke less and less.

Even if no health problems existed, these emotions became barriers to resolution. To determine if something had gone wrong in the birth of her daughter, I asked her if she had:

> . . . fallen asleep soon after the birth? (A new mother is not to sleep for the first four hours.)
> . . . eaten meat soon after the birth? (Only gruel with wine is suitable. No meat for two days.)
> . . . stayed in bed for forty days? (The birth of a boy required sixty-six days in bed.)
> . . . had sex before purification? (The blood must be cleansed both by taking three spoonfuls of briny water every morning and by ceremony.)
> . . . been bled in the arms during her pregnancy? (Bleeding from the foot is acceptable.)

She did not remember how long she had stayed in bed but was certain that none of the other prescriptions had been violated. Other questions were just as painful to ask and most awkward for Mrs. Hutchinson to answer. Nevertheless, she was cooperative.

"Barrenness," I told her, "resulted from a want of love between a man and his wife." She categorically denied that this was an issue.

Had she suffered from irregular menstruation, which was necessary to expel corrupt humors? Again, she insisted this was not a problem.

"Each of us has a natural balance—a physical, mental, and emotional predisposition. For conception to occur, the seed from both the husband and the wife must be released at the same time." She looked away. Perhaps, I had crossed the line of polite discourse. I did not press for a response.

Each month she visited again. Initially, I encouraged her to do more exercise and to eat a low diet of milk and vegetables.

Next, I encouraged her to eat boysenberries and blackberries. She was told to increase her consumption of zinc with leafy green vegetables, fish, and nuts.

Fearing that there might be a problem with Mr. Hutchinson, I gently hinted that his interest and performance could be enhanced by eating peas and beans. I also told her about Aphrodite, the Greek goddess of love, and about what we now call an "aphrodisiac" that increases energy. This assistance could be obtained from eating oysters, sea urchins, and chocolate.

When none of these produced the desired result, I advised, "Follow Dr. William Buchan's treatise in *Domestic Medicine*—take cold baths and consume alum, dragon's blood, and elixir of vitriol."

Sadly, none of these remedies helped Mrs. Hutchinson. In time she might conclude that she had done everything she could and that she would have to be resigned to God's will.

April 20

Some pieces of clothing never wear out and should never be thrown away. I cannot even remember when I got my black checkered shirt, but I have worn it a long time. It has two stains, which I ignore, and is frayed at the cuffs. Hope has mended it several times and thinks it is beyond use for anything but rags. Not me. It is an old friend who has literally stayed by my side. We have experienced and endured together. I feel better, comfortable by just putting it on.

Some things should never change.

May 1

Arnold, who should know since he works at the Warf Distillery, proudly announced at the tavern last night that rum contributes more to the foundation of our economy than any other of our industries—more than agricultural provisions, which we export, more than the growing textile industry, and more than our ship building. He claims that someone has calculated the amount of rum produced here that stays in Rhode Island and has concluded that every adult male consumes 1.5 quarts per week.

We entertained ourselves over a tankard of rum by converting this level to annual, per man consumption into various measurements:

156 pints
78 quarts
19.5 gallons

Then we decided how many men did not drink rum at all. If everyone didn't drink his share, some people had to be consuming barrels of rum per year. We had to do yet another calculation.

In the end, it seemed to us a solemn duty to meet or to exceed this standard in support of our well-deserved prosperity!

May 6
When I got up this morning, I knew this was going to be one of those days when only wearing my black check-ered shirt would do.

June 1
Intolerable! The British marched into Warren, burned the Baptist Church and other buildings. They spiked the cannons and looted. Then they marched on Bris-tol, where they burned thirty houses and set fire to the Anglican Church.

Contrary to their intent, these outrageous acts will not make us subservient.

June 4
The Royal Army pretends to wage this war with intent to solidify existing loyalty to the Crown and to convince others to forego the fanciful notion of independence. During some engagements, the British Army, when

properly observed by their officers, may have exhibited restraint. Often this was not their behavior and, therefore, has generated greater determination for us to stand our ground against tyranny.

In a recent expedition near Fall River, houses were burned and inoffensive inhabitants were taken prisoner. *The Providence Gazette* printed a letter of protest from General Sullivan to General Pigot, who had applauded this British success in the *Newport Gazette:*

Sir—

The repeated applications from the distressed families of those who were captured by your troops induce me to write you upon the subject. As those men were not in actual service, or found in arms, I cannot conceive what were the motives for taking them, or guess the terms upon which their release may be obtained. Had the war on the part of Britain been founded in justice and had your troops in their execution completed the destruction of the boats, and our military preparations in that quarter, without want only destroying defenseless towns, burning houses consecrated to the deity, plundering and abusing innocent inhabitants, and dragging from their peaceful habitations unarmed and in offending men, such an expedition might have shown with splendor. It is now darkened with savage cruelty, and stained with indelible disgrace.

By your leave,
General Sullivan

General Sullivan went on to conclude that the mistaken conduct of the British Army in this country has weaned the affections of the Americans from England, driving them to disavow allegiance to the Sovereign and rousing them to acts of retaliation.

This outrageous behavior toward innocent citizens and the senseless destruction of property is designed to foster fear and force us to sue for peace. However, the anger generated will have the opposite effect.

July 8
Everyone wants to stay well, but rarely does anyone ask me for advice on how to do so. Mrs. Sarah Bartlett engaged me on that topic when she saw me working in the garden. Of those who need advice on staying healthy, Mrs. Bartlett is not one of them. I can't recall when I last treated her for anything. Perhaps, she stays healthy because feeling well is important to her and she just does the right things.

I listed a few important practices for her while I continued to weed around the basil, dill, and marjoram. She was so pleased with the suggestions that she encouraged

me to write them down. She offered to pay for a broad-
side to be published. Now, that is a good neighbor.

Of all those who have written about this topic, I most
admire John Wesley, the Methodist minister, whose
practical advice has stood the test of time. I borrowed
the following:

"The sun and moon shed unwholesome influenc-
es from above; the earth exhales poisonous damps
from beneath. But we can soften the evils of life."

"The principles of health are easily summarized:
the power of exercise and temperance in eating
and drinking."

A few plain rules:

- Abstain from high-seasoned food.
- Drink only water or clear small beer.
- Sup at six or seven, go to bed early.
- Avoid easterly or northerly winds; but if you
  can't, drink warm pepper tea on going to bed.
- Be clean in your house and clothes.
- Eight ounces of animal food and twelve of veg-
  etable is sufficient each day.
- Spirituous liquors are a certain though slow
  poison.
- Coffee and tea are extremely hurtful.

- Walking is the best exercise—two or three hours a day.
- The few clothes anyone uses, the hardier he will be.
- Cold bathing is of great advantage to health.
- Eliminate constipation and promote perspiration with gentle sweats.
- Calm passions that are over-powering, otherwise medicine is applied in vain.

Many of these suggestions for good health will generate vigorous discussions among my neighbors. This is good.

July 11

Until now, Pawtuxet had not been visited by yellow fever. While the environment is not favorable to this fever, the Village is not immune to infection brought by sailors returning from tropical climates. Now that a case has appeared, we are less confident.

By the time Rufus presented himself, there was little doubt that he had yellow fever. His eyes had turned yellow and a yellow hue marked his skin. He was in a stupor and vomited black matter.

I called Dr. Tenny to consult. We debated the best treatments. Since Rufus could not tolerate much of anything in his stomach, we agreed to attempt to lessen the principle causes of the fever by reducing the excessive action in his blood vessels by blistering his sides and neck. We also started a vigorous sequence of bleeding, including the use of leeches. We fought to control his high fever by pouring cold water over his body—first every six to eight hours—and then every two to three hours.

By day three, Rufus began to bleed from his nose, gums, and bowels. He was dead by day five.

July 25

The second case of suspected yellow fever has appeared. Perhaps, this victim had contact with Rufus. Dr. Tenny and I have been unable to determine the likely origin.

We learned that Ethan did not feel sufficiently sick to seek assistance at first. He told us that he had chills and high fever and only came to us because he heard about Rufus and feared yellow fever, which he had seen in the East Indies.

There are many different types of fevers. Deciding which one a particular patient may be experiencing is difficult to diagnose. Dr. Tenny and I decided to treat Ethan as if he were progressing with yellow fever, although his eyes were bloodshot (not yellow).

For his nausea we gave him bowls of chamomile tea. His bowels were kept open and clean by small doses of cream of tartar. His limbs were wrapped in flannels soaked in hot vinegar; vinegar was sprinkled around his bedchamber. We encouraged him to drink Madeira wine diluted with lemonade and to drink gruel and barley tea plentifully. At first, his stomach would tolerate little, but the use of mint helped.

Each day his headaches lessoned and the fever failed to increase. The window in his chamber was kept open to permit the free circulation of air, and we continued to bathe him in cold water.

When our patient survived day five, we believed that the disease had turned. In fact, the fever slowly abated and the yellow of his skin faded. Dr. Tenny and I continued to attend Ethan for another week until we were convinced of his steady recovery.

We decided to publish an article, which we jointly authored, that the *Providence Gazette* printed. We wanted citizens to begin to take precautionary measures. We recommended that bonfires be ignited in neighborhoods, that citizens chew garlic, and that they sprinkle their homes with vinegar.

July 27

Peleg came by the house today to bring me some vegetables from his garden. I was pleased to see that he was wearing his favorite cap again. He was filled with stories about his garden, about carpentry projects that he was working on, and about rumors regarding the war. He said that he had heard that the *Tory* newspaper in Newport had insulted Benjamin Franklin by saying that in going to France he had imitated rats that will abandon a sinking ship and had gone there to live in luxury.

Peleg even had a joke he wanted us to conspire about. He wanted to tell the crowd at the tavern that the British were going to pose a new tax; they would tax fishing. He thought it would be humorous to create a great debate over this latest "insult."

He turned too fast and banged into the garden fence. Not perturbed, he doffed his silly looking "night cap" and, chuckling to himself, he was off on his errands.

August 20

I chose to participate in this battle, knowing that I would be needed to deal with the carnage that surely would result.

Tremendous suffering had already been endured by patriot soldiers. Our own Jeremiah Greenman, who left us to capture Quebec three years ago in what he expected to be a romantic adventure of a lifetime, was one of the lucky ones. He shocked us with stories of deprivation— infrequent or no pay, overwhelming enemy strength, cold, disease, exhaustion, and hunger. He told of men resorting to killing and eating their dogs. Jeremiah was taken prisoner with over 400 of his comrades. Gone were the romantic notions of how we would quickly send the redcoats running back to their ships.

We had faced crushing defeat in Brooklyn and White Plains. More often than not, we had been outnumbered and insufficiently trained to achieve victory. Reports from Valley Forge sickened us. Nearly freezing, living in hovels, few blankets, and dressed in rags, our army somehow survived—just barely. At some intervals that winter, men were reduced to eating bark or they roasted their tattered shoes and ate them.

The war had come to Rhode Island. No longer could we think that the real problem was distant—Canada, Delaware, New York, or New Jersey. The threat was here in Rhode Island. The occupation of Newport since December, 1776, had been devastating in every way. To our shame, Newport had been captured without a fight. Hundreds of citizens had abandoned the city, leaving all that they owned and fleeing north, many to the Providence area. The whole idea of British soldiers enjoying the pleasures of Newport was humiliating. We began to believe that their very existence desecrated our land. The destruction of our flourishing sea trade was profound. The earlier success of our privateers had slowed to a trickle.

We now had a clear sense of what it meant to have been in occupied Boston in 1776. Our fear that we could not stop the British fleet from sailing up the Bay to capture us and Providence kindled a new commitment. It was time to take a stand. My amulet, the philosopher's stone given to me by Dr. Randall, would keep me safe.

Despite my revulsion to war, I must be counted among those from Rhode Island who would free the colony from occupation.

August 29

The air was black with smoke from hundreds of fires ablaze in the fields engulfing houses and barns. The smell of gun powder from muskets and cannons choked our lungs. Worst of all was the reek of the unburied dead whose bodies were festering in the hot August sun.

Nothing could prepare us—even those of us more accustomed to blood and amputations—to the horrors of men wandering aimlessly with arms blown away or screaming in pain on the ground, clutching for a leg that no longer existed. Among the sights that made me nauseous was an encounter I had with a young lad, probably ten years of age, who was most likely a drummer boy. Gone was his drum and sticks and gone was his right hand. In truth, it was almost gone; it dangled by his side attached to a thin strip of skin above his wrist. He made no cries, most likely being in shock. But, he looked directly into my eyes, unmistakably pleading for me to do something.

At first, I was paralyzed by the ugly horror of what had happened to this mere child, caught up in an adult conflict and in a cause he could barely have understood. Forcing myself out of my stupor to attend to his profound need, I sat him down in the dirt, opened my satchel of instruments, and seized my amputation knife. Distracting him by pointing to the battle raging far to the side, I quickly severed the skin that was holding his dangling right hand and threw it out of sight. Still he made no cry. I bandaged the stump, gave him a drink of water and told him to remain where he was and that I would return for him.

Hours later, I did return to the spot where I thought I had left him. He was gone.

August 31

We had General Sullivan's army boxed in at Newport and shaking in their well-polished boots. They abandoned their northern defenses, which we readily occupied and reinforced. Fearing the capture of their ships docked in port and in the harbor, the British had begun to burn their own ships to preclude their being captured.

But then, the momentum shifted. We delayed, waiting to mass our forces. Torrential weather conspired against us, and we were abandoned by the French fleet that sailed off without landing their marines to reinforce our troops.

General Pigot launched an assault on our right flank, which was repulsed twice. The Hessians would have taken the day in their third furious charge had the First Rhode Island Regiment not stood their ground with uncommon determination. I had underestimated their potential contribution and courage.

In military terms the battle was indecisive. In human terms the consequences were devastating. The battlefield was strewn with 400 casualties and a baffling combination of pride in having faced the enemy (even without the French) and of desperate defeat in having failed to win the day. Newport had not been liberated.

I was overwhelmed by the need to provide care for the wounded and dying. I could not attend them all. Their piteous cries drew me from one to another.

September 1

Now, I am grateful that I thought to bring my journal with me. I write because I cannot sleep.

When the battle subsided, the commanders on both sides tended to the wounded, regrouped and decided to withdraw. Our few surgeons' mates attended those we had treated for musket ball wounds and punctures from cannon ball explosions.

Some additional amputations were performed. I focused on treating burns and fractures. Burns resulted from the explosion in the pan of a musket, which the soldier had zealously overloaded with black powder and then raised the flintlock too close to his face when firing. Eyebrows would burn off, an eye might swell closed, and dark powder burns would cover a cheek and fingers. While uncomfortable for the soldier, these burns were easily treated with spirits of wine, a mixture of cold water and camphor in a pint of good rum, and a paste of smooth charcoal or slices of raw potatoes. Since they were plentiful, I used mostly the sliced raw potatoes.

Burns received by cannoneers were more serious.

When cannons are fired in rapid succession, the barrels get extremely hot. Carelessly touching the barrel blisters the hand. Occasionally, while packing a cartridge of gun powder into the barrel, an existing ember can unexpectedly ignite it. If the individual loading the cannon is not standing clear of the barrel, the flash from the explosion can catch his hands and arms. These burns char the skin and can be deep and extremely painful.

Burns from campfire cooking were also common. One of our surgeon's mates brought us a supply of cucumbers from a nearby farmer's garden, which we used to great advantage to cool scorched skin.

Fractures took some time to treat. We would delay treatment until bleeding wounds were attended. Patients would line up outside my tent as soon as the first streaks of dawn appeared. As each entered, I would place him on my cot and reduce the fracture. I removed any foreign bodies and pieces of bone fragments that I could see and provide support for the fracture with a tailed bandage. Thigh and forearm fractures were supported with crude splints. One of the regimental surgeon's mates had cleverly fashioned splints from fence posts and barn boards.

I saw more patients in a few days with General Varnum's regiment near Newport than I typically see in months in Pawtuxet. I saw more devastation to human life than I want to ever experience again. Some patriotic soldiers will recover. However, many have sacrificed their ability to do the work they had done before they enlisted.

The toll is heavy.

September 2

I thought I was made of sterner stuff. I proved not to be. The regimental surgeons have earned my respect. The experienced ones cope with the devastation to human life by detaching their emotions from their duties. Somehow they are able to disengage from the pleas of the wounded, the tortured shrieks of those being amputated, the reek of torn bodies, and the inconceivable carnage that surrounds them.

During the depth of the battle around Turkey and Almy Hills, and for a short while in the aftermath, I was also able to set aside my revulsion in order to do my part. But the sleepless nights that have followed—despite exhaustion—fill every hour with ghastly apparitions of the dead and with nightmares of the tormented living. Each night I seek refuge in the churning of my stomach, despite having not eaten all day.

In ten hours I patched forty musket ball wounds. Little could be done unless I could see or easily reach the ball with my finger. If the ball were deeply embedded, I left it. It is best not to probe beyond the reach of a finger. The wound was flushed with water from my canteen, the soldier was given a drink from his canteen; then the wound was treated with yarrow and bandaged with linen.

Bayonet wounds that were more than superficial were hopeless for the victim. A bayonet charge, the cold steel flashing in the sunlight, and a hoard of yelling infantry-men storming at you, is feared more than the whiz of musket balls buzzing overhead. The triangular shape of the bayonet, when it finds its mark and is twisted by the attacker, inflicts such severe damage that little hope remains. With a prognosis for the soldier of almost certain death from bleeding and infection, I soon learned to follow the experienced regimental surgeons who gave the soldier a square of linen soaked in oil, a quick word of comfort, and moved on to the next casualty. No opium was given. Supplies were too limited to waste on the dying.

Wounds from cannon fire dictated amputation. As the battle progressed, we formed into teams of surgeons and assistants. The surgeons chose the location for the amputation; the assistant lifted the soldier onto whatever makeshift surface we had on hand. No discussion was held with the wounded, though it was apparent to him what was about to take place. Some begged us in most pitiful terms not to cut. The pleading was ignored amidst the screams of those undergoing amputation nearby. The assistants held the patient down.

We would place a fillet and stick tourniquet above the wound to compress the arteries. Selecting a site about four inches below the knee or two inches below an elbow, we would cut the muscles to the bone and then cut the bone with a saw. This was the most difficult time of the surgery since the patient would scream monstrous invectives imaginable against us, the army, and the war. At such moments, the patient is capable of superhuman strength and struggles to throw off the assistants holding him down. When the assistants are brawny enough and when there are three or four of them, the surgery proceeds as planned. If the patient moves while we are cutting, the result is most disagreeable. We would provide the patient with a biting stick, but this did little to help him deal with the pain.

If time permitted, we would tie off arteries with one or two ligatures using shoemaker's waxed thread or hair from a horse's tail, just to control the bleeding; place lint sprinkled with flour over the stump; and then bandage with linen. The soldier's woolen cap would be placed over the stump to keep it clean.

If hot tar or oil were available, a mate would pour it over the stump to seal the amputation and to promote healing and reduce infection. He would remove the stick that had been placed between the patient's teeth to keep him from biting his tongue. Some regimental surgeons give the soldier a bullet to bite during the amputation. I prefer providing a stick for the patient to bite on. The danger of swallowing a lead musket ball is an unacceptable risk. The assistants lined the amputees in a row on the ground and brought on the next patient.

Experienced surgeons could amputate four limbs in an hour's time. Since amputation offered the greatest chance of survival of the most seriously wounded, we focused attention on these cases, ignoring the wounds of the others.

September 10

I was fortunate to be with the surgeons of General Varnum's brigade. Overall in this campaign, there was no coordination of available physicians, no guidelines for treatment, no evacuation plan for the wounded, and very limited medical supply. We soon ran out of linen. The medical situation was chaotic.

September 12

Grotesque in unimaginable ways were piles of amputated body parts left unburied in the small area we had used as our operating theatre. Among the legs that protruded at oblique angles from one another, an arm would rise above the pile as if its owner were trying to work his way out from a premature grave. A totally detached hand, already dark with decay, lay at the edge of one pile, a species of monstrous spider willed into existence by some prehistoric evil force to threaten anything God had created.

Our most skillful surgeons were exhausted. We lost track of the number of amputations performed over the past two days. Looking half-dead with fatigue himself,

Dr. Prescott approached me. "Dr. Carr, we need you to amputate the leg of a young soldier who we thought was recovering from an earlier wound. A black corporal who carried him to us found him only because he was drawn to the private's moans. Others thought he was dead since he was lying flat in his defensive position long after the British had advanced past his position.

"I have never done an amputation by myself, Dr Prescott."

"You are all we have at the moment, Dr. Carr. If you do not amputate, the young private will certainly die."

I continued to protest in vain, finally relenting but filled with a gnawing dread of failing my colleagues and especially this young soldier. Here was my opportunity to prove I was a competent surgeon and could be counted on. But, my past failures swam in my head—the taunts of my brother, the tone of my father's disappointment, the resignation of the vicar that I was unsuited, the first mate's derision and scornful looks. Here the scene would have driven hungry vultures from their watchful perches in the trees. I refused to even attempt to amputate the boy's leg among the piles of broken bodies and the muck of blood red mud.

We created a makeshift hospital in what might have been a farmer's outbuilding. It was ten by ten with a dirt floor and no windows. An assistant I had worked with over the past two days found an old door and two barrels that had once stored corn meal. This became our operating platform. We no longer had full amputation kits. If I had not brought my own scalpel, I would have had to use a barber's razor or an old hunting knife. I borrowed a lantern.

The patient was carried in and placed on our makeshift platform. The tiny room was filthy. Evidence of wild animals having sought refuge here was hard to avoid as I walked hesitantly through the door and into the room. I never learned his name but even in his fevered mind he knew what was about to take place. "You are going to be all right," I told him with little conviction. His wound was extensively swollen. Despite the stench of the man's diarrhea, the sour rot of his wound permeated all of my senses. My eyes watered and I grew dizzy. I took repeated deep breaths, but there seemed to be no air in this tiny room.

My two assistants put their weight down on his upper body and left leg. As I picked up my amputation knife, he suddenly came to life. "Get away from me, you club-footed sons of bitches. Don't cut me." He looked right at me, his eyes red with anger. "Don't take my leg, you misbegotten son of Satan."

He was out of his mind with fever, pain, and fear.

I cut open the wound. To my horror it was alive with larvae. I brushed them off with the edge of the knife. Many landed on the edge of the platform and protested in some hideous dance.

The stick tourniquet we had fashioned from a piece

of old shoe leather kept his blood from flowing out as I enlarged the opening and removed the loose bone splinters. The dim flame from the lantern gave little light, casting shadows that momentarily looked like bone fragments or detached muscle.

Four fingers below the kneecap, I cut the muscles to the bone. One of the assistants held the muscles out of the way as I grabbed for my saw. Dizzy from nausea myself, I dropped the saw to the dirt floor. I quickly retrieved it, wiped it off against my apron and sawed through the bone.

My patient let out a scream that I had heard only once before. It was the howl of a dying horse that had been stabbed by a sword in the heat of battle. I had to hold myself together. I felt my two assistants watching me, questioning whether I knew what to do next and whether I could get through this procedure without loosing the contents of my stomach, which were forcing their way into my throat.

As quickly as I could, I drew out the arteries with a tenaculum; I tied them, removed the tourniquet, and began to wrap the stump with strips of linen. We sprinkled the open wound with flour and wrapped it with tow and linen to hold the dressing. We put his woolen cap over the stump.

The nameless patient had passed out. The entire procedure had taken only fifteen minutes. To me it felt like hours. My assistants carried him off; I know not where, but this gave me time to collect myself.

"The operation probably came too late," I thought to myself. By comparison with many amputations I had seen over the past two days, it was done badly. But I could do no better. At least the young soldier had a chance. I had gotten myself through the test.

September 30

The odor of an army.

Heaps of broken men.

The dying wounded, drained of hope.

The putrid smell of horses ripped by cannons.

The stench of fear as soldiers, who were farmers and merchants only days before, wait for the enemy to appear . . . and then wait what seems a lifetime for the order to fire.

The smells, the ugly tightness in my chest, the panic pouring from those we knew to be strong, their deafening cries of madness. There was no glory during the battles.

In time, the stories will paint a different picture. Not for me. My short encounter with the realities of the battlefield weighs heavily on what I remember. I feel the exhaustion over and over again.

September 31

By chance I encountered private Martin who had assisted with the badly performed amputation of a nameless soldier some days earlier. Without emotion he told me the wound had festered and that the patient had writhed in pain as he fought what was his inevitable death. The private's dispassionate report, nevertheless, knocked the breath from my lungs. A tight knot gripped my chest. He did not seem to notice, but I could not speak.

I joined the Newport campaign with the men of General Varnum's army, certain that we would run the British, at long last, out of Newport, out of Rhode Island. We were confident. I went into battle out of a sense of duty. How could I content myself with treating coughs, fevers, and measles when others faced the musket ball and bayonet? I had convinced myself that this service would make me a better doctor and would give me, incidentally, something to brag about at the tavern. For me knowing that my commitment would be of short duration, the campaign held the inviting seductiveness of a confident spider. . . . But there would be no blessing by a Divine hand. In the end we would retreat, but we could not escape the haunting.

October 4

The power to survive is not contained within the stone I have carried as my mentor Dr. Randall did for so long. I have always known that I would never be a merchant. I did my part, as best I could, to be a soldier, but I did not last long at that. Fame has eluded me as the inventor of Carr's Springtime Soup and Carr's Wonderful Elixir.

Possibly, my true contribution is the small kindnesses I provide for my patients.

October 13

For once, the folks of the Massachusetts Bay Colony have it right. They don't trust the Quakers. It is also no wonder that the British persecuted them in the 1660s. Members of the so-called Society of Friends are as much a threat to our liberty as the Loyalists. I am suspicious that all of their travel back and forth between England and the colonies is not purely to promote missionary work and the standards of Quaker religious practice.

Some say the Quakers are spies; they feed important intelligence to the British officials. They hold secret meetings. Who knows what plans are being hatched.

By claiming not to take sides, they cooperate with the British and raise money to help them. They state that they do not care which civil government is in charge, as if it makes no difference. What warped thinking could lead to that conclusion? Is a government that deprives citizens of fundamental rights—God given rights—equal to one that denies these rights? How can there be any government that serves the common good if everyone is free to defy temporal authority in the name of one's own conscience?

The Quakers claim they wish to remain neutral in the struggle with England. Being neutral when principles of fundamental rights are challenged is just not possible.

These are a most peculiar people.

October 18

The image of the drummer boy without his right hand has left me despondent. His pleading eyes continue to horrify my very being. His loss is so senseless, infesting the darkness of this war and its very human cost. As a doctor I am disconsolate at how little I can do in the face of such tragedy.

October 21

For three days now, I have been looking for the stone. I cannot imagine where I have misplaced it. Every pocket has been searched—twice. Every corner probed. Looked under the bed. Wandered up and down the rows of peas in the garden that I had recently tended. I fear it is lost. Whether it has a special influence over my medical practice or not, Dr. Randall was certain of its power when he gave it to me.

November 28

The *Gazette* reports that a widow has found a three-foot snake, native to Rhode Island, in a jar of herbs on her food shelf. Since it is impossible for a snake that size or any size to slither its way into a closed jar, I would have many questions to ask her.

I would want to know what kind of herbs attracts snakes. Does she believe snakes are evil? If she believes that snakes are evil, is this a warning sign? I would ask her if she believes that snakes like the one in the Garden of Eden are instruments of the devil? Perhaps, she thinks that snakes—even the one in Eden—are on earth to help us to learn and to discover. Are they created by God like all other creatures?

While I had her attention, I would want to know why she did not kill the snake. Most people would have done away with it. Does she think that snakes have healing power and that eating one adds years to your life?

The caduceus, a snake on a staff, is the symbol of my trade. Why then do we know so little about them?

I especially hate rattlesnakes. They display lofty behavior for such lowly creatures. They shout out their presence. They want to be noticed and feared. Most people, except children who view snakes with fascination, hate all snakes and kill any that cross their paths; but not the woman in the newspaper account who found the snake in a closed bottle of dried herbs. She set it free.

What does she know that we do not?

December 3

"What are you thinking about?" Hope asked. I had been starring into the fire for quite a long time.

"Oh, nothing."

"You don't stare transfixed unless you are thinking about something." I think she knew, but in her caring way she was drawing me out.

"Well, to be truthful, I was thinking about Arnold. I was remembering the good times we had together—like the time we went to pick berries. We had a wonderful day, but never found a single berry worth picking."

"I remember him, too. When he dressed up, which was not often, his waistcoat was so short he had to keep pulling it down. I can see him playing with that favorite coin of his. He would keep flipping it between his fingers as if he were doing some magic trick. You are right to think of the pleasant times you shared. He was a good friend."

"Yes, Hope, he was a good friend. Our table at the tavern is empty without him. I miss him."

December 14

How much should we know? For some time I have been committed to learning as much as I can about the human body, the diseases that infect us, and how we can be restored to health.

My neighbor Gilbert Chase, who is the village shoe-maker, tells me that he thinks my probing for such knowledge is scandalous, even heretical. He says that my desire to seek such learning is most prideful. He accuses me of pretending to be God. Gilbert often reminds me that the serpent tempted Eve by telling her that she would not die from eating of the tree in the midst of the garden. "She was drawn into sin by thinking that the tree was good and was pleasant to the eye. She desired to be wise, so she and Adam ate the fruit and, forever, brought punishment down on us. We were driven from Eden."

I tell him, "Being human is to search for understanding and knowledge. We can never expect to comprehend what only God knows."

He is not satisfied with my reasoning. Gilbert says that my search for knowledge about the human body and cures for diseases is not learning a trade like shoemaking. He thinks that I am meddling in matters that are forbidden and that such topics have been purposely hidden from us like the Tree of Life. "To live our allocated time, to suffer as God wills it, and to die when our time has come is the natural order. We are not to interfere," he warns.

I enjoy arguing with him, but there is no changing his mind. If He had not so intended, God would not have permitted us to have curiosity about ourselves, our souls and bodies, nor would He have given us the capacity to discover, to learn, and to exercise reason.

He has given lesser animals, it appears to me, the ability to gain knowledge and to use it in their lives. Each year we see birds and ducks migrating—sometimes long before we are aware that cold weather is coming. Who knows where they go? But, they come back safely in the spring. The buckies, somehow, know how to make the arduous swim up the river to spawn and then return to the sea. Even my cat, Mrs. Norris, has learned when it is time to eat; she comes looking for her food. She has learned the warmest places to cuddle up in the house, and she goes to the same spots as each season changes. She has learned which neighborhood dogs she can trust and which she cannot. If these creatures can learn and use this knowledge, surely God would not deny that we could—and should—do the same.

Nevertheless, the words of my brother persist, "God will never permit you to become a minister." He was right about that. Am I now being kept in my place by an angry God who finds me meddling with the natural order? Just when I believe I am on the path that will prove that I can make a significant contribution with the talents I have, my best friend dies because I forced him to be inoculated and a neighbor berates me for playing God.

December 29
We could learn much from our pets if we would watch and imitate them. They eat moderately and only enough to satisfy their hunger. They just appear when it is their time to eat. If we are delayed in feeding them, we get a gentle nudge, a pleading look, or a petitioning rub against our leg. They are loyal and affectionate. There is never a doubt when Mrs. Norris climbs up on my lap and purrs. Argos wags his tail and comes running to the door to greet me. Affection is simply and frequently expressed. Have you ever seen a pet that was not

satisfied with his home, his family, or the area in which he lives? I have never heard them complain.

To keep fit, since she does not move much or go far, Mrs. Norris stretches every muscle with artistic ease. She pushes out her front legs and then raises her body in a graceful arch. You can see her muscles ripple, the hamstrings in her hind legs quiver with the effort. I have never seen her omit this ritual; she even stretches every time she rises from a peaceful sleep.

Their greatest lesson is in modeling how to relax. If we could sleep as much as they do, we would live forever. They are paragons of contentment. They find a quiet corner, curl up and snooze. For them there are no political issues, no contest with England, no big threat to personal safety or liberty.

1779

January 18

Some slow-witted fools do not learn from their mistakes. While we benefit from commerce in slaves, molasses, potash, and iron, benefits that all colonies do not enjoy, agriculture is vitally important as well. Stealing farm animals is considered a heinous crime; harsh penalties are imposed.

Ward must have decided to make a career out of stealing hogs, regardless of the penalties. In his simple mind, he was likely convinced that he would never be caught.

The first time he was caught he was given twenty-five lashes at the public whipping post. Perhaps, the stripes were not vigorously "laid on" because he soon recovered. Apparently, whipping taught him nothing.

Within a fortnight, he was apprehended again. This time he had stolen two hogs. In a village such as this, concealing two hogs is no easy matter.

He was sentenced to stand for two hours in the pillory. He was jeered. Rotten fruit and worse were thrown at him. When he was released from this ordeal, his ears, which had been nailed to the frame were torn away. Ward would be forever marked as a thief.

I have not seen him for weeks. Perhaps, he has moved to another village to ply his "trade." No hogs have been stolen around here for many weeks.

January 27

Alex has been campaigning to persuade me to stand for election at the town meeting. His advocacy is a pleasant tribute. Alex compliments me on my reasoned judgment, commitment to the Village, and level-headed approach to solving problems.

Becoming a recognized town official is tempting. Most of those elected are accorded heightened respect. Alex points out that almost all of the work is conducted in a short span of time before and after the town meeting in March, and I would be attending the two or three sessions anyway.

While I believe that town meetings are the best way to govern ourselves and, as John Locke suggests, of acting in the common good, I am reluctant to become distracted by local politics. After all, what does meeting do? We debate and then make decisions that affect our schools, who can pasture their livestock in specific locations, what roads need to be repaired, what deteriorations to the bridge should be of concern, what taxes need to be levied, and what we need to do to provide for the poor.

All of these topics need attending, but I have other ways to serve.

February 4
Dear Dr. Wheaton,

Whether we win this damnable war or not—and surely we must with your service in the Continental Army— our toasts in the tavern have grown longer and added much to our merriment:

> To . . . the alliance between France and the thirteen United States.
>
> His most Christian Majesty—King Louis XVI Queen of France.
>
> His Catholic Majesty King of Spain.
>
> The favorable continence of the war,
>
> General Washington and the Army,
>
> The Colonial Navy (as you know, Rhode Island invented it),
>
> Friends of freedom in all parts of the world,
>
> The American victories, that they might drive Great Britain to her senses,
>
> The memory of the heroes who have sacrificed their lives for freedom and independence in America,and
>
> A good and honorable peace.
>
> As our success multiplies, may our toasts get shorter, but one more will always be appropriate:

To you, my good friend.

Your affectionate, most humble and obedient servant.

February 14

I do not know what came over me, but it was, after all, Hope's birthday. We had a quiet dinner. Eliza and Daniel had been put to bed. Hope came over to me after cleaning up, sat unusually close and draped a blanket over our legs. It was one of those wonderfully cozy moments; we have had opportunity for far too few of them lately. We shared the sherry I had poured for myself. Then it just came out:

> "I love that you make the best rhubarb pie on earth. I love that you get a little wrinkle on your chin when you think my idea is foolish (she absently ran her finger across her chin to feel if the wrinkle was there). I love that you can wear the same dress three days a week and still look beautifully handsome each time. I love that you are the last person I want to talk to at night and the first I want to see in the morning. I do not often say it, but you are the most important person who ever touched my life."

Squeezing my hand, she kissed my cheek.

February 16

The seasons come and go so rapidly. Again, we are about to enter Lent, which is not one of my favorite divisions of the liturgical calendar. Yet, I know that it is good to take time to reflect on our purpose here on earth and how we live our lives.

However, I am fond of Shrove Tuesday. The simple custom of eating pancakes today recalls warm memories of my mother and our family eating together before we "fasted" under the dietary restrictions of Lent. Surprisingly, I can clearly remember my mother explaining why we ate pancakes on Shrove Tuesday. Perhaps, she explained this to us children every year. In earlier times there was a lot of merriment celebrated just before Ash Wednesday. The Christians turned from self-indulgence to confess and repent their sins of the past year. This included a dietary shift. The recipes for the stacks of pancakes my mother made and we all heartily ate called for wheaten flour, eggs, butter or lard, water, milk, ale, and spices. Under strict rules, she told us, all dairy products had to be used because they were prohibited during Lent.

My family here in Pawtuxet no longer follows the old practices of making merry on Shrove Tuesday nor do we think of it as a day to prepare for the more religious observations of Lent. But we do continue the tradition of eating pancakes.

Hope makes delicious pancakes, which she sprinkles

with sugar and spices. We cover them with molasses or maple syrup.

The symbolism for this practice is lost in the hazy past, and I make no attempt to instruct my children about its origin. We just call it Pancake Day, and we sure do enjoy them.

March 5

General Washington loves the play. I hear he has seen it six times. Against the will of Congress, he had it performed at Valley Forge.

The student players at the College of Rhode Island performed it last night. We have had little public entertainment since the beginning of the war; this was a welcome diversion.

Perhaps, "Cato" is not a diversion at all. General Washington (and the rest of us for that matter) finds many lessons that echo down from Caesar's time to our own. Numidia and the Colonies share a common concern about the need to resist tyranny.

Like the Numidians who wanted to think of themselves as Romans, before this conflict we preferred to think of ourselves as British. Rome had its loyalists in Numidia. There are those here who, like Sempronius or Juba, have a much narrower view of what is worth fighting for. London decided to send troops to put down rebellion here in much the same way as Rome sent Caesar to Numidia in North Africa.

The play has stirring lines that could easily be used to rally support for this conflict. This is probably why General Washington likes it so much:

"I regret that I have but one life to give for my country (Act 4)."

"Give me liberty or give me death (Act 2)."

Despite the popularity of this play and the enthusiastic performance at the College, we are reminded that politically Cato made a costly decision when he chose to side with Pompey in his unsuccessful civil war against Caesar. We can admire Cato's role model—his stalwart and courageous stand on principle values. The circumstance he faced was overwhelming. Victory was certain for the Roman legions and for Caesar, one of the most powerful military leaders of all times.

Must we, too, face a hopeless situation and die in an effort to resist tyranny? Must we risk everything?

While it is of little immediate comfort to us, Caesar eventually pays the ultimate price at the hands of members of his own senate. Shakespeare would have us believe in his play about Caesar that he is destroyed by his vanity and desire to exercise power as if he were king. In this respect his lack of popularity may be akin to what we see in George III.

Today we remember Caesar's tragic ambition, but we celebrate Cato's heroism.

March 9

I have been thinking more about "Cato" as a model for our own thought and behavior. Standing on principle for liberty did not get Cato anything but death. Numidia was not awarded independence from Rome. Others in the play are quick to see what they must do to be allied with the winning side. . . .

This is precisely the dilemma I face in practicing medicine. I can sail the same sea by following the currents and tides that my colleagues do. They take satisfaction by safely drifting in tradition and common practice. They go with whatever winds are blowing.

Or, as I would prefer, I could chart my own course. To do so is a greater risk, but there is a chance of making new discoveries and through exploration finding a better route.

Neither Cato nor Caesar are very good models to help me ride out this stormy decision.

March 29

"Nice shirt, Luke," Peleg sneered with a wry smile. "Are you going to wear that checkered piece of tattered cloth until we win the war?"

"I will wear it until it wears out. It has years left.

"You could make a major contribution by donating it to oil down muskets or swatting cannons."

"You mean 'swabbing' cannons, don't you? Stop pestering me. You are not exactly the height of fashion yourself."

With a glint in his eye, he touched his stained night cap and lifted his tankard in an end of discussion salute.

April 7

Just for the fun of it, Hope and I created a set of rules for the household. We used military metaphors to give Daniel and Eliza a sense of the structure and discipline of a soldier. Each became a "private." Hope is the major commandant and I am the captain-commanding.

Each officer and private shall be ready for breakfast and dinner as soon as the same is notified by order of the major commandant. No officer or private shall appear for dining without his hair neatly combed, face and hands washed, and shoes cleaned. No private shall run about in the parlour. The duty of reading every evening is to be regularly performed by the Corps and to whom that duty shall be by general order assigned (when each member of the Corps becomes capable of performing this task).

Cleanliness, being of great importance and which promotes good health, everything contrary thereto will be considered highly reprehensible and treated as such.

Members of the Corps will keep their sleeping and work areas neat and tidy. Inspections can occur at any time.

Eliza and Daniel took great delight in these rules. They liked playing soldier. We shall see how long this stratagem works.

April 16

An outrageous satiric advertisement recently appeared in a London paper and, naturally, got widely circulated through the colonies:

"Lost by Mistake"

Thirteen Provinces in America with all appurtenances

More than 20,000 well-trained European Soldiers

Our natural influence on European affairs

The integrity of our ministers

Freedom of the subjects and the virtue, justice, and good sense of our King

Anyone capable of producing these or knowing of some means by which the aforementioned items can be restored as a whole or in part should notify the Royal officers who are appointed over these items, which have by mistake been lost . . .

There should be promised a rich reward for said service.

Someone of intelligent perspective and courage still lives in London!

April 30

The newspaper reported on news printed in Philadelphia. "On April the 19th Spain declared the American states independent."

Pressure mounts on King George.

May 3

Those who thought about making a quick profit by employment in the Salt Works may have to rethink that decision. The need for salt both for the army and for the rest of us warranted the establishment of our salt works on Post Road. When they enlist, each soldier is promised a quart of salt with every 100 pounds of beef. Financially, the Salt Works has prospered. Little was predicted, however, of the human consequences of working day after day mining the salt.

Living by the sea, we know that salt water—even salt air—will pit metal over time. Iron, if left unprotected or unpolished, will sustain ruin.

Few of us would worry about salt having ill effects on our bodies. Fishermen, after all, spend their entire lives on the sea without harmful consequence from the salt air.

Evidence that I have now suggests that prolonged exposure to over 4,550 square acres at the Pawtuxet Salt Works is detrimental to health. Evaporation fills the whole atmosphere. Breathing this concentrated, corrosive air creates fermentation in the stomach, produces leg ulcers, and weakens muscles.

When Christopher Cowell came to me he complained of all sorts of ailments that were impossible to associate with any particular disease. He told me he had headaches, chest pains, toothaches, and tired arms. As usual, he presented his symptoms with a great flourish.

If you do not take his dramatic monologues too seriously, he can be quite entertaining. He missed his calling by not going into the theatre.

"There is no doubt, Dr. Carr, I have contacted a rare disease from the East Indies.

"Have you been there recently, Mr. Cowell?"

"No."

"Have you been in contact with sailors who have recently been to Papua, Sumatera or somewhere else in Indonesia?"

"Well, no, but sure as I am standing here I have one of those diseases I have heard about."

"Have you often had headaches and toothaches?"

"Most of my adult life I have experienced headaches, but ulcers and weakness are new to me and I am afraid I have caught something really bad."

"To cure these problems you will have to quit your work at the Salt Works. Something in the air is causing these problems."

"I can't do that," he protested. "It is not my fault that I work at the Salt Works. I have eaten something I should not have."

I suspected that his ailments were associated with the unique environment of his occupation and that concentrated salt air might be a source of his ailments. I told him this, but it was evident that he would have preferred to have some tropical disease. I gave him a salve for his leg ulcers.

When he returned in a few days, the ulcers were less bothersome but his weakness was increasing. His melodramatic flourishes had not in any sense diminished.

"Content yourself with creating whatever story suites for the cause of your ailments, but you might try some of the following to counteract the agitation in your stomach. Eat foods rich in fat, like pork sausage, and use lots of oil and butter." He agreed to nothing that I suggested, except the consumption of full-bodied wines. He undoubtedly will tell many that he has a sensational doctor who cures strange and unique diseases by telling his patients to drink lots of wine.

May 7

For some reason, perhaps the abundant rain, we have been visited by a large infestation of spiders. They do not seem to bother anyone but Caleb Hollingworth. He hates them. They must know this because they do whatever they can to terrorize him. He feels they are out to get him and they often do. He has been bitten again this year. The bite reinforces his conviction that he is singled out by these "evil creatures" and that he is ordained to suffer this burden.

Several of his neighbors have tried to convince him that a spider bite is not purposeful punishment for some sin that he cannot recall. Frankly, he rather enjoys frustrating those who show concern and want to help. He would rather complain.

Caleb gets a significant swelling at the site of the bite and usually an inch or two above and below it. He complains of severe itching. He also complains of fever and weakness, though I suspect exaggeration and desire for sympathy.

As usual, I applied vinegar to the bite and told him to cover it for three days with tobacco juice and rub it with salt. These treatments seem to be just what he craves. Of course, he need not come to me to get relief from the itching and swelling, but he comes every time that he is bitten. He enjoys the attention that I give him.

May 8

With Hope's assistance I have prepared a dozen bottles of my molasses-based tonic. Mr. Sheldon has agreed to put them on the shelves in his general store, providing that I split the selling price with him. A deal like his is usury, but I must begin marketing somewhere.

May 11

She came into the room to tell me—Nel had run away. I had been stewing about this and feared that she had stolen something. Hope was distressed. She knew, before I did, that I didn't want to discuss this. I had concluded that we must have done something wrong to warrant her abandoning us.

Hope drew near but paused—said nothing. I was not going to initiate the conversation. To the left of the hearth, a spider had spun its web between the stone and the wall.

Hope began, "I have discovered that Nel has taken all of her possessions." Silence.

The spiderweb gently fluttered in a draft from some unseen source.

"I think she has run off with her boyfriend."

The web was not perfectly formed, though amazingly intricate in design. One strand floated to the right side like a scout out looking for a victim.

"She stole a cooking bowl, our forks, and my satin bonnet."

I made no comment. The web had trapped a fly—dinner for tonight or tomorrow or a random act of fate without any particular relevance. The spider was nowhere to be seen.

Where could it have gone and why had it deserted its web?

May 16

To Mr. Sheldon's astonishment and more especially to mine, half of the bottles of Carr's Wonderful Elixir have been sold. I cannot believe it! The label with what looked like a rum bottle that Hope created must have drawn attention. When word spreads how powerful the elixir is my fame will explode.

May 28

As Argos and I walked along the Knightsville Road out into the country, I troubled myself with the recurrent thought I had buried some time ago. . . .

High above, an osprey circled. At first, it swept across the field, looking. It could not have been hunting this far from the ocean. What was it doing here? Soon it climbed to considerable altitude and glided, wings fully extended, a marvel of effortless movement. It had found some supporting current—or the current had found him.

A picture of ultimate freedom.
Unburdened for the movement without any need to hunt.
Satisfied to drift wherever the air current would take him.
I fantasized, envying the osprey. He was above it all.
  Liberated from responsibilities.
  A solitary creature in harmony with nature.
  Independent.
  Autonomous.

Like me, he has somewhere he wants to go. For now, he will pause to enjoy this moment. He probably does not wake up at night thinking that Fenner's Farm is no longer interesting or that Pawtuxet is too small to challenge his spirit of exploration. He probably has no longing to engage in communal excitement and conversational stimulation with the osprey of New York or Philadelphia. He isn't planning how to avoid another long winter.

On a whim, he controls the timing of his life. In an instant he breaks out of the lazy circling and heads off. I watch him for the longest time as he fades from sight. Tonight he will be someplace else.

Argos barks at me. He thinks it queer that I have spent so much time watching a bird when we are out for a walk. He races ahead to remind me that we have some distance yet to go.

June 2

Mrs. Barnes came by early this week complaining of poor vision. She had no fever nor did she complain of pain in any body part. Convinced that her deteriorating eyesight was not caused by some malady, I told her I would try treating her with eye stones. I had been given these special stones by Dr. Eastor as a gift after I had assisted him by successfully bleeding one of his patients.

These stones, I had discovered, were useful for sore eyes and for drawing out redness, but were of little help for poor vision. However, Mrs. Barnes pleaded with me to try.

Laying her flat on a bench, I placed the eye stones on her lids and let them rest there for some minutes. When I removed them, she joyfully proclaimed that she could see much better. Such are the miracles of physic!

She was back two days later with the same complaint, now with her son Ron, who seems destined for leadership with the Rangers. I told her that I would try the eye stone treatment again, if she wished. "Rarely, would a single treatment bring permanent improvement," I advised.

Again, after the treatment, she felt her vision was clearer.

Today she returned yet again, now much discouraged. She asked if I could give her a tonic, prepare a salve, or concoct a tea that would help her. Sorely tempted to give her each of these—and charge her for each of them—I tactfully advised that the change in vision was probably the result of her advancing age. I suspect that she was much insulted, but tried to hide it from me.

"Can nothing be done?" she lamented.

"Next time an itinerant peddler comes through the Village," I told her, "ask him if you could try on various spectacles that he carries until you find a pair that improves your sight."

"If you find the right pair, you will know instantly that spectacles are what you need."

Delighted with this prospect, she thanked me and bid me good day.

June 5

Even with little meat these days we can enjoy an ample supply of quahogs. A favorite tradition around here is to dig our own. Benjamin and I went clamming today. He

uses his special rake, which he swears finds more quahogs, but I harvested as many as he did by uncovering
them with my feet. We gathered six bushels between us.
Mrs. Waterman down the street taught us to chill them
to relax the mussel in the shell so we can more easily
shuck them.

Hope will apply her genius to this bounty to make
clam cakes, grind them, and bake them in the shell as
"stuffies," and with her mother's special recipe she will
make the best chowder in all of Pawtuxet. Daniel doesn't
much like quahogs but eating them sends me into rever-
ie—a gift from the sea.

June 25

If the army could only take better care of its soldiers, they
would be healthier, better able to endure long marches,
and fight with more determination, but many of them
suffer from dysentery or the bloody flux. Soldiers bring
it home when they get a furlough from their service or
on returning after their enlistments.

Recently, I have been treating Ezra Hazard, who
came home exhausted and emaciated. He enjoys the
excitement of being in the army and is determined to do
his part to change the world. Even in his compromised
physical condition, he could not stop telling me about
the battles that he had fought in, the thrill of watching the lines of lobster backs advancing, the whizzing
of musket balls, the roar of cannon fire (especially our

own), the dense smoke which sometimes covers the entire scene like a heavy fog and then suddenly lifts to reveal the dramatic destruction, the acrid smell of gun powder which he claims is intoxicating. Like the Greek Ares, Ezra loves the adventure, the lust of battle, seeing new places, and taking risks.

Ah, he is young.

I admire his confidence and am grateful that we have young men who will follow General Greene and, at peril to themselves, win independence for us all.

He told me that he dreads being sick; it keeps him out of the fight. He sees this bout with the bloody flux as a temporary interruption and expects to be back in the army and back in action as soon as I can cure him.

I prepared a decoction of sassafras roots and told his mother to keep giving it to him until he felt stronger. "He will not be himself for several weeks," I cautioned. "Then he will need your good cooking to fatten him up." She was pleased to consider how she could contribute to his recovery, yet was fearful about his going back into the army. She knew she could not stop him.

"I want reports of his progress and," I told her, "I will visit him in a few days. If the sassafras is not sufficient, I will prepare a powder of white oak or a decoction of dried elderberries."

She wanted to know what caused her son's dysentery. "There are a number of conditions in the camps that might have been responsible: unripe fruit, uncooked vegetables, the damp ground, or wet clothes. Some suspect that bad water is the blame. Do not hesitate to let me know if he does not make steady progress."

July 7

"Luke, what will death be like?" Seth wanted to know. "I have been puzzling every day over the approach of my own death. Will there be more pain?" He choked on these words. "Will it be like a laborious trip where I will be wearier with each step?" He hesitated. I said nothing, waiting to hear what else he wanted to know. "Will I fear the bend in the road or that the next hill is hiding some undefined place that is filled with horrors?"

"I am not sure what death will be like, Seth," I admitted. "You certainly have been thinking about it. Your illness has taken over your life, changing nearly everything that you once were able to do, and I admire how you have faced those changes."

"But, now, Luke, I sense the end is near and I want to know what the final journey will be like. I want to know where I am going."

As I listened, I began to be absorbed in my thoughts and uncertainty.

"You read the Bible and have heard the pastor. The answer may be there."

"Perhaps, I should be satisfied with those answers, but I am not."

"This is a time, Seth, to think about all of the good

things that you have done, to see in your mind the bright reds and oranges of the sunset, the tender green of new growth in spring, the rosy streaks of dawn. Imagine smelling the bread baking on the hearth and the acrid smell of the sea as the tide goes out. Listen in the evening to the lively chirp of crickets. Think about your family and friends and the pleasant times you have spent together. And when you are ready, close your eyes. Move beyond. Be content in the silence."

As I spoke to him, he did close his eyes and seemed to be drifting. His breathing was shallow as he rested.

Each time I encounter the death of someone whose life I have admired, I wrestle with my own life. What will death bring? Will I have achieved something of value? Like Seth I want to know. It is the ultimate piece of knowledge.

July 29

A letter published in the *Boston Evening Post*, July 24, has struck terror into our hearts. There are days when the war seems distant. Our small village, despite its active and often illegal engagement in commerce and trade, would seem an unlikely target of British military attention. Providence was the focus following the burning of the *Gaspee*. Pawtuxet went unnoticed. Boston's tea party drew far more ire than our own. But, the events reported in the *Post* reminded us that we are not immune to the ravages of war. Fairfield's letter was written in Connecticut:

I am sitting down to describe to you the sad and horrible events which have taken place in our beautiful and pleasant town, but now a sad place, a devastated heap of ruins, horrible sight of most terrible destruction. We became aware of the approaching British fleet but it appeared as if they intended to pass by. Between 9 and 10 of the clock, however, after the fog had lifted, we again saw them to our right below us . . . Some troops began to disembark and marched to the center of our town where they separated into small groups and began their hellish business. Few of our militia could be summoned; our forces much too weak. A few women had lost too much time with a view of saving their most precious possessions. The ladies may have thought that meeting the invaders with a kind and submissive demeanor would secure them against coarse behavior, but they were badly mistaken. The Hessians were the first party that was let loose to plunder and destroy; they broke into the houses, brutalized friend and foe without difference, broke open chests, trunks, closets, boxes, and took everything of value. They not only abused the women with the most disgusting language but also stepped on them and put bayonets to their breasts. The English came last and devastated what had not been destroyed.

Shortly after sunset, the fire broke out. The women

begged that some houses and particularly the churches be spared; General Tryon refused. On the next morning the fire consumed the city. But then came the rear guard, the most savage band that has ever been let loose on humans. They set fire to everything left standing. They can rightfully be called the sons of plunder, destruction, and devastation. The report in the Hartford paper, according to which a man was cooked in brandy and later burned, is false.

With our location between Newport, with its easy access for the British fleet, and Providence with its developing wealth and political obstinacy, are we not subject to the terrible fate of this Connecticut town? May God have mercy on us.

August 10
More and more I see the need to give patients who have terminal illness something positive to cling to. These aphorisms might prove useful:

Fatal Disease
It cannot erase friendship.
It cannot extinguish what you have already contributed to family, friends, and community.
It cannot overcome your love for the things that please you.

It cannot steal today.

It need not shatter your faith.

It cannot destroy your place in heaven.

August 15

The tide has turned. Opportunity knocks at last. I have been given permission to set up a stand at this year's fair to sell my elixir. All I need is enough bottles and a few testimonials to entice the fairgoers into purchasing. Perhaps, like Spain recognizing American independence, my reputation as a great doctor will soar with sale of my Wonderful Elixir.

August 23

Locke was a brilliant thinker. I have been most fortunate in being able to borrow *Human Understanding* and *Two Treatises of Government* from John Curven's personal library in Providence. I wanted to read Locke because I understand that he had studied medicine. Perhaps, his thoughts would benefit both my own practice of medicine and my occasional uncertainty regarding the struggle with the Crown.

Consistent with the teaching of my mentor, Dr. Randall (during my apprenticeship with him), Locke contends that we learn through experience. We must use our five senses in keen observation and exercise a process of reflection to write on the "tabula rasa" of our minds. This philosophy, it seems to me, requires active reasoning and encourages discovery. My belief is that this is the only way we can advance our knowledge of medicine.

Locke disagrees with Hobbes, who felt that a supreme monarchy was preferable for government. Too bad that Locke had insufficient influence on George III! Locke saw no need for government with great powers. He believed we give only some personal freedom and power for the common good to ensure our own peace and security. I wish he had said what level of government was necessary: village? state? national?

There is danger in the government becoming too large with wide geographic dispersion, diverse environmental considerations, and social traditions. The public welfare and common good become extremely difficult to define. Abuse of power is invited in the interests of the few. Certainly, England has lost Locke's concept of government by popular consent, as it has built an empire.

August 28

The air was filled with the alluring aroma of freshly baked pies. A band was playing a march in a nearby field. My booth at the fair was near the baking competition and the row on row of canned jams and other preserves. Being next to the pens filled with cattle and pigs would neither have encouraged visits nor buying my elixir. There seemed to be a lot of children running around, dancing with excitement. In my mind I rehearsed the salesman's pitch I had prepared, and waited for the crowds to assemble in front of my booth. The sun had broken through the clouds. A perfect day for the fair.

By noon one young couple had stopped. They did not stay long enough for me to get into my sales pitch. An old man stood patiently as if waiting for me to convince him to buy. I practiced on him but all he did was shake his head and walk toward the squealing pigs. By late afternoon I had spoken to no more than two dozen people. I had sold only three bottles of the elixir. Others who were selling their wares told me that attendance had been poor and that few people were buying. The war had taken its toll. People came to the fair primarily to enjoy the free entertainment.

As the late afternoon shadows created an uncharacteristic chill in the August air, I packed up my elixir bottles. Heavy with discouragement, I lugged them home. Reluctantly, I might have to concentrate on Hope's plan to make candles.

September 2

The fishermen knew long before the rest of us. There was a major storm lurking out at sea somewhere in our region. They repeatedly scanned the horizon for signs of what was to come.

At noon an eerie calm hung over the Village. The leaves on the oaks barely moved.

2:00—Heavy sea swells began to crash ashore. The tide was high. Winds were north–northeast. The sky clear. Fishermen brought small boats ashore and tied down the rest. Hope gathered mops and rags for our windows and door.

3:00—Large waves, now from the southeast, created a distant roar. Winds were still blowing from the north–northeast. The limbs of trees were thrashing. I retreated inside, bolted the door, and nailed the shutters closed. Then I helped Hope put rags around the windows. We checked our supplies of food, candles, and oil.

5:00—The howling winds continued to increase. Even inside we could hear the surf—wild and noisy.

6:00—We saw timbers and huge tree branches flying through the air. One beam that must have been sixteen feet long crashed through Peleg's house across the street. Hope huddled the children in a corner, reassuring them that we were safe. Neither of us was very certain of that.

9:00—There were no signs of the storm letting up. Occasionally, there were intense flashes of lightening. We had abandoned keeping the fire going but took solace in the one candle that we could protect from the wind that had invaded the room. The whole house quivered. We tried to block out the explosive sound of splitting limbs and the thud of debris hitting the roof and the sides of the house. Two of our shutters were ripped off. The storm was directly over us. Wild torrents of rain drowned out our ability to talk to one another. We were numbed by fear. Like a monstrous living thing, the wind seemed intent on tearing the house apart. Hope and I avoided looking directly at one another.

10:00—The fury abated. The tone of the wind changed. The rain seemed to end. We sighed with relief, but we had only twenty minutes of grace before the attack began again. The wind screamed. We feared that the enraged giant, who was intent on breaking in, would succeed. The house crouched against the weather.

11:00—We lost track of time. At some point the storm, frustrated by failure to wreck total destruction, moved on.

As if reluctant to appear, the dawn finally arrived, but it was later and dim.

September 5
In retrospect, I should have known something was about to happen. There had been an unusual number of complaints about headaches, yet I did not recognize a trend at the time. Falling barometric pressure can precipitate

this condition in some people. The newspaper reported that John Winthop of Harvard, who makes a hobby of recording the weather, had noted pressure as low as 28.96 inches during the storm.

Argo had been restless. He kept staring at the door but would not go out when I opened it. Mrs. Norris was nowhere to be found. She did not even appear at her usual feeding time.

Flocks of ducks appeared in the cove; I had joked that they must be holding a convention. Scores of gulls sat on the piers, on waterfront buildings, and on the surrounding banks, facing the wind. I never linked all of these forebodings.

They turned out to be premonitions of the impending storm.

Fortunately, there was no loss of life in Pawtuxet due to the storm. I treated Mrs. Haskill for a wound to her head when a beam in her kitchen fell on her. I set many broken bones. All of the Dexters had bones broken when their house collapsed around them.

Neighbors took care of one another.

Barns will need to be rebuilt; fences mended. Small boats that had washed ashore will need repair and will be dragged back to their moorings. Repairs to the piers and the clean up of mud that invaded businesses along the river will take some time. Some of our roads washed out. Debris from upstream has contributed to the flooding. Other roads are flooded with four or five inches of water. Trees are uprooted. Even large pines were split in the middle—a fearful thing to behold. The bridge survived. I walked out on the point. I found hundreds of fish, many with their eyes popped out due to the decreased pressure.

A few houses will need extensive restoration; most will need some repair. We lost shingles from our roof, experienced some water damage in the upstairs bedrooms, and we will have to replace a window that was destroyed by flying debris.

Much damage is being reported in Connecticut. We are grateful to have been mercifully spared.

September 18

She is one of the most unique pieces of work that God ever created. She is charming, intelligent, and manipulative. And she can aggravate me at will.

Despite being younger, she insists on proving to her brother that she is in no way his second. Whatever toy he is playing with, she wants, grabbing it if he will not share it, which he only occasionally will do. He protests loudly; she ignores his complaints. If he puts the toy down, she takes it. When he yells at her, she is obstinate. This infuriates him, all the more—exactly her intent. She really doesn't want the toy. She wants to make him angry. He will lecture her with words that he has clearly memorized from what his mother often has said to him about being nice and sharing. His lecture has no impact on her. Daniel looses control. She is victorious!

"Eliza," he will scream, "you are mean. I am never going to play with you again. I hate you."

She is not bothered by this, but I am.

"Daniel," I reprimand, "you may not talk to your sister that way." My face reddens, my voice gets louder, my anger is blatant. "Eliza, stop pestering your brother," I add.

He is in tears. She has succeeded in getting him into trouble. A satisfied smirk on her face, she goes off to plan a new scheme.

If Hope hears me yelling, she will caution me to have more patience. "They are only children, Luke. They are just formulating their relationship and learning to cooperate."

"Nonsense," I retort. "They have no interest in cooperation."

I worry about how manageable she is going to be as she grows older. While I love her dearly, she knows how to trigger my frustration and anger.

October 4

Solitude—a place of your own—precious space. At first the stillness just rests peacefully. Then, I become aware of how quiet the world has become. Days normally filled with comings and goings, filled with sound—often just noise—fade. The quiet itself invades, takes control, dominates. It envelopes and refuses any distraction. There are no borders. It tightens the mind, squeezes out the clutter. Eventually, I stop thinking about it and begin to relax. I give in. The fear of being alone dissolves. The disturbing sadness of isolation no longer bothers me. My mind clears. I embrace the present. I feel open to new energy and possibilities. Such moments are fleeting.

Yet, without them some inexplicable vitality would be lost. New insights rarely appear on these occasions. No new epiphanies launch me in far or out deep. The answers I am struggling to find do not just float to the surface.

But, I feel refreshed . . . ready . . . not just to go on but to move ahead.

October 12
While I was in David Jeckes bookshop browsing for any new medical treatise, I encountered Dr. Isaac Senter. I briefly introduced myself, sympathized about his capture in Quebec and expressed my pleasure that he was back in Pawtuxet. We pledged to meet to discuss the war and medicine. Then I got cornered by Unity Rogers who wanted to discuss a medical problem but didn't want to do so where others might overhear.

We went outside and strolled down the street. She told me she could not sleep. She felt tired but lay awake reviewing the events of the day and planning activities for the morrow. I asked her if other things were troubling her. She denied any other problem. She only admitted to being very busy. As I questioned her, she got more and more agitated. Her speech became more rapid and elevated. She even began to walk faster; I could hardly keep up. She went on and on about all of the activities she was engaged in, had organized, and often led. She exhausted me just listening.

"Why do you take on so much?"

She blurted out, "Someone has to do it." She told me she liked to do these things herself. "They make me feel that I am needed, that I have something to contribute."

"Are your friends working as long and as hard as you are?"

She said that they were content to just take care of their families. She found this boring. She also confided, with some reluctance, that her father had worked extremely hard—her mother had not—and he had always expected her to excel.

Asked what she would most like to be doing with her life, she told me that she would like to run a tavern. "Organizing all of the details of providing food, drink, and lodging, while joking with the male patrons, would be perfect," she thought.

For now, she was weary from lack of sleep.

"You have too much blood in your brain. Read the Bible," I told her (she was doing this but could not concentrate for long). "Drink some warm milk—perhaps with a little rum."

She smiled. The warm milk had been tried, but not

the rum.

I told her she might try a little angelica root, a mustard footbath, tea of lady slipper root or poria which grows on the trunks of pine trees. "Poria is a mild sedative, but take it sparingly," I warned, "because it also promotes the flow of urine."

She shook her head at the poria but said she would try the rum that very night and off she trotted.

October 27

We learned that the British have finally abandoned Newport. We would so much have preferred to have driven them out by force last year, but failed. From the reports of those who have passed through Newport by stage, the British may have decided to leave because there is nothing left to loot.

Travelers say that the British nearly destroyed everything when they evacuated: burned Long Wharf and other wharfs, destroyed the barracks and the light house on Beavertail, filled wells, demolished 180 buildings, and pillaged the library. Dr. Ezra Stiles told me, "The town is in ruins."

Others give us contrary reports, saying that the British went off quietly. I doubt it. I will have to go down there to see for myself and to offer medical attention to those that have survived this long ordeal.

November 6

While down on the wharf, I chanced to watch the *Sloop Providence* pull into port and was surprised to discover Dr. Zuriel Waterman on board. Curious to discover the extent of his adventure and particularly interested in learning about his practice of medicine at sea, I invited him to the tavern. Noted for his affability, he readily accepted and soon proved his love for copious gills of rum. He tried to make his two-month privateer voyage to Newfoundland sound exciting, but the ship came back empty. The adventure sounded dull to me.

"Why did you go off on this adventure?" I asked.

"I am determined to see the world. I want to roam and have some fun. Besides, when we capture British ships and recapture American vessels, I will make a lot of money—more than I could ever make in this sleepy Village."

"But, when you return with nothing, all you have done is waste time."

"Next time I will select a captain who is more adventurous, who will take some risks. Captain Godfey was disappointing."

"My understanding, Zuriel, is that the Continental Congress authorized privateers for defense of our coast, for reprisal and for retaliation, but privateers indiscriminately hunt down any ship they can find—not just enemy war and supply ships. That is just piracy. How does privateering help our cause when the hunt is for private profit off Newfoundland, Nova Scotia, or the West Indies?"

"You miss the point, Luke. Being out to sea, giving chase is a great thrill. Having a high time in ports where you have never been is more exciting than tending to common sickness in the dull villagers of Pawtuxet."

"There must be day after day on board with nothing much to do but count the days you have been away. Do you not fear being captured by the British and spending the war on a notorious prison ship?"

"Being on the sea is a lot more promising than being a surgeon for some land-based artillery regiment. There is little loss of life, food and rum are almost always plentiful on these short voyages, and there is the promise of personal profit. A good captain can elude capture. I will be on another ship that is headed in some new direction just as soon as I can."

"Tell me about what medical practice you encountered."

"Truthfully, not much. Seamen are generally healthy, and we get into port frequently. I dressed a man's scalded foot and treated a few mild fevers caused by exposure to the cold."

"What a waste of your medical talent."

"And what great diseases have you treated—coughs, measles, sprains? What have you accomplished by bleeding and preparing poultices? How dare you, sir, pretend to be superior to me. My brother George continues to serve Pawtuxet. My ancestors can be traced on this continent from the 17th century. There was a Waterman with Roger Williams when he founded this colony. That is a lot more than you can claim." His eyes darkened with accusations. "I don't need your approval or your rum." He slammed his chair against the wall as he stood and stomped off.

Compared to Zuriel Waterman I am not wasting my god-given talents. But I am not confident that I am living up to His expectations or to mine.

November 22

On the second Saturday in December in past years, Obadiah Follet and I anticipate winter by preparing meat for storage in his smokehouse. We are planning to work together again this December. I am fortunate that Obadiah has permitted me to use his smokehouse and to take advantage of his butchering skills. With some foresight he built this solid structure twelve by twelve—much larger than he needs. He sells or trades space to neighbors, which, I suspect, more than covers his costs. Like me, many of those who use his smokehouse also contribute to cutting apple wood used for the fire. He does the butchering and we help him hang the slabs of hog.

After the firewood is ready and the hog butchered, the process begins by mixing twenty-five pounds of salt and two pounds of brown sugar into the meat. Our own Pawtuxet Salt Works conveniently is the source of the salt. To retain the pinkish color in the meat we add in salt-peter. The smoke is fed each day for one or two weeks. We add corncobs to ensure all the smoke needed.

This is a long process since the meat ages in the smoke-house for two years. Insects are discouraged by coating the cured meat with pepper. We inspect for molds and a buildup of creosol.

For the use of his smokehouse, my arrangement with Obadiah is to trade herbs from my garden, which Mrs. Follet uses in her cooking and medicines. Hope spends a lot of time curing and drying these herbs and, this time of year, her daily efforts are also dedicated to canning fruits and vegetables for the winter. Soon we will need to work together to restore our own supply of candles.

Good planning ensures sufficient supplies.

December 8

The British think that we are all alike. They do not dis-tinguish between the hotheaded rebels like Adams and Otis in Massachusetts Bay and those of us in Rhode Island who just want to be left alone.

Captain Wallace, who has been blockading Newport, has threatened to cannonade the city of Newport if it does not supply him with food and clothing. He did can-nonade Bristol to force them into submission and burned Jamestown.

The people are in terror. We are in dread suspense. Our own security can no longer be taken for granted. The roads are crowded with people abandoning their homes and businesses in an attempt to find safe havens.

An army officer in Rhode Island told me that we have established fourteen coast guard stations and six beacons to provide warning of further encroachment of British troops and ships. Booms and chains have been stretched across our harbors and thirty-nine forts have been constructed along the Bay.

I worry about how I will be able to care for the wounded and dying if fighting erupts on a large scale. There are too few of us with medical skills, no hospitals, and few medicines.

December 23

This war is tiresomely endless. For those who have endured with General Washington since the Continental Army was formed in Boston—and not many have continued to serve—the war must be interminable.

This is unlike any other war. The British hate it because we are so unconventional and they add "ungentlemanly." We do not surrender. Our survival strategy is aptly summarized by the word "persistence." When we cannot win or are in grave danger of being taken prisoner or of annihilation, Washington withdraws—sometimes requiring clever deception.

Our other famous strategist is Ben Franklin. Like Washington he practices patience and perseverance. Long ago others would have given up negotiating with

the French. Not Franklin. As a chess player, Franklin has
provided the following principles:

> Look ahead. What will be the advantages or disad-
> vantages of a move? What can my adversary make
> of it to annoy me? Consider the whole situation—
> the entire chess board. Like Washington, Franklin
> is not inclined to respond in anger or frustration.
> He encourages seeing the possibilities or a favor-
> able outcome.

> Do not move too hastily.

> Do not hurry your adversary. That displeases and
> shows rudeness.

> Be moderate in victory. You may want to "play"
> again.

We might expect the master of the Almanac to observe
present appearances and the lessons of the past. How
often we think of living only in the current instant. Perseverance permits the emergence of events that might
allow us to extricate ourselves from supposed insur-
mountable difficulty.

. . . I would that we all could behave with Franklin's
"generous civility" to earn esteem and respect.

1780

January 1

Without the usual anticipation and rejoicing, this New Year's Day was ushered in with somber reflection.

I believe it will be a sorrowful year for many people. The clouds hang low on the horizon—dark, heavy, foreboding. We are within the cycle marked by the Great Plague of London that killed 100,000.

January 24

Cold, bitter cold again today. Endless freezing rain. Icicles hang on my beard when I must venture out. The winds chop about—moist and ugly—dangerous to the constitution. The scar on my thigh itches persistently. I am beginning to appreciate how seamen feel who cannot ward off the constant, soaking chill as they round Cape Horn.

February 9

An enjoyable way to beat the winter doldrums is to go

down to Notly Pond to watch the skating. Gray, over-
cast skies, even cold, snowy weather does not seem to
matter much when I am down at the pond. There was
a time when I did a lot of skating on that pond. These
days I am content to watch the kids chase one another
around. They never seem to tire of inventing new games
and contests. Someone always builds a bonfire; it is most
inviting. The fragrant smoke and the crackling sparks
that burst from dry oak or pine are a welcome part of
the scene.

These troubled times do not cast a pall over the skating pond; it is a world of its own. As if by some unspo-
ken agreement, my neighbors and I do not talk about the
war or politics. We smile with one another as we delight
in the antics of the children.

Occasionally, a pet dog will scamper out onto the ice
only to discover that four paws and no skates present a
formidable challenge to staying upright. Argos always
comes with me. He has learned to stay off the ice and
near the fire. He visits with his friends.

Children trying out new skates that their fathers have
carefully crafted face the same challenge as the inexpe-
rienced dogs, but they persist until their skill and confidence improve. A cup of hot mulled cider by the fire
when I get home completes a perfect winter outing.

February 16
It took Peleg searching each of his pockets twice before

he found it, but I am glad he read it to us at the tavern. It was a letter from an officer who had been captured and placed aboard a prison ship in Falmouth off New York. In part the officer deplored:

> ". . . a most dismal prison where we have no room to lie down. When we go to bed, we have to lie down at the same time and whenever one of us wants to turn, all have to do so. This is a hellish, confounded hole, of which no one can form an idea. Never have people been locked in such an abominable hole that can be compared to Hell. This is the British way of treating us."

Such reports must instill a strong motivation for our troops to fight—or to retreat—but certainly not to surrender.

March 16

Nothing seemed to be wrong with her. She had a positive spirit. No bruises or discoloration appeared on her arms or hands. Yet, Mrs. Humphrey complained of constant soreness. In the morning, she told me, her fingers were so stiff that she had to rub them vigorously before she could dress herself. At night her legs hurt and were stiff.

Mrs. Humphrey was not old enough to have these ailments of old age. She told me that she was a weaver and was working on a very special set of linen bed curtains that had to be finished in three weeks time. She agreed to let me observe her at work.

Her loom sat in the corner of the room where the family ate. There was light from the embers glowing in the hearth and from a couple of beeswax candles on a side table to her right. The accumulated wax drippings testified to frequent use. She sat on a plain wooden chair without a cushion. But, she was anxious. Not only was she committed to finishing the bed curtains for a wealthy family in Providence, who had suggested that she might get other work from them, but the flax she was using had been especially imported from Ireland. She had conducted the retting process herself, beating the stalks to get perfect fibers for dyeing a special color of yellow with turmeric, a spice from India. She had set the linen seeds aside to create flaxseed oil, which Mr. Humphrey would use in varnishing. She had twisted the fibers by hand. Progress on the loom had been slower than she had anticipated. Despite her usual skill at throwing the shuttle over and under the warp strings when she was using cotton thread, she felt she had to work with greater care with the flax fiber so it would not break. When the weaving was completed, she still had to embroider a floral design that her customer had sketched for her.

As I watched her work I was impressed by her diligence and concentration. Hannah may have thought that her weaving was uncharacteristically slow, but for me her speed in throwing the shuttle back and forth made me dizzy.

I focused on her hands. Her fingers were calloused, gnarled. She had perfected the process to such an extent that only her fingers moved. She sat very upright, legs stationary. Because her work was on a strict deadline, she often worked without a break, even for the noon meal. After an hour, I was tired, bleary eyed and stiff from just watching.

"Mrs. Humphrey," I told her, "you are troubled by what many sedentary workers—tailors, cobblers, jewelry makers—experience. Your limited movement for prolonged hours causes an accumulation of unwholesome humors. The monotony of your weaving taxes not only the muscles in your fingers and legs but is having an impact on your whole body."

"What . . . can I do?" I could hear the tremor in her voice. She trembled at the thought that she might not be able to complete the promised bed curtains and that future work would be lost.

"Exercise, exercise, exercise. Stand up, walk around the room, pour yourself a cup of tea. This will only take a few minutes but will stretch and relax your muscles. Each morning and evening walk outside for at least half an hour to prevent further soreness. Rub your arms, thighs, and legs with oil of sweet almond. Continue to rub those parts that are sore to excite the blood and distribute the humors. Two other remedies will help: bathe your hands in aromatic wine and take the tonic, which I will provide. This tonic is so safe that it is given to children to ease the pain of teething."

March 29

Why we think this war with England is going to achieve some great benefit is beyond my comprehension. The world just cannot seem to do without resorting to violence. We have been at this darkening of our hearts for over four years now, and what have we accomplished? We have lost brave men. We have deprived ourselves of English goods. We have created a scarcity of food, clothing, and other items needed to support the army. Our churches have now painted this violence as something sacred, as if God were on our side, exclusively. Is this not a fight of brother against brother—of Osiris and Set?

While hoping to reserve our liberty, we are losing it through occupation and imposed depravation. We are thinking small, tribal, parochial. Like Abraham, who was told to sacrifice his son in testimony of his faith, we need to think big.

We could create a more promising world with England—world stimulated with new possibilities, rich in moral principles, and wealthy in goods shared through cooperative trade. Violence and destruction should not have the last word.

April 3

He is a smart lad and well he should be! Since it may be some time before we could engage a tutor for Daniel and there are not immediate prospects for the education of Village children at public expense, Hope and I have initiated a systematic plan to teach Daniel. So far, he loves it. Eliza will not be neglected in this tutoring process.

Hope and I spent a lot of time discussing what to teach them—not always agreeing. More specifically, we discussed how to teach them. Our main objective is to instill in them not only the knowledge they will need but also a curiosity for learning and a continuing interest in reading and mathematics. We agreed to be patient with this development, knowing that pushing too hard could result in just the opposite desired effect.

Hope began teaching Daniel mathematics by first having him match like size coins. "Find a shilling that looks like this one." He liked this game and wanted to know what each coin was called. Like her mother, Eliza excelled at mathematics. Her skill probably urged Daniel to learn quickly as well. In time he began to learn about equivalent combinations. He knows, for instance, that one pence has the same value as four farthings. Much sooner than I had thought likely, she had him using mathematics. He can tell you how many pence equal eight farthings. Interest in mathematics reached a new height when she took them to a shop where they could pick out a toy worth up to one shilling with the coins that they had been awarded for solving previous problems during lessons at home. Now they ask for problems to solve.

April 6

My success in teaching Daniel has been more modest than Hope's. I picked out a couple of maxims from Franklin's *Poor Richard's Almanac:*

> "Early to bed, early to rise makes a man healthy, wealthy, and wise."

> "Never leave that till tomorrow which you can do today."

Daniel was quick to memorize these and would eagerly repeat them. My expectation was that we could use these to shape his thinking and behavior. No matter how many examples I gave him about activities he could and should do today rather than delay, the idea made little sense to him. Whether folding his clothes today and putting them in his chest or doing so tomorrow or sometime later escaped his sense of urgency or desirability.

He did not like the idea at all of going "early to bed" and was confused that there could be any relationship between sleep and making him "wealthy." He said that he was already "healthy" so did not need to sleep more.

I decided that teaching him maxims would be a fine exercise but expecting him to understand them was premature.

April 11
The Rhode Island Almanac does not always get its predictions right or its advice acceptably cogent. *The Almanac* is, nevertheless, widely read, reread, and believed. The information on roads and court dates is useful. Stories and antidotes are entertaining. This year's *Almanac* has two interesting pieces of medical advice:

"For treatment of wounds caused by rusty nails wash with equal measures of turpentine and soft soap. Make a plaster to extract the poison."

Recipe for Health:
"Take each morning a good portion of forethought, in regard to the benefits of the day, reserving a little time and strength for contingencies, and endeavor to adjust the benefits to the constitution, beginning moderately. At meal time eat a little less than appetite seems to crave and drink sparingly. At evening have a care of the damp air. Thus, care may prevent the necessity of cure."

If my fellow Villagers followed this sage advice, I would be out of business.

May 2

Daniel and Eliza learned many games at home. I became quite popular by organizing neighborhood children and teaching them tag, marbles (we found round stones in a nearby brook), hide-and-seek, and leap frog. Both girls and boys would squeal with excitement when they were "found" playing hide-and-seek and would plead for "just one more game." The boys especially liked leap frog, probably because they were better at it than the girls. Some of the children were very competitive and would take great pride in winning the hoop races. Their parents would tell me how they would boast of the winning achievement for days.

On rainy days Daniel and Eliza would invite a couple of friends to the house to spin the wooden tops that I had carved. It took awhile to develop the necessary skills, but the children caught on and got so good at spinning the tops well that it would occupy them for hours.

Another favorite activity has been making cornhusk dolls. Girls and boys enjoy this. I thought we could decorate some of them to look like Rangers and hold mock battles, but Hope refused to permit this.

May 5

Daniel first learned the alphabet by using a sampler with large letters, which Hope's mother had made. Some letters like "Q" and the difference between "U" and "V" perplexed him.

His grandfather Tucker had also given him a horn-book with the Lord's Prayer written on it. Since Daniel already knew the Lord's Prayer, which we practice every night just before he goes to bed, he began to hear what the letters sounded like when formed into words.

Grandfather Tucker had a battledore, which looked a lot like his hornbook, made by a sailor from one of the ships that often came into Newport. The battledore spelled out DANIEL, which instantly became his favorite word to copy and read.

Besides the first line of the Lord's Prayer, Daniel likes to copy maxim number thirteen "Kill no Vermin as Fleas, lice, ticks in the Sight of Others." He thought this was a fine joke and would giggle all of the time as he copied it. He paraded around the house endlessly reciting this maxim.

The boy has a boisterous curiosity and is as lively as a cricket.

May 19

Judgment Day is upon us. Until today, I have not held much credence in the Book of Revelations' prediction of Armageddon nor of those "prophets" who predicted, from time to time, the end of the World.

Today we are all shaking in terror that hell-fire and damnation are upon us. What have we done to provoke such wrath and indignation against us? Of what cataclysmic sins are we guilty? How have we angered our God?

Is it the war? Like Cain and Able we are set upon one another. Have we offended His holy laws? Have we erred and strayed from His ways like lost sheep? Have we sinned in Thought, Word, and Deed? Could it be punishment for the sins of slavery?

Today the sixth seal has been opened—there was a great earthquake, the sun became black, the moon became as blood, and the stars of heaven fell. Like the great men and every bond man reported in Revelations 6, we cry out to be hidden from the face of him that sittith on the Throne.

In the morning at 10:30 of the clock the darkness descended. By noon the darkness was ominous. Lightning flashed, thunder rolled. Men returned from their labors in the fields. Students were dismissed from their studies. Birds sang their evening songs. Frogs began to peep. Cattle walked back to their barns, thinking night had descended. Those of us who gathered to pray observed that so black a darkness had never been seen before. At 1:00 of the clock, it was too dark to read the Bible. The rain was thick, dark, and sooty. The air smelled like a malt-house.

The Darkness could not be more complete. The earth is without form and darkness is upon the face of the deep. Is this an Egyptian darkness—a prelude to a plague of locusts? Is the End at hand?

May 20

The signs of doom witnessed yesterday have abated. We are alive. The sun shone on the Village this morning. We are reminded of the seven seals that were opened by the Lamb in Chapter 6 of the Book of Revelations. "They who have passed through the great ordeal never again feel hunger or thirst nor scorching heat. God will wipe all tears from their eyes."

Our prayers have been answered. Praise and Thanksgiving be unto thee, O' Lord.

June 3

At the tavern there have been no shortage of explanations for our darkest day on May 19th. The more gills that got consumed the more scandalous the rationalizations became. I sense a false bravado among my friends because those fourteen hours of darkness are inexplicable. Some say they heard reports of massive wildfires to the north and that the winds drove ash south darking the skies. When I asked our minister, he paused for several moments. "God does not explain, but we need to be warned."

June 12

Ephraim had suffered from consumption for years. Over time, I had gotten to know him well. He loved to fish and was acknowledged as the best buckies fisherman in the Village. We often saw him fishing on the bridge or at Copp's Cove. A faithful attendee at church, he generously gave of his labor to help neighbors repair roofs and leaking barns.

Until the consumption curtailed his movements, depleted his energy, and tormented him with pain, Ephraim's optimism and playful humor made him a joy to be around. Consumption ended all of that. Since his wife died, he lived alone and rarely associated with anyone.

Increasingly, I found it disagreeable to visit him. His disease was beyond my skills as a surgeon. Perhaps, I could have bled him profusely. Perhaps, I could have given him more powerful purgatives. In his final days, I chose not to visit him at all. When he died, no one was at his bedside. I had left him to die alone.

As I mourn the loss of his once vital spirit and our many conversations, I consider how weak and small I had become as his neighbor and surgeon. Strangely, I am also relieved that he is gone.

July 4
Today, the 4th of July, was observed with pride and conviviality in celebration of independence. The Rangers took the lead in the festivities, having planned activities for ourselves and the community for weeks prior. The Company paraded at an early hour and having performed various evolutions, escorted a respectable

procession. Formed at the bridge, we marched to services accompanied by a band of music that played such stirring tunes as "March to Boston" and "Yankee Doodle." The Throne of Grace was fervently addressed by the Rev. B. Jacobs, an eloquent and patriotic oration pronounced by Joseph Tillinghast, Esq., after which we repaired to M. Joseph Aborn's Inn and partook of a sumptuous entertainment with the citizens. After dinner, a number of appropriate toasts were given, and the day passed with the utmost harmony. Among our traditional toasts on this splendid occasion was one to General Washington:

> "T's Washington's health, fill a bumper all around
> For He is our Glory and Pride . . .
> There cannot be found search all the World o'r
> His equal in virtue.
> Huzzah!"

July 29

Old man Bucklin came by today to tell me that his rheumatism was much improved since he started carrying horse chestnuts in his pocket.

August 11

My first impressions of Dr. Solomon Drowne were of an imposing man, strong willed, so self-assured that he had a quick response for every question, an unequivocal statement for the slightest of challenges. I heard him at a lecture at Rhode Island College. He is continuing to serve as a surgeon in the Continental Army. Dr. Drowne believes that natural history is the basis of all science, and the study of botany is of the first importance. He told the audience that he has learned more from plants than from medical textbooks and dreams of one day creating a classical botanical garden.

He surprised me by admitting before a room full of doctors that "nature has the power of operating alone the cure of the most part of diseases." While he might believe this, I am told he is not passive in his treatments.

After the lecture, I waited and spoke briefly with him in private. He almost seemed to know who I was. I suspect that making others seem familiar is one of his talents.

"What other advice do you have for a village doctor?"

"That is too broad a question, Dr. Carr. What specifically do you want to know?"

Having been put to the test, I thought quickly. "Do you advise administering tonics with multiple material medical ingredients in anticipation that some of these will cure the patient?"

His dark grey eyes narrowed. His posture became rigid. The tone of his response made it clear that he thought I had asked a naïve question.

"Never give a patient anything you are not thoroughly convinced is needed," he intoned. Our conversation was over.

My deficiency in not having studied at a university stalks me. I yearn to be wiser.

August 14

I have been reflecting on my unsatisfactory meeting with Dr. Drowne. Perhaps, it is my training with Dr. Randall or perhaps it is just my nature, but I cannot espouse medical theory or treatment advice with the driving force that Dr. Drowne makes his statements. He might always be right but if I have learned anything from my reading of classical literature it is that clearer understanding can come from someone who is blind like the Theban seer Tiresias and that the hubris of confident boasting, like Odysseus' taunting of the blinded Cyclopes, can only lead to further calamity.

August 21

Crickets can be hypnotic. This time of year they sing half of the night. I wonder what they are talking about, what they have to share? During the day I look for them—there must be hundreds in the tall grass—but they are well hidden.

Some say crickets predict good luck. They announce that the corn is ripe and anticipate the apple harvest. Their melodious song is louder this year. I hope they have some providential insight that will be good fortune to our Cause.

Sat with Hope on our garden bench to enjoy the

cool evening. We silently listened to the chirping of the crickets.

This is the mating season. No wonder they sing half of the night.

September 8
Violent showers today. The river rose over a foot.

September 30
We may not have much of a navy. In truth we have nothing worth calling a navy. But we may cause some havoc yet. Our privateers have out-maneuvered the Royal navy, sneaking in and out of ports under the cover of darkness, making use of our knowledge of local waters and using the tides to extreme advantage.

We have a new advantage. The French have refitted a ship which is now renamed *The Bonhomme Richard*, a tribute to Benjamin Franklin, and presented it to our own John Paul Jones. Some think of him as a Scot, some as a Virginian, but we know he is a Rhode Islander.

In what we are told was an audacious act of courage, *The Bonhomme Richard* attacked the British ship *Serapis*, a forty-gun frigate, at close quarters. Jones had men firing down on the *Serapis* from high in the rigging of his own ship and lobbed a deadly projectile that exploded below the *Serapis'* main hatchway. The *Serapis* lost her mast and began taking on a threatening amount of water. Her captain lowered her flag in defeat.

Our first naval victory!

October 5

"You are a scoundrel, a poor excuse for a doctor, an instrument of the devil himself. You killed my beloved husband with your incompetence, torturing him to his untimely end."

She was on a tirade, furious, out of control.

"Madam, you are thoughtless and rude. Your memory is deficient. You have forgotten your active participation in the decision to operate on your husband. I told you that I would not, did not want to operate. You begged me to reconsider. You sent Mr. Lockwood's brother to persuade me. He even offered me a special compensation to attend his brother. I still refused. You wept. You implored me. You prayed that God would change my mind.

"I told you that the operation was fraught with uncertainties, that Mr. Lockwood's condition might resolve itself without intervention, but, if I did operate, we ran many risks, including his death. You urged me to proceed."

When Mrs. Lockwood called me out of a sound sleep to rush to her husband's side he was in extreme discomfort. Even by candlelight he looked pale. He could not rest on his back because of the ache. I asked about his less obvious symptoms.

"I am flushed with the fever, Dr. Carr." The sweat dripped off his chin. The chest of his nightshirt was soaked. "And, Doc, I have not been able to pass any water."

"You probably are afflicted with the gravel, Mr. Lockwood. Keep trying to pass water. Small stones often will be expelled on their own. Force yourself to drink water constantly. Mrs. Lockwood, prepare him some barley water—that will help him. If you can get him up, some gentle movement may force the gravel to pass out of his body."

"I will try," he whispered with lips clenched, "but I hurt terrible bad."

"Shouldn't he be bled?" she inquired.

I felt his pulse. It was fast but weak. "If I thought his sweating was a sign of too much blood, Mrs. Lockwood, I would bleed him; however, his pulse is shallow. We will wait and observe."

"Doctor Carr, have I caused this problem? Is my cooking at fault?"

"We are not certain what causes gravel," I admitted. "Strong wine, being sedentary, or sleeping on his back could all contribute, but probably not your cooking." She looked worried but relieved.

The next morning I checked in on him. His pain had increased and the little urine he had passed was cloudy and contained blood. For a strong man he was being reduced to a sapless seedling.

"Please," he wined "make the pain go away."

"Keep drinking water," I urged, "and get up and

move. We will discuss the pain tomorrow."

Some months ago I had spoken with Doctors Tenny and Carpenter about bladder stones. When I was an apprentice, Dr. Randall mentioned that these painful stones were common, but he had never removed one. Dr. Carpenter knew of stones being passed on their own by patients but had not undertaken to remove one himself, cautioning that the operation was painful and dangerous. Dr. Tenny thought differently. "I have seen patients in such excruciating pain that I felt as a doctor that I should do something. Providing laudanum for the pain could only furnish temporary relief."

When I asked him if he had ever removed a stone he admitted that he had not, though he said he saw the operation performed successfully in Newport. Dr. Tenny went on to describe the procedure in detail, drawing me diagrams and sketching the design of the instrument. He said that if the stone migrated to the penis it could be readily reached, grasped with the instrument, pulled out or crushed.

The thought of performing such a procedure filled me with intense fear, yet I was sympathetic to Dr. Tenny's conviction that as a doctor I ought to be able to help a suffering patient. Caleb, our blacksmith, crafted me the tool to match Dr. Tenny's sketch.

When I returned to check Mr. Lockwood a day later, I found him sitting in the kitchen in apparent good spirits. Mrs. Lockwood also appeared eased of a great burden of her own.

"I feel much improved," he rejoiced. "The pain is gone. You were right. You said it might go away by itself."

"That is good news," I said. "Did you pass the stone in your urine?"

"Well, I don't know for certain. To be truthful, I haven't passed much water and I didn't see no stone."

"You should continue to drink lots of water," I encouraged. "If the flow of urine doesn't increase in a day or two or if you are not feeling well, send Mrs. Lockwood to get me."

She came for me in two days.

When I examined him, he was in terrible pain. His bladder was bloated, stretching the skin on his stomach so tight it was shiny. He looked pregnant. He told me that with great effort he could only dribble a few drops of urine.

Again, he pleaded for relief. I explained to both of them the possible procedure that Dr. Tenny had described to me, where I would insert an instrument into the penis and attempt to extract the stone that was blocking the flow of urine or crush it. I made it clear that I did not want to do this operation, had never done it before, and believed it was dangerous to even consider. Mr. Lockwood moaned when I told him he should think about it overnight.

At their insistence, I performed the operation. I even amazed myself. The instrument that Caleb had fashioned for me, oiled with animal fat from the kitchen, entered the penis with relatively little trauma and grasped the stone like a hungry fledging. I slowly eased it out. We all cheered, especially Mr. Lockwood.

Two days later, Mrs. Lockwood was back, banging at my door and shouting in great panic for me to come immediately. As we hurried to the Lockwood home late in the afternoon an early October chill replaced what had been a few days of unseasonable but pleasantly warm weather. Rain was not far off. Dampness hung in the air. Threatening lightning flashed in the east.

Mr. Lockwood was in serious trouble again. He was shaking with chills, despite the two blankets covering him, yet his chest was hot to the touch. His heart was racing at a disturbing pace. His breathing was labored. He gasped for each breath. I quickly opened the bedroom window to give him more air.

What could have caused such a sudden and catastrophic reversal? What insult could he have experienced? I had precious little understanding of what was happening.

Dr. Tenny had cautioned that some doctors suspected that the instrument could cause problems, but mine was new, never been used, taken right off my table where I keep all of my instruments.

Mrs. Lockwood said that her husband was confused. He kept asking where he was and why she had not prepared his dinner. He called her by his sister's name. She was devastated. She showed me that the small sample of urine she had collected from him was cloudy and foul. He writhed in the throes of pain. He kept trying to rub his back as if the sharpest pain were centered there. He shouted out blasphemous curses, held his ear as if it too ached. He lost control of his bowels, filling the room with a terrible stench. His hands and feet were abnormally cold and beginning to turn gray.

In terror he fought the angel of death with all of his waning strength. By sundown, as the thunderstorm reached us, he had lost.

"You will pay for this," Mrs. Lockwood warned in a most menacing tone. "I will spread the word how you forced your incompetent procedure on my unsuspecting husband. You will not practice in this Village for long."

If Mrs. Lockwood wanted to provoke a fight over my reputation, a fight she would get. She had unnerved me with her insults and threats to sully my good name, but a new choleric temperament rose to dominate my thinking.

Hope tried to calm me, "Mrs. Lockwood is in grief and is all talk."

I am not so sure.

While it is said that things—especially bad things—happen for a reason, I am befuddled to know what possible good could result from this tragedy.

October 11

The war has moved south. While the British army has a large force and is supported by a formidable fleet, America is a big piece of geography to occupy. Their new focus in the southern states brings some relief here, but we are not secure. The British are fond of returning to occupy New York. They could return to Boston or to Newport, though much of the available wood, housing, and cattle have been devastated.

If the British navy could navigate Narragansett Bay, Providence could become a target. Yet, the limited number of loyalists still there may not invite occupation. The Rangers and other local militia units do not intend to abandon the defense of the Bay. We continue to prohibit importation. I wish we had access to medicines from England and I fear we are losing out on medical discoveries that are being made in Europe.

We must make due.

October 23

Sooner or later I knew it would fall down, and the time is past due when I should have replaced it. Otherwise, one of us will be inside the privy on that fateful day.

Decisions need to be made for our temple of convenience, the "necessary," if improvements are to be made. In the end, we are not going to enjoy the water-flushed troughs that ran beneath the streets of ancient Rome.

I would like to disguise our "necessary," whose

purpose is more than apparent as it stands prominently behind our garden. Could I build one of brick and make it an octagon? Hope gives me that look of hers and tells me not to be foolish. "Just duplicate what we have." I will dig a deeper pit this time to control odors, somewhat, and I will cover the wood with tar to retard decay.

The big question is whether to build a two-seater or three-seater (a small one for Eliza and Daniel or for some other child who is visiting)? Hope insists that one adult and one child seat is sufficient. "We do not go there to visit. It is intended for a private function."

I never suspected that replacing our necessary would generate such interesting discussions.

October 26

Just when I thought that I had discovered all of the pleasures of this Village, I discovered another. Fall is such an incredible season. We have sweated our way through the hot days of summer and we know we are about to struggle for the next five months against bone-chilling rains, endless snow storms, and biting winds. But, October is magnificent. . . .

The trees blossom in spectacular reds and yellows. Huge flocks of ducks and other birds temporarily visit our cove to remind us that this is a special place. We gather chestnuts, go "apple-ing," press cider, and split the last of the wood for the hearth. In addition to all of this, there is frost fishing. While I had heard about this village tradition, I never paid any attention to it until my neighbor Bernon decided to invite me to walk the shoreline with him. Fishing has never been a passion for me; I prefer to let others do it. Fishing takes too much patience. It always seemed boring—throw in a line and wait. Frost fishing is very different. Unlike ice fishing, it is not a contest between who will freeze first—you or the fish!

The night I went frost fishing with Bernon, we had a beautiful October night under a full moon and nearly a flood tide. At first, I carried the lantern to illuminate our way and to help spot the whitings that get stranded by a receding tide. Bernon carried the spear and expertly thrust at the fish. We just continued this process until our buckets were filled. I caught several myself. I can see why this tradition has been going on for a long while.

At home, Bernon gutted the fish, oiled them with bacon grease, rolled them in corn meal, and quickly fried them until brown. They were delicious.

November 13

"Do you believe in witchcraft?" Amos wanted to know.

Before I could answer one way or the other, he made it clear what he thought. "Witches are the cause of many of our current problems," he pronounced. "They will destroy all that those of us who are God-fearing have created by our hard labor in these colonies."

Amos reminded me of a story about a woman who

was tried some years back who had been charged with causing a neighbor's sheep to dance and hogs to speak and sing psalms. Two men who had seen the trial recreated the scene in vivid detail over a gill or two at the tavern.

The witch was placed on a great scale with the Holy Writ in the balance. The scale teetered for several minutes as if trying to make some grave moral decision. First the witch appeared to be heavier than the Bible. Then the Bible appeared to be heavier. This shifting back and forth lasted for several minutes, with the crowd cheering each time the Bible appeared to be winning. In the end, the men at the tavern reported with considerable disappointment, "The Bible was not heavier than the accused. Guilt was not proven."

"Those of us in the crowd were not satisfied with what we were certain was a faulty test. We insisted on a trial by water."

"We cheered as the witch was bound hand and foot and was lowered into the pond. For some inexplicable reason, the witch floated light upon the water. The magistrate declared that the trial was without conclusion, but most of us continued to believe that she was guilty as sin."

Amos, who had only heard the story as had I, was convinced of the witch's guilt. While there are, God protect us, evil forces at work and there may be witches in a few places in these states, the stories of hysteria that reach us strike me a perverse entertainment designed to distress the mind.

November 20

Daniel appeared disheartened. Most unlike his usual, playful self, a cloud of gloom hung on his face. "Why are your spirits so low? You look very sad. Is something wrong?"

"Nothing is wrong. I am just not feeling well."

"Are you sick?" I put my hand on his head to see if he might have a fever. He did not. "Well, something is wrong. Are you fighting with your friends?"

"Well, sort of."

"Tell me what happened."

He went on to lament that his friends made fun of him because he always lost at checkers and was always the first to be found at hide-and-seek. "I step on the line every time when we play scotch hopping."

"But, Daniel," I reassured him, "you are good at lots of games. You are better than most of the boys at leap frog and at hoop racing. Besides, you are very smart. For instance, you are very good at mathematics for someone your age."

"Still, they make fun of me, especially Oliver Rhodes."

"We can't be the best at everything we do. Each of us is given certain talents; we need to be content with that." He looked unconvinced. "Let me tell you a poem about the peacock and lark. Do you know how fancy a peacock looks with its tail all spread out?"

He nodded.

"Well, this is a story that reminds us that peacocks and larks are both special, but very different:

> "The peacock with its varied plume,
> Would above all other birds presume.
> The skylark heard and made reply
> Your coat is fine I can't deny,
> Whilst I in homely russet clad,
> Make everyone that hears me glad."

"Next time Oliver laughs at you, challenge him at racing hoops." Daniel smiled and ran off. I suspect he went looking for Oliver.

December 15

Aaron, a young man from Pawtuxet just returning home having completed his obligation of a year in the Continental Army, came to my house for attention, his arm wrapped and supported in a sling.

He told me that he had been wounded in a battle at King's Mountain when wood from a fence post splintered by cannon shot entered his arm (he had been crouching behind the fence for protection). The battalion surgeon had pulled out the wood fragments and bandaged the arm. Aaron thought he was mending because the wound swelled with what the surgeon called laudable pus, though the arm continued to hurt him. The wound got red and discolored. The young soldier decided to delay any other treatment until he got home since his enlistment was nearly up. He reported that he felt feverish from time to time.

His wound was now ugly looking and painful to the touch. A dark spot on the wound suggested that gangrene was setting in. I opened the wound further and incised it—the blood was a yellowish brown with a frothy discharge and had a putrid odor. I applied a poultice of elder blossom tea and created a paste from a slice of bread powered with comfrey, which I had stirred into boiling milk.

I told the young man that a delay of treatment for even a week would have given the gangrene such an advantage that no option would have been left except amputation.

The young man turned pale, promising to strictly follow my instructions.

1781

January 10

No one bothered to ask me or any other local surgeon that I know how to alleviate Moses Brown's suffering. He received advice, I learned, from Dr. Abraham Choock. Certainly, all of the skilled men of medicine are not living in Philadelphia.

Moses' persistent chills, fatigue, and vertigo have been diagnosed as palsy and apoplexy from "too great an attention of the mind." No wonder. He has been obsessed with the issue of slavery. Dr. Choock prescribed tonics with powered rhubarb and cinnabar of antimony. I predict those will bring no effect.

Fame and wealth do not necessarily provide good health.

January 15

We should do our duty and not grumble, but the quartering of French troops has had disagreeable consequences. Even the opening of an army hospital for them in University Hall has taxed our resources. We have endured damaged and stolen property, including crops. The soldiers disturb the peace with parades and firing. They sound reveille a half hour before sunrise and tattoo at ten at night. Many of us are already asleep. They parade four times a day.

Most disturbing has been their contribution to moral decay. The tippling houses and grog shops are over-run. At the start of the war, we had twenty-seven licensed establishments. We have nearly fifty now.

Bread is in short supply as is sugar and salt. We had already been strained by refugees from Aquidneck, Newport, and Portsmouth. Now we have to support the French. Even the workhouse is occupied by soldiers. General Sullivan promises to restore order. He has chastised the troops and set curfews.

As unpleasant as this is, we must resign ourselves to this contribution to the war effort.

January 23

Today I was told that General Washington had been mortally wounded at the Battle of Cowpens, South Carolina. Lord help us if that is true. We were also told that Patrick Henry had been seized and hanged without trial. Many would like to silence the boisterous and argumentative Mr. Henry, but would anyone dare seize him?

Some weeks we cannot sort out the truth. When we know the source of the news we can better judge. But much of what we hear is repeated from a newspaper account that is old by the time the reader receives it. Newspapers are notoriously wrong to begin with, and the reader embellishes what he reads or quotes the item incorrectly. By the time the "news" gets passed down to us, the facts are a jumble.

February 6

Mrs. Briggs presented herself today, complaining of a constant headache and cough. She had tried all of her home remedies without any relief. She said that Mr. Briggs had the same problem but was continuing to work. He had recently been unloading ships and she feared he had gotten some disease from the sailors. I told her that she and Mr. Briggs probably had a bad cold. I suggested a tea made of lemon, boiling water, and ginger, as well as lots of liquids and as much rest as possible.

February 9

Mrs. Briggs appeared again today. She looked worse and felt worse. "The lemon-ginger tea has not helped me," she complained "I am feeling achy. Mr. Briggs is improving. Two members of the Metcalf family, who lived near me, are also sick." I suggested she take sassafras to help sweat out this problem and that she should take measures to keep her bowels open.

February 19

Again, Mrs. Briggs came for advice and treatment. "I am much out of order," she complained. This time she reported that her vision was blurred; I could tell that she was having difficulty in focusing. She had trouble finding the chair I offered her. Her eyes hurt, and her headaches were worse. Her face was flushed and felt warm. I bled her with leeches of a small amount and told her to be consistent in applying the other remedies. Since she looked so puzzled about the cause of the headaches, I told her that sharp sides in salt particles are carried in the blood to her head so she should forgo salt and red meat.

Mr. Briggs seemed to have overcome his discomfort. The Metcalfs further down her street had also recovered.

February 20

Three other patients reported today that they were experiencing symptoms similar to those that Mrs. Briggs had described. They all lived near Mrs. Briggs and had attended a social together. None of them knew of any one else who was sick. I prescribed the lemon-ginger tea or chamomile tea, sweating, and rest for them.

February 21

In speaking with Dr. Samuel Tenny in the market, I discovered that he was also seeing an increased number of patients with severe colds. "Some years we get more than others. Just let these isolated cases run their course," he advised.

February 23

Today's cases did not present with identical symptoms to those I had seen before. Of the five patients I saw today—two of them in their homes—all had fevers. Perhaps, they had intermittent fever, I deducted. But, three of them complained of nosebleeds and two of extreme sensitivity to light. These symptoms were not typical of a severe cold or of intermittent fever. There was swelling and redness. If they were bleeding from their noses, I reasoned, because of too much blood, I should accelerate this process. So, I bled each of them.

In truth, I have never known the body to bleed itself without a wound.

February 28

Reports of cases from my colleagues in Providence and Bristol testify that this "cold" is not a local, Pawtuxet problem. I had begun to keep track of where my patients lived and worked, expecting to find a site with noxious fumes or putrefaction. But the cases in Providence and Bristol did not support the conclusion of an environmental cause from a single source.

While the numbers are estimates, there have been sixty patients treated in this area besides the twenty patients in Pawtuxet. Still, no one seems worried.

March 2

The news today gave impetus to my worry. An article in the *Providence Gazette* revealed that hundreds of soldiers were being hospitalized in their camps because of severe headaches, high fevers, body aches, respiratory problems, and nosebleeds. I think the nosebleeds are particularly troublesome. There is something unusual about this disease. So far, many treatments have been tried, but no doctors are claiming that they have found a cure. No one has proposed a preventive measure.

March 4

A train arrived today from Valley Forge filled with soldiers. Fourteen of them were taken immediately to the new military hospital at the College of Rhode Island. Most of the remaining soldiers were crowded into dormitories and halls that had been occupied by students until the start of the war. I am greatly disturbed by an influx of additional sick into this area. There are few individuals to care for the sick at the military hospital. Many of our doctors have joined the Continental Army. Perhaps, the army will send more medical help.

March 5

Every day brings bad news. Misfortunes never come singly. Each ship that docks here has several sick on board that require treatment. The *Storm King* docked today with six very sick seamen. One was in such agony that he could not be touched. Two were coughing up blood. All appeared to be suffering from constricting respiratory problems.

Several of us did what we could to comfort the men from the *Storm King* by finding them homes to stay in. The military would not take them at the college. Townsfolk have been most Christian in their willingness to tend these sick. Wives whose husbands are in the army have been especially generous in taking an individual into their homes.

March 6
Six soldiers have died at the college hospital. These were young men, robust and previously healthy. This disease does not respect age, location, gender, or occupation. Very disturbing is that children, sometimes very young children, are also susceptible. This is frightening.

I continue to check on those individuals who are staying in private homes in the Village. We could try to contain the spread of this disease by refusing to permit any new person with symptoms arriving in the Village to stay here. Or, we could isolate those already suffering. There is no political support for this suggestion.

So far, I am at a loss regarding effective treatment. Nothing has worked. Some lucky individuals—the majority of those afflicted so far—have recovered.

March 10

Our neighbor's child who is eight has come down with the disease. She has been a frequent visitor to our house with her brothers and sisters. I am beside myself with worry.

Three more soldiers have died. One was reputed to be in such agony that he was delirious. Another had soaked his linens with blood. He even bled from his ears.

March 11

There was talk today at church, in the tavern, and on the street that this is not influenza. The newspaper has denied that we are seeing an epidemic. Some people, including medical personnel, think this is a form of the plague. The newspaper refuses to use this term. There appears to be a concerted effort not to panic the populace. However, the most frequent term being used is influenza or *la grippe.* Reports say that the spread of the disease in some army units has leveled off and that everyone is recovering.

I am chilled by the thought that those who have died have done so in some awful and unexplained way.

March 12

I am treating five new patients—some with mild symptoms; some more severe. All of the usual remedies have failed to cure: nourishing soups, special teas, sweating, bleeding, forced vomiting. I have given up trying to find a pattern. There is no time to keep statistics. There are too many afflicted. The symptoms are too diverse.

I now believe that some people recover on their own regardless of what I do. My philosopher's stone has provided no inspiration. As a doctor on whom so many depend, I should be able to figure out this malady and be of some help. I have never felt this helpless.

March 14

We have seen epidemics before. Many children have experienced measles and seem to have spread them within their families, schools, and neighborhoods. No child has ever died of measles in this Village. We now have a death of a four-year-old from influenza, or whatever this disease is. Such a death is tragic, heart-rending, and heart-breaking.

I have run out of remedies to try. I have examined urine and blood, which provided no clues. I have always relied on my reason to figure out alternatives. This is now insufficient. My excellent observations, which have always helped me to find a solution, now provide only inconclusive possibilities.

None of my colleagues have answers. Some are less humble about what they are doing, nevertheless. I am beginning to feel that the method of inquiry that all of us are using limits the possible solutions.

Something has inflicted this terrible tragedy upon us. We are forced to face how little we really know.

Why does such a crisis occur? I am beginning to fear that the natural order is being supplanted. Are we being punished?

March 16
Two men, who arrived by ship and who have been staying in homes here, have gotten worse. One has turned blue; the other a very dark color, as if he were a member of another race. These are the worse cases that I have seen. I am frozen in fear. The disease is getting stronger, more efficient at killing. The sick are everywhere in the Village . . . someone is sick in most households. This disease is acting like a pot of soup heating over the fire. Like the soup it begins to come to a boil—a single bubble comes up from the bottom of the pot . . . then three or four . . . then a dozen. Unattended, the whole soup comes to rolling boil. If you do not take the pot off the fire, the soup begins to boil away. If you ignore the pot, the soup burns; it cannot be salvaged. If we cannot find the cause of this disease and a cure, we may all be destroyed.

March 19
Other stories of patients turning blue or even black have reached me. Some are labeling this the Black Death. Could we be facing a plague? Nothing I observe in my patients is conclusive. I fear that the disease could be explosive, intent on overwhelming us in this desperate battle.

March 20

We must change how we are thinking about this disease.
It is not like anything we know. My colleagues and I
have little time to correspond with one another. Those
nearby cannot stop to compare what we have seen and
tried. We are tired . . . I am tired. I cannot take time to
think more deeply about what I have seen. But, I must
do something more than what I am doing.

March 22

My theory, based on the patients who have turned blue
in their struggle to fight off this disease, suggests to me
that the most dangerous aspect is respiratory. Certainly
that is what kills them. Patients who cannot breathe are
having some terrible problem with their lungs. I wish
I could actually see their lungs and examine them to
determine what is happening. This is, of course, impossible.

What can I do?

I will offer suggestions to the political leaders in the
Village that might save some lives.

March 28

I spoke to the Village fathers. Several of my medical colleagues had already pleaded with them to take action.
Our elected officials have done nothing. I suggested the
following:

Fire muskets and cannon in the populous areas to

permit the gun powder to cleanse the air. Prohibit all
public meetings. Close the schools and courts. Encourage the churches, businesses, and taverns to close. The
Village fathers balked at the last suggestion to close
businesses and taverns. They felt this was unnecessary
and that it would be impossible to achieve compliance.

I went to the newspaper. The editor was most pleased
to publish advice, though he had been providing read-
ers only with optimistic reports up to this point to avoid
creating panic. Privately, the spread of the disease had
him nearly as concerned as I was. I did not admit to the
full extent of the terror that I felt at what I feared would
come. The advice he printed:

> "Households should wash their walls with
> vinegar.
> Individuals should wear a clove of garlic to ward
> off contagion.
> Avoid crowds.
> Cover coughs and sneezes.
> Chew food well, avoiding meat.
> Avoid tight clothes.
> Get plenty of rest and fresh air."

April 1
We are fearful of attending services these days—fearful
that whatever contagion is about will seize us. Attendance was definitely down today. Despite our customary

pew assignments, we dispersed throughout the meeting house. Conversations between us after services were guarded, amounting to brief greetings and wishes for sustained health.

The pastor chose as the topic for his sermon: Exodus 15:26: "If thou wilt diligently hearken to the voice of the Lord . . . I will put none of these diseases upon thee which I have brought upon the Egyptians, for I am the Lord that healeth thee."

It was a comforting sermon. The message suggested that our faith may have already protected us from the prevalent scourge and we might look in confidence to the healing power of the Lord.

I am sure there were others in the congregation who, like me, wondered why so many of our fellow parishioners were suffering from the widespread disease that has struck many families. Not many of us would boast of being more devout or deserving of being especially chosen by the Lord for protection. Yet, we were there on Sunday in case the Lord was checking on us.

It is also troubling that we do not have any reference in the Bible to some more current illness that the pastor could discuss. Surely, the Lord has protected his people from diseases since ancient Egyptian times. After all, a lot has happened here even since last Monday.

At any rate, the pastor was mercifully short in his sermon today. Those of us present were, appropriately, there to give thanks for having been spared the miseries of this disease—so far—and to offer our prayers for our neighbors.

April 3

We had success in reducing the impact of small pox by vaccinating with a small amount of puss from a patient with active pustules. Could we not develop some material from cows, some other animals, or from patients with the disease that might serve to fight against it? I wish I had time and skill to determine if such a vaccination were possible. I do not.

April 5

We are now inspecting those who come to our docks and isolating anyone who appears sick. Schools have closed. The Baptist Church has cancelled services and encourages families to pray at home.

April 6

There is little time to fully document my observations in this journal. I am too tired, anyway.

April 11

Many people with this flu have recovered—even some who were very sick and who were expected to die. Can we attribute recovery of some to anything besides God's intervention? How can we explain why many pregnant women die or have still births? The numbers of those who have died have been predominately in their twenties—most often they had been, otherwise, healthy people. Something that should be a part of their defenses is destroyed by the disease. While some people can overcome this attack—despite anything I do or fail to do—others cannot. How can this be? I am baffled.

Whatever I do does not make much difference. Perhaps, I give too much medication, bleed too little, and instigate vomiting too often. Nothing seems to reestablish the necessary balance of humors. I feel under intense pressure to help those afflicted, but I am doing something wrong . . . or not enough. I am depressed . . . humbled . . . nearly defeated.

April 12

We are going to need outside help to care for the sick if this disease continues. Everyone with medical skill is consumed already. Where could help possibly come from?

April 14

Townsfolk are isolating themselves. They avoid conversation. They cross the street to avoid contact.

April 15

I am not feeling well. Every day, I find it harder to tend to my duties. Few patients come to my home—I prefer that they do not come. But then I must travel to them. There are so many of them. I am tired all of the time, out of sorts, under a bad digestion. Hope and the children are patient with me, but I have no patience with them.

April 17

Today the headache was intense. I have an unproductive cough. My eyes hurt.

April 18

This morning I felt worse. I am unwell. My problems are intestinal—not respiratory—thanks be to God. I am exhausted. I fear that I have contracted the disease.

I will lie down and rest.

April 28

I have been in bed for ten days. Hope tells me that I have been delirious. She thinks my fever has been intermittent.

There are few memories of these days. I have been enveloped in an impenetrable fog. My thoughts were devoid of any concern about my patients or about the disease. Mostly, I remember feeling that I was totally alone. I ached. I don't recall eating or drinking anything, but Hope, the angel that she is, fed me.

I am alive. Spared. However, I am weak. I can sit up but have no energy.

April 30

When Hope tended me today, her eyes were red. I asked her if she had been crying. She told me not to worry that she was doing all right and that I should rest, get stronger.

When she brought me dinner, she had obviously been crying. I insisted that she tell me what was wrong. Finally, she admitted that Eliza was sick. When she reviewed her symptoms, it was clear she had the flu. Hope tried to assure me that Eliza was strong and would ward off the disease. She was unconvincing.

Dr. Carpenter had come to the house twice while I was dominated by my own illness and had treated her as best he could.

I was beside myself with guilt and worry. I dragged myself out of bed and went to examine her.

She was pale, shaking with chills, despite being wrapped in a quilt. She couldn't stand the light of the candle that I had brought to her bed. She moaned in pain, obviously so when I touched her.

Fear came, overwhelming me, and stayed. I prayed. I kept cool cloths on her forehead. I continued to pray. Sleep was impossible. I refused to leave her side.

May 2

Despite my efforts to do what little I could, Eliza got worse. She died this morning as I held her in my arms.

May 7

She is not gone; she is just visiting—somewhere. I cannot believe that Hope permitted her to be away from home so long. She denies that Eliza is with her grandmother. Perhaps, she is with neighbors. Eliza so did love to play with the Crandall and the Aborn children.

While I am certain that she is happy playing with friends, I am anxious to show her the new set of alphabet cards that I bought; I want to teach her the letters.

Yesterday, I found Martha, her favorite doll, which her grandmother had made for her. Eliza always carries it around the house and never visits without it.

May 13

My muscles tensed. Redness swept across my face. I could feel the heat. How could she defend him? He had to be blind, incompetent, and ignorant not to see that Eliza was failing.

Why did he do nothing? She was much too small to ward off this disease on her own. She was much too young to die. Dr. Carpenter's failure to visit me is proof alone that he knows he is to blame.

I yelled at Hope for insisting that Dr. Carpenter had done all that he could.

Whatever he did was not enough.

May 21

There is no purpose in going on. I am shrouded in joy-less existence. The bitter smell of despair torments me.

May 27

Our pastor insisted on seeing me today. I told him that I felt God had forsaken me. His assurance of God's continued love brought me no comfort. Others had advised me, I told him, to put my mind on other things and to keep busy. Such advice infuriates me. My loss is not theirs.

The pastor advised that I read St. Paul's letter to the Colossians—cut off your anger and let God rule your heart.

June 4

Today, I heard a bell toll from somewhere in the Village. To me the ringing of a bell had always announced an important meeting, an event, or was a call to worship.

Today it mourned. It was spiritless, lonely, and dark.

June 8

The shutters have closed on my life. I cannot work. Despite Hope's urging, I eat little. I am smothered in despondency.

June 19

My world is filled with shadows. What are left are

shades—only silhouettes. I have no command of myself.

June 26

The darkness hangs heavy upon me. I am tired all of the time. The nights are long, followed by endless days. Light has faded. There is perpetual fog and gloom. . . .

June 30

Hope appears to be dealing with this much better than I. The loss is not less for her. She is busy with Daniel and continues her community activities.

My neglect of Daniel is not fair.

July 6

I was briefly checking the garden today when Peleg spotted me. Our conversation was quite awkward. He did not seem to want to talk about events or my disposition; neither did I. We discussed the weather and the garden, instead.

As he was slowly leaving (his leg seemed to be troubling him), he invited me to return to the tavern for a game of darts.

I declined.

July 12

Hope mentioned that Mrs. Whipple had come by again today. She says that Mrs. Whipple is pleading to have me examine her. She has been to see Dr. David but feels no better. She even sought advice from our charlatan apothecary. She told Hope that I am the only one who can help her.

I do not really want to see her or any patient for that matter, but Mrs. Whipple has been loyal to me for some years. If she is confident that I can help her, I suppose that I should see her.

July 14

When Mrs. Whipple left today, she said that she was already feeling better. That is encouraging.

I am feeling somewhat better myself.

August 10

As I walked through the garden today, I was startled by a clear vision of Eliza gently playing among the flowers. She would have been four and a half years of age. Her image was so clear that I almost called out to her. She was admiring the daises—her favorites—bright and sunny. I picked a bouquet for her and placed them in a glass on the table near where she often sat, playing with Martha and Mrs. Norris.

My heart aches.

August 21

Having received a plea in a letter from Mrs. Greene, Hope has been tireless in her effort to organize the women of the Village with L. Egan and J. Knowles and, through friends, the women of neighboring towns and churches. The Army of the South, now under General Greene's command, is desperate for clothing. Hope's army of sewers and stitchers, as I call them, is diligently at work making shirts and socks. They also repair any piece of clothing that is salvageable. As Mrs. Greene has asked, we will send this clothing to a new camp on the Pee Dee River that is being established in the Tidewater. If this effort is duplicated between here and the Carolinas, our troops might be decently clothed.

General Greene's acceptance of the command of the Southern Army surprises me. He does not like to be far from home; this assignment will give him no opportunity to visit Caty and his family. Nor will it be easy for a native New Englander to find comfort in the unfamiliar terrain of the south. Besides out-smarting Cornwallis, he will have to slosh through habitats of snakes (rattlesnakes that are six feet long, I am told), avoid the water moccasins that thrive in the numerous swamps, and fight through dense forests where moss cascades from cypress trees like hay intended for some huge prehistoric cattle which no longer exist. We also hear that he will encounter brutal civil war—neighbor against neighbor—to which the principles of the revolution against the Crown are only vaguely connected.

My understanding was that he wanted to command West Point. Congress and General Washington must have seen it differently.

September 4

Why doesn't the letter come? The committee has had more than enough time to render a verdict. Something must be wrong. I toss and turn at night. Hope asked me three times whether I was going to visit Mrs. Weatherbe to check on her condition. I never heard her question. I cannot even recall what Mrs. Weatherbe's condition is. I pace around the house during the day. At night I am too tired to sleep. Reading does not distract me. I check the arrival of the post in the morning. Nothing for me. I check again in the afternoon. Nothing.

Why don't I hear? Something must be wrong.

Hope baked me my favorite blackberry pie. I nibbled at it. Left most of it on my plate.

At 1:00 of the clock I thought I would check the post. I knew it was too early. At 2:30 I decided to check. At 3:00 I checked again. At 3:45 I thought I heard the stage rumble by. No mail. I paced some more. Another day with no word.

Today I was there when the stage arrived. I asked the driver myself for my letter. He had none. I accused him of not picking up the mail. He looked scornfully at me. I had to apologize.

I went to the hearth to pour some hot water for tea. There was none in the kettle. I sputtered, cursed under my breath. Hope must have heard me; she chose to ignore my impatience. Not only did my letter not come, I cannot even get a cup of tea.

September 6

The letter, at long last, came today from the Society for the Promotion of Knowledge and Virtue. I was so nervous that I could not open it. I carried it home as if the letter had no immediate importance. My hands shook as I opened it.

I read it twice but did not understand what it said. The committee applauded my desire to join the Society. They acknowledged my work and my desire to promote the spread of practical knowledge. They felt my character was upstanding, and they considered that I would be compatible with other members. In a terrible tone of condescension, whoever wrote the letter (it was signed by the secretary) suggested that *some* day I might make a significant contribution to the reputation to the Society. Some day? I do not know what that means.

What is clear—upon the third reading—is that I have not been elected. With all of the praise lavished in the first part of the letter, I am at a loss to know why. They did not say. Someone must have blackballed me. They made it clear that the decision was final.

It is not fair.

October 14

The hot talk in the taverns this week has been our spectacular victory at Yorktown. Cornwallis actually surrendered—or he would have were he man enough to present his sword in person to General Washington rather than fain illness and send his second to represent him.

To our amazement, the French finally came through. We couldn't rely on the French fleet and soldiers to help us rid Newport of the British or to push them out of New York, but Admiral Francois, Count de Grasse, surprised us all by offering Lafayette his full support and 3,000 infantry. With 17,000 Americans we pinned Cornwallis and nearly blasted him into oblivion. Yorktown must be the decisive blow of this war.

Every night the tavern celebrations have been more raucous than the night before.

October 25

I was not even thinking of her, but my eyes filled with tears.

In apple season we had often walked through the orchard, Argos running ahead of us, marveling at the ripening fruit. We would chat about the new cider we would get and anticipate the delicious pies her mother would prepare for us.

I long to lift her again into the branches to touch the fruit and to dream with her of the days that were to come.

October 28

Today was a prodigious and warm autumn day. We rented a boat from Rhodes and Gardner's and gently rowed up the river as far as the grist mill. I love the variety of each season: the fresh sheen of early spring, the deep green of summer, the autumnal coloring of crimson and yellow, and the white mantel of winter. Unlike the cove or the bay, the river provides us far more opportunities for peaceful meanderings.

November 22

Isolated on a hill on the old road to Scituate sits a weather-worn farmhouse where the spinster Hutchinson lives. We never see her. Sabrina Hutchinson and perhaps the house itself have a sinister reputation. Vines and rambles intertwine from the road to the porch. Anyone foolish enough to walk up to the porch would be entangled, attacked by those killer weeds.

The windows are shuttered, but flickering light has been seen and an occasional wisp of smoke from the chimney. You can feel the chill when you see the door that hangs by a single hinge. The place is insidious.

The spinster is said to create a fever in anyone who looks her in the eye. Children are warned to stay clear of the Hutchinson place; they do. The villagers will avoid taking the road that goes by this old farm or will walk across the adjacent field to put some distance between it and themselves. They whistle while they walk in the belief that this wards off the evil. No one walks by the place at night. Wild strawberries grow near the road, but they lay untouched. Even the birds seem to ignore the berries.

We speculate about what might have brought the spinster to the Village and why she stays—jilted by a lover when she was a girl . . . abandoned by a sea captain who never returned for her . . . possessed by the house that traps her.

Some Villagers say she has always been there and always will.

December 2

Sometimes it takes an innocent voice to make you see clearly.

Daniel and I, hand in hand, with Argos running out ahead, were out walking along the Pawtuxet River on Saturday, my mind drifting with the gentle breeze and the aroma of wet grass along the river bank.

"Why does not Mrs. Norris come on walks with us, Father?"

"Well, she is a cat, Daniel," I answered, hoping that would end it.

"Does she not like to walk?"

"She scampers around the house, once in awhile, but she prefers to find the sun or any warm spot and just sleep."

Daniel seemed to be puzzling over the difference between Argos and Mrs. Norris, but said nothing.

And then, after a long pause, he asked without looking at me, "Where has Eliza gone?"

Now it was my turn for a long pause—the unexpected

question catching me unprepared. Deciding not to engage in a complicated discussion with him, I simply answered, "She is visiting with God."

He looked puzzled. "When will she be coming home?" he wanted to know.

This question drew my breath away. I had to stop for a moment.

"Sometimes, when people go to visit God, Daniel, they just talk to him in prayer as we do in church and at home when we read the Bible together. Sometimes, they talk to Him in a special way, like we are today, by walking along the river and appreciating all of the beauty of His creation. Sometimes, when people visit God, they go to heaven and they stay there with Him. That is what Eliza has done."

Daniel was content with that. Perhaps, I need to be as well.

Now I realize that the difference I can make will not be as an inventor or merchant of a magical elixir. When this war is finally over, I will not be known as a lionhearted soldier or as a distinguished civic leader in this Village or in Rhode Island. The contribution I can make is as a father to Daniel, a better husband to Hope, and as a competent surgeon for my patients who depend on me.

December 3
When I shared Daniel's and my conversation about Eliza with Hope, she broke down in tears. She cried

inconsolably, her whole body suddenly consumed with soulful trembling. It wasn't until then—and only then—that I realized how she had been withholding her own grief. She had been pretending to be strong for Daniel . . . and for me. I had been absorbed by my own selfishness. I had been the one to withdraw into a protective cocoon. I had left her to suffer alone.

Moving to her, I held her in my arms as she shuddered in pain. "Please, forgive me, Hope. My behavior has been callous, cruelly insensitive. I am ashamed."

The innocent wisdom of a child is truly one of life's great gifts. It can shock you into new insight. In time, by the Grace of God, perhaps Hope and I will be blessed with another.

The world is fresh with new possibilities.

Acknowledgments

To authenticate the story of 18th century medicine, events of the Revolutionary era—especially as they were seen in Rhode Island's Pawtuxet Village—and a clear presentation of the manuscript required the collaboration of many.

For reading and commenting on many aspects of the practice of 18th century medicine: Dr. Stanley Aronson, former dean of the Brown University School of Medicine, my thanks.

With great appreciation for assistance with the research: the library staff at the National Library of Medicine, the Rhode Island Public Library, Cranston Public Library, the Providence Public Library, the Belvedere-Tiburon Library, the Swen Library at the College of William & Mary, the Redwood Library and Athenaeum in Newport, the Library of the Royal Society of Medicine, the Library of the Royal Society of Surgeons, Wellcome Library, Library of New South Wales, British Dental Association, the Old Operating Theatre, and Herb Garrett at

the original site of St. Thomas' Hospital, the Medical
Library at Yale University, the Rhode Island Historical
Society Archives and the Yorktown Victory Center.

For teaching me through their living history presentations as "surgeons:" Rory McCreadie, Geoff King and
Mr. Cousins in England, David Downs in Massachusetts,
John Currier in Rhode Island, Alonso Chattan in California, the "surgeons" at the Colonial Army encampment at
the Victory Center in Yorktown, Virginia, and the many
others who share their knowledge and passion for this
aspect of medical history.

Special thanks to those who helped with the language
of the manuscript: Fran Cadieux, Holly Powell Kennedy,
Charlotte Scherer, and Janis Newman..

About the Author

Richard Kennedy, a former hospital administrator in Rhode Island and California, is a retired Army Reserve colonel who commanded five hospitals in Desert Storm. A Fellow of the American College of Healthcare Executives, he now teaches at Quinnipiac University. He has lectured worldwide on 18th century medicine and has conducted living history presentations at universities, elementary and high schools, and at community events. He serves as "surgeon" to the Pawtuxet Rangers and the 6th Connecticut Regiment of the Continental Line.